PRAISE

"Fight scenes, action, mystery all come together into a taut thriller... *The Morgenstern Project* blew me away."

—*Fantasio*

"A real treat for readers who love a fast read with action and conspiracies. The Consortium thrillers offer a roller-coaster ride into the past, racing back to the present. They are all action movie with a touch of *X-Files* thrown in, and some dark humor to remind us that this is entertainment."

—*Phoenix Magazine*

"This book is for readers who love testosterone-filled pages-turners and World War II stories."

—*Meelylit*

"Might remind some of Ian Fleming's Bond novels or Adam Hall's Quiller series."

—*Library Journal (The Bleiberg Project)*

"A fun, fast-paced thriller."

—*Shelf Awareness (The Bleiberg Project)*

"Fast-paced, a chilling thriller that leaves you biting your nails."

—*Mystery Sequels (The Shiro Project)*

"Suspense done to perfection."

—*Le Monde (The Shiro Project)*

"An impeccably written thriller."

—*Page̶   Shiro Project)*

"A thrill-a-minute̶   ̶ro Project)*

"Fluidly written and̶   ̶ed, the book is a fast-paced adventure... L̶

—*Booklist (The Shiro Project)*

The Morgenstern Project

A Consortium Thriller

David Khara

Translated from French by Sophie Weiner

LE FRENCH BOOK

First published in France as
Le Projet Morgenstern
by Editions Critic
©2013 Editions Critic

Published by special arrangement with Editions Critic in conjunction with their duly appointed agents L'Autre agence, Paris and 2 Seas Literary Agency

English translation ©2015 Sophie Weiner
First published in English in 2015
by Le French Book, Inc., New York

http://www.lefrenchbook.com

Translator: Sophie Weiner
Translation editor: Amy Richards
Cover designer: Jeroen ten Berge

ISBNs:
Trade paperback: 9781939474353
Hardback: 9781939474377
E-book: 9781939474360

War is horrible, but slavery is worse.
—Winston Churchill

CHAPTER 1

POLAND, DECEMBER 1942

Bundled in the thick gray coat swiped from an SS guard, the boy felt neither the wounds inflicted during months of abuse, nor the bitter cold of the Polish winter. The raw night air that filled his lungs as he raced on gave him unspeakable joy and fueled his drive to escape his torturers.

He wasn't feeling tired. His gait, in fact, was growing stronger and faster as he gained distance from that monstrous place. Eytan paced himself to the sound of his steady breathing. In his mind, he replayed the events that had led to his escape. Eytan saw himself seizing the gun that the guard had shoved in his face and firing the bullet into the man's forehead with cold accuracy. He had then taken aim at the gas container he had seen on his many trips to the lab and pulled the trigger. The German soldiers had panicked. Eytan would never forget the furious look on Bleiberg's face. Bleiberg, the scientist who had enslaved him and forced him to endure dozens, maybe hundreds, of injections and brutal tests.

Of all the kids subjected to this very same treatment, he alone had survived. Why had the experiments killed all the others but made him faster, more agile, and stronger? Each time the guards carried away the wasted body of another child, his guilt grew. But over time, anger replaced the anguish.

Now his rage was as icy as this December night.

It would keep him alive no matter what, and he would use it to strike down those responsible for all the suffering.

~ ~ ~

THE CANADIAN FOREST ON THE US BORDER, PRESENT DAY

The solitary traveler was struggling to make his way through the forest. With each step, his muscular legs sank deeper into the thick blanket of snow. The cruel and relentless gusts of wind refused to let up for even a second. Snowflakes collected on his face, and the cold stung his cheeks. Again and again, he had to wipe his protective goggles dry. He readjusted his hood, tightened the straps of his backpack, and looked at the compass clenched in his gloved hand to make sure he was still heading south. Despite the violent elements unleashed on him, Eytan stayed the course.

The wind rushed past his ears, and he swore it carried the voices of long-lost friends. Vassili, the silent Siberian titan. Karol, the scrawny teacher from Krakow. And of course, the charismatic Janusz, with his sandy-colored beard. Eytan even thought he saw them emerging from behind the trees, guns in hand and their faces worn down by sorrow and combat.

Eytan stopped and leaned against a tree. A lump was rising in his throat.

"I miss you guys," he told his visions.

He took a deep breath and gathered himself. This was no time to reminisce. Mental weakness was out of the question. He had to keep going, no matter the cost.

The lives of loved ones depended on it.

CHAPTER 2

IRAQ, SPRING 2003

With one elbow pressed against the passenger-side window and both eyes glued to his binoculars, Sergeant Terry scoped the dunes in search of the enemy. All five senses were on high alert. A low-flying backup chopper was whipping up ochre sand clouds along the tortuous route taken by the recon unit's Humvee.

Timothy Terry ignored the sweat trickling down his cheeks and onto his lips, chapped by the scorching afternoon sun. The seasoned soldier had only one thought on his mind: bringing his three team members back safe and sound.

Since the start of the US invasion of Iraq three days earlier, they had completed no fewer than eight missions, five of them under enemy fire. On top of that, they were dealing with all the ordinary hurdles accompanying a disorganized war—meager supplies, shitty equipment, and inconsistent orders, to name a few.

Tim Terry was the veteran member of his unit. The once-shy high school student from Ohio had come out of his shell during his ten years as a Marine, when wars had broken out in the Balkans, the Middle East, Africa, and Persia. The years had toughened him and given him nerves of steel, plus a real compassion for his fellow Marines. This had earned him the respect of both his superior officers and those who served alongside him. And to top it off, the guy had killer aim.

Good thing. Killing was his job, as much as he disliked it.

In their stories and news clips, embedded reporters liked to make heroes of the Marines. And many were, whether they were serving on the front lines or working behind the scenes as engineers, medics, or communications specialists. At the heart of it, though, they were all there to do the same thing—kill on command. And Tim Terry carried out that assignment like no one else.

Still, this stint would be his last. He had put in his time and had no intentions of re-upping, even though he knew he would be promoted to master sergeant if he stayed in the corps. He had no desire to climb a chain of command that was more preoccupied with its own advancement than getting the job done. How many times had his unit gotten caught in friendly fire? How many absurd orders had he been forced to obey just to give the journalists a story to send back home? Too many. In any event, too many to fill another three to five years of his life.

"You know what they say about guys with big guns: the bigger the gun, the smaller the dick," the driver cracked, breaking up the two Marines in the backseat.

Hansen had gone five minutes without making a stupid joke. A new record, Terry thought as he looked at his wise-ass buddy wearing a stupid grin. The scrawny troublemaker with the maturity level of a teenager was a regular standup comedian. He didn't take anything seriously. His humor was usually borderline or straight-out lewd, so Terry and the other guys had to keep him as far as possible from the officers just to avoid any drama.

Terry and Hansen were together most of the time, both on and off duty. This meant the sergeant was frequently at the butt end of the comic's jokes. If Terry took a one-liner the wrong way, it was usually because he was fatigued. Someone who didn't know the two might have thought they had nothing in common, but in fact, they were both driven to excel at their jobs. Hansen, the twenty-three-year-old goofball, was unparalleled when it came to operating a Humvee in difficult terrain and he had almost superhuman stamina. He could drive for three days straight. Granted, he downed vitamins by the handful.

"Keep your eyes on the road. I'm scoping the surroundings. And you newbies back there, quit laughing at his lame jokes," Terry ordered. "You're just egging him on."

The remark set off another round of guffaws. Baker and Charlie were hard to tell apart. They were tall and buff, and despite their efforts to look brave, their eyes betrayed a certain amount of fear. The boys were fresh arrivals from Parris Island boot camp.

"I mean seriously, what the hell are we doing here?" Hansen said. "There's nothing but fucking rocks and sand that'll wreck this tin can. I spend hours cleaning the engine every time we get back to base. Why'd they send only one team to check out the area if it's a danger zone? Isn't that messed up?"

"You're a Marine, man. You knew what you signed up for," Terry teased. "We're a recon unit, so..."

"Chill. I know what we're supposed to be doing. But does that mean we have to like being out here all by ourselves with our asses exposed? This is the perfect setup for an ambush."

"We're not exactly by ourselves. They've assigned us a back-up chopper. So shut up. I'm trying to focus. And you two in the back, stay alert."

Twenty minutes went by with only the steady roar of the Humvee engine and the whir of the helicopter blades.

Too many hiding spots for the enemy, Terry thought as he inspected the dry rolling landscape. They could surge out at any second.

An abrupt swerve threw all four passengers against the side of the Humvee. Hansen slammed on the brakes, inciting a chorus of protests.

"Just a small technical problem! Instead of giving me shit, how about you cover me," he ordered.

Hansen opened the door and leaped out of the vehicle, followed by his fellow Marines. The newbies stationed themselves on each side of the Humvee. They lowered themselves into firing position, one knee on the ground.

Hansen made his way around the vehicle and opened the hood.

"God dammit! Shit!"

"What's going on?" Terry barked as he approached his partner, his eyes still fixed on the surroundings.

"Broken drive shaft and an oil leak the size of Niagara Falls, Sergeant," Hansen said, kicking the bumper. "And the tires are blown."

"Did you hit any rocks?" Terry asked.

"No, I swear I didn't!"

"Can you get us out of here?"

"Not in this piece of junk. It's a good thing our loving commanders provided us with... Hold up, where'd the fucking chopper go?"

Terry looked up and searched the sky. Preoccupied with the vehicle, he hadn't noticed the disappearance of their aerial support.

"I can't believe it," he grumbled as he held down the switch on the transmitter attached to his protective vest. "Vanguard to command, our vehicle is immobilized in the middle of unfriendly territory."

"Command to vanguard, copy that loud and clear," a choppy voice confirmed.

"Would you be kind enough to inform us of the whereabouts of our backup chopper?"

"Command to vanguard, we're checking on that."

"That's right. Check on it, asshole. And take your sweet time," Terry sneered after cutting off the transmission.

Beneath the wrecked Humvee, Hansen was cursing up a storm. When he came out a few seconds later, he was wearing a worried look, one that Terry had never seen on him before.

"Dude, there are shards of metal under there. Something busted up our ride."

"Are you serious? What? A mine would have vaporized us."

There was no time to get to the bottom of it. Terry knew they couldn't stay out in the open.

"Guys, we'll station ourselves in twos behind the rocks on either side of the hill over there," he ordered. "Hansen's with Baker. Charlie's with me. We'll cover each other while we wait for the cavalry. Go!"

The men started running toward their posts.

The first shot snagged Charlie in the arm. He fell to the sand with all the weight of his massive body. Seconds later another blast caught Baker and sent him flying through the air. He landed on his back, a hole in his belly.

Cut off before they could reach the hill, Terry and Hansen dashed back to the busted vehicle, their only shelter under what was now heavy fire. They hoped to cut off the invisible assailants' field of vision.

The fire power shrieked as it hit the vehicle. The two men tucked their heads into their shoulders like turtles and prayed for the storm to pass. When the gunfire finally died down, they could hear the newbies crying in agony.

"Vanguard to command, under enemy fire. Two men hit."

Only static met the sergeant's call. Terry peered out to check on his teammates' status. Charlie was twisting in pain, his uniform coated in blood. Baker wasn't moving.

"We can't leave them like this," Terry said.

"Are you nuts?" Hansen shouted back. "These aren't some amateur schlubs defending their village. We're dealing with pros here. It looks like a Republican Guard ambush."

"Do you really think they'd be waiting for us out here? Let other assholes do the analysis. Just cover me on my signal. Now!"

Sergeant Terry left his hideout and crawled toward Baker while Hansen pointed his M4A1 into the distance and kept firing. Tim grabbed the wailing soldier's jacket, and using all his strength, he pulled him back to the Humvee.

Hansen shot Terry an angry look. "Not the best timing for your little rescue and recovery mission."

"Can you think of a better time? I'm going back out."

"Just give me a second to reload!"

But his commanding officer had already sprung into the open.

"Fucking hero," Hansen muttered as he stepped out of hiding. He took aim and got ready to shoot another round. A snap. A splatter of blood. Crawling toward Charlie, Terry heard Hansen cry out and turned to his buddy. He saw Hansen's assault rifle fall to the ground. The severed hand was still attached to the weapon. Terry fell to his knees like a puppet whose strings had just been cut.

Terry didn't know what to do. It was a moment of hesitation he immediately regretted. What summed up the life of a soldier? A hundred good decisions. One bad decision, and it was over.

The dreaded bullet and the countless others that followed shredded his thigh. He collapsed, dizzy from the burning metal. With his eyes lost in the blue sky, he saw a helicopter soaring out from behind a hill. He sank into a delirious state where time stood still.

Dangling between coma and death, Terry heard muffled voices. A childhood memory flashed in his mind. He saw himself, his ear glued to the door of his sister's bedroom, where she often spent entire afternoons with her boyfriend. Terry had giggled at their moaning and groaning. It wasn't until much later that he understood what those sounds meant.

The memory faded.

Now it was he who was groaning, and it felt anything but good. In the middle of the increasingly dense fog, a figure leaned over him.

"He's beat up bad, sir, but he's alive."

"I sure hope so," another ghost-like figure said before squatting beside him. "You're gonna be all right, kid. Prepare him for the evacuation, and be careful."

Terry struggled to stay conscious, despite the pain in his legs and spine that felt like jolts of electricity. He clenched his teeth as hard as he could. He feared his molars would shatter.

But as the men fussed around him, blessed relief arrived. A wave of heat rushed through his arm, and he was liberated. He had the sense of floating on air.

In that moment, each and every shortcoming of the Marine Corps vanished. The cavalry had saved him, Hansen, and the two rookies.

God bless America!

"What's the status on the other three?" asked the man leading the operation. He was walking alongside the stretcher as it carried Terry toward the helicopter.

"Two seriously wounded, and the driver is in critical condition, sir. What are your orders, sir?"

The superior officer placed a hand on Terry's sweat-drenched forehead and wiped it with an unexpected tenderness.

"*Semper fi*," Terry stammered, swept away by the morphine that filled his limbs with protective numbness.

Semper fidelis. The Marine Corps motto.

"Sorry, boy," the man mumbled.

After a long silence, he gave the order.

"As for the other three... Finish them off."

CHAPTER 3

He could already hear the commotion inside. Michael Dritch smiled as he gazed at the storefront window, behind which lived hoards of novels, comic books, and miscellaneous pieces of merchandise, including superhero figurines and *Star Wars* T-shirts.

He pushed open the door to the small indie bookstore, his favorite hangout whenever he had a free afternoon. He looked forward to breathing in the vanilla aroma tinged with must. It meant that he would soon be transported to another world.

Lining the walls of the narrow shop were shelves tightly packed with works of science fiction. Rare comics filled a set of racks running down the middle of the store. The precious collector's items were in airtight and light-resistant cases.

The steady influx of new stock conveniently justified Michael's frequent visits to this place, which he kept secret from his coworkers. They didn't know that behind the hard-nosed face, which put off more than a few people, there was an introvert who dreamed of pirates, outer space, and caped superheroes.

But Michael found so much more in this wonderful shop called Morg's Universe. It provided him with a community of fellow enthusiasts who were like family to him. And as was true for most biological families, differences of opinion often led to heated arguments.

Seconds earlier, in fact, someone had thrown down the gauntlet.

"Hey guys," Michael called out, greeting his fellow patrons.

He was rewarded with a couple of distracted heys before the argument picked up again. The insults were flying so fast, he could barely tell who was saying what. Watching the verbal joust between the two geeks hyped on Red Bull made him feel like he was attending a WrestleMania match at Caesars

Palace. In his head, he could hear Michael Buffer introducing the two contestants.

"On one side of the register, in baggy black jeans and Iron Maiden sweatshirt, we have the brainy computer engineer with the celebrated bulging belly and buzz cut: Greg Nadjar! And behind the register, in gray trousers and blue button-down shirt, we have the undefeated owner of this bookshop. The angelic baby face, blond hair, and blindingly bright smile could only belong to the one and only Jeremy Corbin!"

Michael weighed in.

"Gentlemen, far be it from me to intervene, but try not to lapse into any petty name-calling."

"This numbskull doesn't know what he's talking about!" Greg fired.

"Well, don't waste a minute of your time listening to that numbskull over there," Jeremy shot back. "He's making an ass of himself."

Michael could tell that Jeremy wasn't about to back down. "Could one of you explain why you're quarreling?" he asked.

"I made the mistake of giving His Highness an opinion that he didn't like," Jeremy said.

"You can keep your ignorant opinions to yourself," Greg answered.

"We're not getting anywhere," Michael sighed as he noticed the Captain America figurine behind the cash register.

"All I said was that I thought the first hundred pages of *Lord of the Rings* were a little boring. There's no reason to throw a hissy fit," Jeremy explained.

Uh oh, Michael thought. Any criticism of *Lord of the Rings* was sure to get a rise out of Greg. The stubborn programmer was a ringer. He owned several editions of Tolkien's trilogy. He had Peter Jackson's movie adaption on DVD and Blu-ray, along with *The Hobbit*. Greg also had an array of books and essays on Tolkien. Michael even suspected that the devotee was fluent in Elvish.

Diplomacy would be necessary to defuse the situation.

"Greg, we both know that Mr. Corbin is trying to fill in the gaps in his cultural knowledge. Wouldn't you agree?" he asked as he nodded at the owner of the store.

"I guess," Greg conceded. "But hey, you're not a good liar—what do *you* think about *Lord of the Rings*?"

Yikes.

"All things being equal…"

Michael stopped himself. The two combatants were watching him with impatient eyes. He gave them an embarrassed smile and glanced at his watch.

"Oh jeez, look at the time! I've gotta run."

"Answer the question," Greg insisted.

"Yeah, I want to hear your thoughts too," Jeremy chimed in.

These guys were such a pain. He had to say something. There was no getting out of it.

He mumbled an inaudible response.

"Huh?" the bookstore owner asked.

Michael cleared his throat, took a breath, and braced himself for the rebuttal.

"I said that I also thought it was a little…"

"Ah ha!" Jeremy gloated, clapping his hands.

"Jesus, what backwards universe am I living in!" Greg huffed.

And with that the two disputants hopped back on their verbal merry-go-round, which was spinning so fast, Michael was getting dizzy. So much for his valiant attempt to restore order. Maybe he was stuck in the middle of a crazy amusement park, but he had to admit he loved it.

"Hey boys! How's it going?" The melodious voice of the beautiful blonde in the tight sheriff's uniform silenced the men.

"Hey Jackie," Michael replied with a friendly wave.

Jeremy walked over to her, slipped an arm around her waist, and kissed her gently on the lips.

Even though Michael had grown close to the couple, their past was still a mystery to him. They were always dodging questions by making jokes that might have fooled their other friends but didn't fool him. He couldn't say exactly why, but he had a hunch that Jeremy and Jackie had come to this quiet little town to start a new life.

"Hi Jackie," Greg said as he threw his black backpack over his shoulder. He carried that thing everywhere, and no one knew what was in it. "You really married a jackass."

"I know that better than anyone else," she joked as she gave her husband a big smile. "But I love him anyway. Are you still coming over tonight to take a look at my laptop? I'd like to figure out why it's so slow."

Greg gave Michael a pat on the back and opened the door to leave.

"Yeah, around eight. First I have to finish up a website." Still standing in the doorway, he took out his phone and read the screen. He put it back in his pocket with a worried look on his face. "You're lucky you've got those muscles," he shot at Jeremy. "All right, fools, I'm outta here. You all need to brush up on the classics."

"If you want guns like mine, try lifting boxes of books or even spending a little time in the gym instead of sitting behind your computer and stuffing your fat face with chips, psycho," the bookseller fired back.

Greg's response was a classy flip of the middle finger.

With Greg gone and Jeremy preoccupied with his wife, Michael could finally explore the sci-fi displays. He had his heart set on a recent book called *Battle of the Beggars* by Thomas Gota, a *Star Wars* parody that all the geek blogs were raving about. It promised to be a fun read that would cheer up an otherwise dreary late-autumn evening.

"It's on the house if you watch the store for me Saturday morning," Jeremy said, still glued to Jackie.

"Planning a hot Friday-night date? Don't think you'll be up in time?"

"No, not really. Jackie is working, and the little one has a doctor's appointment at ten. And since there's always a huge wait, I need someone to cover the store. But if you're not free, I can ask Greg when he comes by the house tonight."

Michael didn't hesitate. "No, don't bother him. I'll do it." The offer was a huge honor. Plus the idea of being in charge of this nerd paradise during its busiest hours was the adult equivalent of spending an entire night locked in a toy store.

"How old is Annie now?"

"Exactly six months. It'll be our first Christmas together," Jackie said, smiling.

The woman was almost always in a good mood, except on the rare occasion when some jerk committed a serious crime. Almost all of the infractions in their small New Jersey town involved a teenager shoplifting a lipstick or a distracted office worker running a stop sign.

But one time, when he and Jeremy were having a friendly argument over a cup of coffee, Michael did see the deputy sheriff in action. He was schooling his friend on art house films when the sound of a crash interrupted his lecture. A car had rammed into a telephone pole across the street from the bookstore, and the driver had dragged himself out of the smoking vehicle.

The man, who was wearing a Stetson and waving a revolver, was clearly hammered. He stumbled into the middle of the street and started singing Willie Nelson's "On the Road Again."

Michael panicked. His hands over his ears, he ducked behind the cash register.

"Get down!" he yelled. "It's the twenty-fucking-first century, and a cowboy is about to shoot us dead. A fucking cowboy who doesn't even have a fucking horse! Fuck Willie Nelson, and fuck 'On the Road Again.'"

Jeremy was watching the whole thing from the doorway of his shop.

That's when Jackie zoomed onto the scene in her patrol car. After executing a controlled slide, the tiny law-enforcement officer sprang out of the vehicle and lunged at the man with lightning-fast speed and an impressive show of aggression.

"She's crazy! We have to call for help!" Michael shouted after summoning the courage to get up and look out the window.

"She's not the one I'm worried about," Jeremy replied, his arms crossed in front of his chest.

A minute later, the drunkard's wrists were bound in handcuffs, and his nose was gushing blood. The woman's reputation was established in Michael's mind.

Michael brought himself back to the present. "Annie's six months old already? It seems like she was born just yesterday. All right, I'm out of here. I'll be back tomorrow for the keys. Have a good night. Oh, and in the future, try to avoid discussing Tolkien with Greg, unless you want to reawaken his inner demons."

"Lesson learned."

Michael gave a Japanese-style bow before leaving the store. He was eager for the arrival of Saturday morning, which was forty-eight hours away.

~ ~ ~

"Alone at last," Jackie said. She gave Jeremy a pat on the butt.

"Hey, you think just because you're a sheriff's deputy you have the right to harass innocent citizens?"

"Do you expect me to believe that an ex-sex addict such as yourself doesn't enjoy some mild discipline administered by a woman in uniform?" She batted her eyes.

Jeremy smiled and whispered, "What do you mean 'ex'?"

"And he doesn't even hide it," she sighed as she disengaged herself from her husband's hold.

Jeremy walked to his computer behind the register, and after quickly checking his e-mails, he gave her a disappointed look.

"Are you still hoping to hear from him?" Jackie asked.

"It's almost Christmas," Jeremy said.

"It's highly unlikely that..."

"I know," Jeremy interrupted. His tone was sharper than he meant it to be. "Sorry, honey, but you know how much I miss him. Shit, I feel like... Anyway, I owe him everything. You, our little girl, this store. He gave me—he gave both of us—a second chance. I can't just snap my fingers and forget him."

Jeremy certainly wasn't the man she had met almost two years earlier—an arrogant and thoroughly unlikeable stock trader who hated himself and was drowning in booze. Even though she never talked about Eytan, Jackie also missed him. The courageous and generous Mossad agent hadn't merely protected them during their crazy adventure in Europe. By way of example, he had helped them grow up. And, in fact, he had brought them together.

Jackie felt a lump in her throat and thought it best to change the subject.

"Can I ask you a favor?" she said.

"What is it, honey?"

"Could you pick up Annie from the babysitter's tonight, after you close the shop? I have a mountain of paperwork to finish."

"Um, let me get this straight. I screw around with my friends all day. My banging-hot wife pays me a surprise visit at work. Then my banging-hot wife says she has to work overtime and asks me to rescue our little girl. Pretty much your average day."

CHAPTER 4

Jackie parked her cruiser in the lot and entered the colonial-style building that housed the sheriff's department and courthouse. Those with business in the building were straggling out, as the offices and courts would soon close for the day. The young woman smiled politely at a guard manning the information desk and headed toward the department.

She entered the perfectly organized space and gave it a satisfied look. When she joined the sheriff's department, the offices were a pigsty. Official statements and sandwich remnants were strewn all over the desks. A search for a simple stapler could turn into an hour-long treasure hunt. But Jackie, trained by the CIA, followed the place-for-everything-and-everything-in-its-place maxim. And the new recruit eventually succeeded in creating a haven of tidiness.

She hunkered down at her desk and got to work on her reports. While only a few thousand people lived in her small town, the department's jurisdiction encompassed a much wider area of one hundred thousand residents. And even though Jackie didn't see many felonies, she always had paperwork to do. The former field agent considered it a huge pain and did it as quickly and professionally as possible. In the end, she realized that this task was her job's only downside, compared with what she had faced during her years in the intelligence agency.

She had had her fill of adventure on her last assignment, when she was charged with protecting Jeremy. They had fallen in love during the mission and had almost died. After that, Jackie was more than happy to end the CIA chapter of her life. These days, she took pleasure in the simple things and her family.

Jackie yawned. She glanced at her watch and gasped when she realized that she had already been there for two hours. She was resting her eyes when her cell phone started playing the theme from *Dora the Explorer*. The four deputies who were working on their own reports guffawed, and she shot them an icy stare. Jeremy loved messing with his wife by regularly changing her ringtone to something that was sure to get her teased.

The jerks were probably paying Jeremy to do it, she thought. Irritated, she answered the call. She didn't recognize the voice.

"Mrs. Walls-Corbin?"

"This is she."

"Listen to everything I have to say before hanging up." The voice was deep and husky. "I strongly suggest that you walk over to one of the windows on the back side of the building. The attack is about to start... Right *now*."

Before Jackie had a chance to respond, her computer went down, along with all the electricity in the building. Only the red exit sign was still lit. With the phone still fixed to her ear, she heard a muffled gunshot in the lobby.

"Everyone on the ground!" she yelled to her colleagues.

They turned toward her with confusion and alarm written on their faces. A much louder bang went off. Chips of wood went flying, quickly followed by countless sheets of papers swept up in a storm of bullets—bullets that destroyed everything in their path, including Jackie's four fellow officers. Unable to escape, they fell one by one.

Jackie instinctively crouched under her desk. She removed the safety on her weapon and pointed it, ready to fire.

"They're coming to get you, Jacqueline," the anonymous speaker continued calmly amid the uproar. "There's nothing you can do for the other officers. Get out as fast as you can."

"Wait. Why are you telling me this? What's going on? How do I know I can trust you?"

"Model 2003, Jackie. Do you remember it?" The call ended.

"Model 2003? Oh shit!"

It was like a punch in the gut. Without wasting a second, Jackie shoved the phone into a pocket and, sensing a lull in the gunfire, sprinted to the designated windows. She had just reached one of them when she felt a pinch in her right calf. Shielding her face with her arms, she soared through one of the windows. She tumbled to the ground, surrounded by shards of glass.

She opened her eyes with great effort. The pain radiating through her leg was less worrisome than the strange fatigue that weighed her down. As she fought against the lethargy, she heard what sounded like an explosion and glimpsed a white flash. She couldn't move. She felt someone grab her by the collar, and as she was being dragged toward the parking lot, she faintly called out, "Annie... Jeremy..." She drifted into unconsciousness.

CHAPTER 5

"Pour two and a half cups of honey into a bowl. Add the same amount of barbeque sauce, then two crushed cloves of garlic, and top it off with two spoonfuls of soy sauce. Now mix it all together."

New York celebrity chef Rocco DiSpirito was reeling off the instructions as he prepared the dish before a studio audience.

With one eye on his state-of-the-art refrigerator with LCD television and the other on the utensils and ingredients on his stainless-steel countertop, Jeremy was imitating the culinary wizard's every move.

Even though he wasn't blessed with the creative skills of a master chef, Jeremy excelled in reproducing Food Network recipes. And so, after returning home from his store every night, the bookseller would tie his favorite apron around his waist and set up shop in front of the oven, ready to concoct tasty little meals for his adoring wife. Today's main dish: honey-glazed spareribs.

For Jeremy, cooking was a substitute addiction. After numerous attempts to rid himself of his cigarette dependency, which included the patch, acupuncture, and even hypnosis, Jeremy had taken up food—not so much the eating of it, but the preparation. When he craved a cigarette at the shop, he would jot down recipe ideas or go to the Barefoot Contessa website. His tobacco intake had fallen considerably, and Jackie no longer fretted about his smoking.

At this stage in the recipe, all he had to do was marinate the meat and wait for his lady love before throwing the dish in the oven. If all went as planned, they'd be feasting at seven thirty. Jackie hadn't called with any updates, and according to their communication system, that meant she wasn't running late. After wiping down the countertop and soaking the dishes, Jeremy decided to sneak just one cigarette, which he intended to enjoy on the porch.

He went to the living room, grabbed his black coat, and searched its pockets for his cigarettes. On his way out, he picked up the baby monitor, which was equipped with both audio and video features. Jeremy smiled as he opened the front door, his eyes on the miraculous device that showed his bundle of joy soundly sleeping.

Once outside, he raised his collar to shield his neck from the winds that had been sweeping the Atlantic coast for several days. A flame. A puff of smoke. The delicious sense of happiness.

Sitting on the steps of his white frame house nestled in a neighborhood inhabited mostly by New York City retirees, Jeremy reflected on the journey that had led him from his personal rock bottom to salvation as a husband, father, and simple business owner. Who would have believed that just a few years earlier, he was a hotshot trader on Wall Street? Who could have imagined that one night, after getting hammered, he had slipped behind the wheel of his Aston Martin and caused the death of a small child?

Not many people.

Definitely not Greg. The computer geek was trotting up to the house, carrying his beloved backpack. His hands were shoved in the pockets of his puffy North Face jacket, which made him look even heavier than he was.

"You're super early," Jeremy hollered after taking another drag of his cigarette.

Greg didn't respond. The grim look on his face was a stark contrast to his usual jolly appearance. He hurried up the steps before taking Jeremy's extended hand. Jeremy squeezed it with enthusiasm, relieved that there were no hard feelings from their little dispute earlier in the day. But Greg didn't let go.

"Fuck, let go. What are you doing?"

"Shut up and get back in your piece-of-shit house," Greg whispered in a tone that sounded menacing.

He underscored his words by drawing a gun equipped with a silencer and waving it in Jeremy's face.

Jeremy was shocked. Then he burst out laughing. "You're such an idiot. You almost had me there. Are you taking up paintball?"

"I can assure you, this thing's not loaded with paintball ammo. I'll prove it."

Greg pointed his weapon at a tree in Jeremy's front yard and pulled the trigger. The sound took Jeremy back to the shootouts he had lived through in Europe with Jackie and Eytan.

Greg was definitely holding a real pistol.

Instinctively, Jeremy lifted his hands in the air.

"L-l-look," he stammered, "I'm sorry, all right? Tolkien's first one hundred pages aren't boring at all. You were right. Are you happy?"

"I don't give a shit about *Lord of the Rings*," Greg said. He was clearly growing impatient. "Now get in that fucking house, or I'll punch you in the face."

"Don't tell me you're working for the Consortium," Jeremy burst out. Now he was furious.

Greg hit Jeremy with the back of his armed hand.

"I warned you," he sneered before giving Jeremy a rough shove. "Now shut your ugly face and get inside."

~ ~ ~

The mission itself was a cinch. Capturing a civilian was child's play. The only obstacle was the location: a home in a gated community. While discretion was key, leadership accepted a certain number of casualties as long as the objective was achieved. The three men in the back of the white van passed around the photograph of their target. Lieutenant Delgado took back the picture and slipped it into the pocket of his black combat pants. He readjusted his earpiece and made sure his mike was securely fastened. He put on his facemask, as did his team members. They loaded their machine guns and one by one gave the thumbs up. The driver started the vehicle and pulled onto the road, heading toward their objective's location.

As usual, Delgado was in the dark about his boss's motives. But he didn't care, and neither did his men. As far as they were concerned, national security took precedence over all else.

Five minutes later, the vehicle stopped. Delgado gave the commando across from him a nod. He slid the side door open and leaped out. Weapon in hand, Delgado bolted toward the house and mounted the front steps. His three subordinates followed. He scanned the perimeter and lingered a few seconds on the smoking cigarette butt in an ashtray on the window ledge. The subject's file had mentioned that he was a smoker. The lieutenant tested the front door and smiled as it gave way without resistance. In two minutes tops, Operation Jeremy Corbin would be completed.

Delgado and his men continued silently and swiftly. Their synchronized movements allowed for optimal coverage and limited their target's ability to escape. They checked the kitchen, the living room, the laundry room, and the bathroom. No dice. There was just one door left on this floor. It was beneath the staircase. And it refused to budge. While his accomplices surveyed the surroundings, Delgado got ready to break the lock. He stopped when he heard a baby whimpering upstairs. The crying was soon lulled by what sounded like a nursery rhyme.

~ ~ ~

The basement was a dream man cave. Taking up half the space was a bar with a zinc countertop that looked like it was straight out of a nineteen-thirties Parisian bistro. Across from the bar, a recently purchased pool table sat under a stylish light fixture. Four crimson leather chairs were positioned in front of a monolithic flat-screen TV. Superhero movie posters decorated the walls, along with a few black-and-white prints of legendary jazz musicians.

Jeremy was holding Annie in one of the chairs and keeping a close watch on Greg. For his part, Greg was shifting his focus from the father and daughter to the door at the top of the stairs and then back again. In light of the computer geek's unforeseen abuse, Jeremy thought it wise to comply with his commands, even though they were as weird as shit. His latest instruction had Jeremy pointing Annie at the camera of the baby monitor, which Greg had snatched from her crib. Greg had then callously pinched the little girl's calf to elicit the desired response. The nutcase was now asking Jeremy to croon a lullaby.

Jeremy tried to shake off his fear. At the nutty ball, this guy would definitely be eating all the cashews.

~ ~ ~

The four commandos slinked upstairs and arrived in a hallway. Hugging the wall, they followed the crying all the way to a dimly lit room. Delgado entered first. The baby's bedroom looked like the display window of a toy store. Tons of early-learning games and stuffed animals filled the shelves all around the room, which had a whimsical border of farm animals. In the center was a round crib with bubblegum-pink bedding.

The lieutenant walked past the changing table and approached the crib. He grabbed a corner of the quilt and raised it carefully to come face to face with... The receiving end of a baby monitor! The screen showed the face of an unhappy baby, and the speakers relayed her sobs. At the same time, muffled cries were coming from the hallway. Before he had time to turn around and shoot blindly, blood splattered the little wallpaper duckies.

"No prisoners," Delgado heard someone behind him whisper just as he felt a knife pierce his neck.

~ ~ ~

All right, it's official. He's totally lost it, Jeremy thought as he listened to Greg talk to himself. For two minutes, the guy had been saying, "Yes... Okay... Got it." From what Jeremy could tell, Greg wasn't wearing a mike. The man was losing touch with reality, probably from spending his life playing *Call of Duty*. Jeremy swore that if he got out of his ridiculous hostage situation alive, he'd change the theme of his store to attract a more boring clientele. Right now, botany sounded like a safe bet.

Fortunately, the loony tune seemed to be calming down. He stuck his gun in his belt and turned to Jeremy, who was trying to soothe his daughter.

"It's all good," Greg declared, clearly relieved. "We can go back upstairs."

With his eyes still glued to the wacko, Jeremy stood up slowly. He carefully placed his now-sleeping little girl on the seat of the leather chair and without warning rushed at Greg.

The bookseller had mastered the tackling stance: knees bent, arms open wide, head lowered. Greg, however, managed to react with surprising speed for a guy of his tubbiness. He spun around, successfully dodging his attacker. Jeremy went flying into the bar. Luckily, no damage done. He got back up, shook it off, and prepared for a second assault.

"It would be real swell if you showed up one of these days. I'm gonna have a hard time calming him down," Greg yelled seconds before ramming Jeremy with a flawless corkscrew punch. But he lost his balance and fell to the floor, along with Jeremy. Greg also lost the upper hand. Jeremy mustered up a second wind and subdued his abductor by pressing a knee to his throat.

"Who the fuck are you talking to, you psycho freak!" Jeremy shouted.

Greg let out a series of unintelligible sounds as he pointed to the leg threatening to crush his windpipe. Jeremy eased some of the pressure.

"To him," Greg spit out between coughing fits.

"Who's him?" Jeremy insisted, adding a bit more weight.

"I believe he's referring to me." Jeremy looked over his shoulder. The voice was so familiar, but so unexpected.

"Eytan?"

CHAPTER 6

The clanging of metal and the grunts of the swordfighters filled the large hall of the fancy Berlin mansion. The combatants' parries and thrusts quickly intensified as two servants, both fascinated, watched behind a wooden kitchen trolley holding towels and a pitcher of water. One of the servants was a large sixty-year-old man, and the other was a cute young woman with a round face and brown hair.

Both swordfighters were adamant and refused to give any ground. In fact, the training session looked more like a death match. The swordsmen had the agility of wolves in their prime.

Karl-Heinz Dietz, his hand fiercely gripping his weapon, was taking voracious delight in the combat. It had never been a friendly lunch-hour match, as proposed. His renowned guest—and opponent—deserved a little lesson, an overdue lesson, considering his high rank in Hitler's hierarchy. A reality check would do him some good.

These times of madness and uncertainty in the world demanded intellectual, cultural, and physical superiority. As far as Karl-Heinz was concerned, his opponent, Reinhard Heydrich, was his inferior in all three areas. Described by many as the brains behind Reichsführer-SS Himmler and the uncontested chief of the Reich's main security office, the Reichssicherheitshauptamt, Heydrich was in need of a healthy blow to his ego.

While Karl-Heinz relied on his extraordinary speed, coupled with a natural sense of craftiness, Heydrich took advantage of his longer reach and experience. But he wasn't able to counter a lightning-fast assault. Karl-Heinz struck his right arm with the blunt saber. Wild with rage, Heydrich ripped off his mask and threw it to the ground, then rubbed his arm.

Karl-Heinz removed his own mask. He wiped his sweaty forehead with the back of his sleeve and smoothed his short jet-black hair.

"That makes it eight to two if I'm not mistaken. Perhaps you'd like to stop here, Reinhard," Karl-Heinz proposed as he tested his blade's resistance.

Heydrich's clear blue eyes flashed furiously at the suggestion of a dishonorable surrender. He angrily slipped his mask over his face and assumed his on-guard stance.

Colonel Karl-Heinz Dietz couldn't decide whether to admire this man for his tenacity or hold him in contempt for his inability to accept defeat. An accomplished athlete, he appreciated a warrior's total commitment, but not if it clouded his judgment. Karl-Heinz was driven by survival instincts. He understood the importance of reevaluating a combat situation without letting pride supersede reason. He applied this philosophy to other areas of his life, as well, especially in situations where the stakes were too low to make much difference. For him, it wasn't about winning or losing. It was about being shrewd enough to survive until it came time to kill.

If only we were fencing with real swords. That would spice up this competition, he thought as he inspected the tall, lanky figure with blond hair. The man was breathing heavily and appeared to be wearing out.

"*En garde*," the general ordered.

Karl-Heinz pulled down his mask again, after giving the arrogant prick a smirk. Heydrich's aggressive moves failed to conceal the fear in his eyes. His posture was stiffer than ever.

Without further ado, Karl-Heinz took full advantage of his opponent's rigid stance and lunged. His wrist was strong yet relaxed as he orchestrated simple swings at the arm he had hit before. Heydrich bumbled on until a delayed counter-parry destabilized him and opened up a prime pathway. Karl-Heinz heaved his sword at the vulnerable torso and pinned the tip of his weapon on the general's upper abdomen. The defeated party planted his knee on the ground.

"Enough!" Heydrich yelled.

How could anyone be afraid of a man with such an embarrassingly high-pitched voice? Before Karl-Heinz had time to think about it, his opponent's mask went flying across the room. It hit one of the many paintings, which crashed to the floor. Heydrich was taking his defeat quite poorly. The general broke the heavy silence with a snap of his fingers. The butler grabbed a towel and hurried to Heydrich. The young woman approached Karl-Heinz, her head lowered.

"I assume our session is over," the colonel said.

The general replied with a string of curses muttered under his breath. Defeating a character like Heydrich required not only talent, but also bravado, as he belonged to an elite group of fencing masters. These men were the best in the country, maybe even the world. Humiliating him put one's life at risk. A single glare from this man could kill just as quickly as a bullet.

Most people would never cause Heydrich to lose face.

Karl-Heinz Dietz, however, wasn't most people.

The man's unrivaled hunting skills gave him great power. They made him far superior to the higher-ups in the system—a system with an ideology he despised as much as the way it operated. Most of those in the top ranks would have benefited from reading even a few of the books that had perished in the regime's book-burnings. Their intellectual gaps would eventually lead to the demise of Germany's empire.

Reinhard Heydrich stormed off toward the stairs and leaned on the massive railing as he struggled to climb the steps. Reaching the top, he disappeared down the corridor leading to the guest bedrooms.

The servants returned to their regular tasks, and the now solitary master of the house stood before a mirror by the door. He straightened his chin and celebrated his victory by making his signature salute.

With the tip of his sword, he traced a perfect "J." It was the first letter of the title used by those who knew Karl-Heinz and even those who had just heard of him. The title was solidified with each victory in battle, and it would follow him to the grave.

Der Jäger. The Hunter.

~ ~ ~

Half an hour later, after cooling down under relaxing showers, the two men reconvened with a carafe of wine in one of the mansion's sitting rooms. Seated on the chesterfield sofa, Heydrich had regained his composure and was masking his cold and dangerous persona behind a wall of feigned pleasantries. His host was not fooled. Their shared meal and the fencing match had served as *hors d'oeuvres* for the day. With his legs crossed on an ottoman across from his guest, Karl-Heinz was awaiting the main course.

"Lovely décor," the general said as he examined the numerous military and hunting trophies on display. "I believe they sum up your career quite nicely."

Alongside the paintings and military plaques, animal heads, from bears to antelopes and zebras, were mounted on the walls. Heydrich took a particular liking to the lion's head, its ferocious fangs on full display.

"These are mere trinkets," Karl-Heinz replied. "My most prized conquests are in my cave of wonders, but I rarely show them off."

Karl-Heinz was growing weary of looking at the man's face. How long would it take him to get to the point?

Heydrich placed his glass on the table next to the sofa. He stood up and walked over to a record player on a sideboard near double doors that led to the garden. He spent several seconds observing a swan as it glided across a man-made pond. Then he turned back to the sideboard and started going through his host's stack of seventy-eight rpm records.

"Ah, Schubert!" he exclaimed. "Would there be any harm in playing one of his sonatas during our discussion?" The first notes floated from the record player before Karl-Heinz could answer.

"I haven't come here to enjoy your food. And certainly not to give you the pleasure of schooling me in the art of fencing," Heydrich said, returning to the sofa.

Finally they were getting somewhere.

"I heard about your mission in Greece," Heydrich continued. "You managed to succeed where the Italian army fell short. I'd like to personally congratulate you for your remarkable effort."

"Flattery doesn't work on me, Reinhard. Our Italian friends have managed to make an art form of negligence and inefficiency. Cleaning up after them was a bore. I'm tired of such inconsequential assignments."

"Yes, heaven protect us from our Italian friends," Heydrich sighed as he picked up his glass of wine. "Meanwhile, our troops are facing guerilla warfare in several occupied territories."

"The Wehrmacht is a well-oiled machine as long as the enemy bends to the rules of engagement. Our large army is useless against these small movements. They're scattered, invisible, and determined."

"Hence the need for a unit as special as yours, which I'm quite proud to have created, if I say so myself."

As usual, the man was taking credit where it wasn't his to take. Karl-Heinz had single-handedly built that group. It was yet another example of Heydrich's shamelessly distorted take on reality.

"Anyway, the majority of our soldiers are busy removing Jews from Germany's sphere of influence and fighting on the Eastern Front," Heydrich continued.

"The Russian campaign is an embarrassment," Karl-Heinz interrupted, ignoring the general's mention of the Jews. They weren't his concern. "The plan is a rogue strategy. It's military suicide. The Russian winter will crush our forces. Quick battles and minimal losses, that's my idea of an intelligent war. You don't need a genie's lamp to know how the invasion to the East will end."

"You are aware that such comments border on treason?"

"Of course, but we're speaking in private, and I know you well enough to understand that you share my point of view. We both respect efficiency. Bootlicking, however, is one of the rare sports in which I do not excel."

"The generals the führer has dispatched to Russia are incompetent," Heydrich said. "Sadly, I am not steering this war. Well, not yet, in any case. But that is not why I'm here. There is another problem that requires your talents."

Heydrich picked up the black leather briefcase at his feet. He placed it on the coffee table and searched its contents.

"Reichsführer Himmler has authorized large-scale medical experiments on Jewish children."

"Sounds like an utter bore. You'll have to do better than that if you want to arouse my interest."

"Read this," Heydrich insisted as he handed him a file. "You'll be begging me for command of this mission, I assure you."

"Let's see," Karl-Heinz said as he began going through the file. He still wasn't interested. "Research center at Camp Stutthof. Jewish... Polish... Subject of experimentation... I see our scientists are having a field day with this one. A ten-year-old child? Come on, Reinhard, you can't be serious."

"Keep reading," Heydrich ordered in a tone that would not permit any further delay.

"I'm only doing this to humor you."

He scanned several pages, skeptical of their content, and then closed the document before handing it back to the general.

"Simply stunning. And it's all true?"

"Every word of it. I was indifferent when the reichsführer recruited me for Project Übermensch. But the experiment's success has persuaded me to take action."

"What kind of action?"

"The reichsführer wants to see how this guinea pig develops. I do not."

"Oh my, a difference of opinion? That'll cause a stir in the upper ranks," Karl-Heinz mocked.

"Spare me your little quips. The experiment wouldn't have upset me if the first genetically superior human were Aryan. But this is a Jewish child. The symbolic implication is morally unbearable and politically disastrous. And so I'm charging you with the task of eliminating him. Of course I am counting on your discretion. Otherwise..."

"No need for threats. You have provided me with a unique challenge. That is more than enough to guarantee my full cooperation. When shall I act?"

"You will wait for my signal. The subject is still undergoing tests. It would be unwise to intervene in the middle of the research. The scientists predict their creature will be ready for combat in a few months. Perhaps his death could take place during a training session."

"I hope the boy is as dangerous as you think he is. Killing a ten-year-old child isn't something I'd brag about."

"According to what I've read in this file, he will give you a run for your money."

Karl-Heinz stroked his lips and smiled, giving his assent.

"Very well," the general concluded, slapping his thighs. "I am returning to Prague with the assurance that this matter will be taken care of."

With his briefcase in hand, Reinhard Heydrich stood up. Karl-Heinz followed him to the door, where the butler helped him with his long leather coat. Finally, the general put on his cap with the Panzer insignia. He had reclaimed the proud bearing that had been wounded in the midday face-off.

"When the time comes for you to go to Poland, you will have complete command over the local authorities. Do your best not to make a mockery of this mission."

"You know that's not my style," Karl-Heinz said.

As soon as Heydrich's car arrived to take him to his Messerschmitt aircraft, the colonel returned to the sitting room to go over the file left by his guest. He felt an uncustomary excitement. Was he holding the very thing he had been waiting for all these years: a mission worthy of his abilities?

"Maria, come in here!"

The servant presented herself in the doorway.

"Shall I clean up, sir?" she asked. She had always seemed a little frightened of him. There was nothing bad about that, Karl-Heinz thought.

"Yes, you shall," he confirmed without taking his eyes off the precious file.

The young woman passed by him, picking up the wine glasses and placing them on her tray. She then walked to the sideboard and put the record back in its sleeve. In her haste to get the job done, she knocked over a lamp but caught it before it crashed to the floor.

"Nice reflexes," Karl-Heinz remarked, amused.

He now saw the young woman in a new light. A pretty little face, small waist, and generous bosom. She certainly had her strengths.

"Pardon me, sir," she said, sounding anxious.

"No harm done. While you're at it, get rid of that cheap wine," he ordered, pointing to the carafe. "Find a nice bottle of Bordeaux in my personal reserve, and bring a glass to my bedroom."

Maria complied and slipped away, head lowered. He grabbed the file and followed her, playing with the key hanging from the gold chain attached to one of his belt loops. His eyes rested on the young woman's lower back.

Such a natural beauty would deserve his full attention one day soon. But for the moment, his excitement over the mission trumped his desire to conquer his housemaid. As the latter veered off toward the kitchen, Karl-Heinz headed down a narrow corridor beside the staircase. He reached a door, which he opened with the key that he kept with him at all times.

He entered a room darker than night and searched for the switch.

A simple click, and light flooded his cave of wonders. He closed the door just as quickly and gazed at the walls, his hands on his hips. He was overcome with the pride he felt every time he visited this holy haven.

A dozen mummified heads displayed on heavy wooden plaques bore stupefied and grotesque expressions. On each forehead the letter "J" had been carved with a knife. Below each trophy was a metal plate with the vanquished person's name.

What a collection! Only exceptional prey deserved a place in this hall of honor. Every one of them had given him a run for his money. All nationalities and religions were represented. In the colonel's eyes, every man was created equal. At least that was the case when faced with death at the hands of the Jäger.

He searched the walls for just the right place. He stopped at a spot between a recently vanquished member of the Romanian resistance and an Iranian soldier. Both formidable opponents.

"If that fool Heydrich is telling the truth—if the new target lives up to the general's promises—he'll be a fine addition to this prized collection," he told the mute heads.

He opened the file and skimmed the pages for the target's name. Finding it, he patted the empty space on the wall.

"You shall be up here quite soon, Eytan Morgenstern."

CHAPTER 7

Jeremy didn't know what to do. He couldn't contain his excitement or his bewilderment. He had a thousand questions to ask the grinning bald bloke in front of him. But the questions were all tangled together, so he didn't do anything. He just stared at his friend in combat pants, matching jacket, khaki crew-neck T-shirt, and lumberjack boots. The Jolly Green Giant was back, all right.

"Looks like you're in pretty good shape," Eytan said, helping Greg to his feet. "In the future, I'd appreciate it if you didn't try to kill my agents."

Agent? Greg? The information didn't compute.

"Jeremy?" He could see Eytan's hand moving back and forth in front of his face, but he was still feeling entirely out of it.

"He's in a state of shock," Greg said with a half smile.

Yes, I need to reboot, Jeremy said to himself. He blinked, shook his head, and drew a deep breath.

"Uh, yeah, sorry. I'm here," he managed to get out.

"Wonderful," Eytan responded. "Load up the little one. We're leaving, pronto."

Jeremy started to protest. He wanted to enjoy their long-awaited reunion.

The giant put a friendly yet firm hand on his shoulder. "I realize you have a million questions. But for now, you need to stay quiet and get your little girl ready to leave. Greg, you and I are expected."

"By whom?" Jeremy asked.

"You clearly missed the part about waiting till later to get your questions answered. What you need to know now is that we're going to meet up with your wife. Get a move on. And grab that bag by the front door. I've packed it with clothes for you and your family, diapers and all. I even have Annie's car seat."

Upon hearing mention of Jackie, Jeremy swept Annie into his arms and raced up the stairs on the heels of the unlikely duo.

~ ~ ~

The smell of gas attacked her nostrils, filled her lungs, and made her stomach queasy. She could barely hold back the urge to vomit. She felt dizzy, as though she were waking up with the world's worst hangover. She tried to open her eyes but reconsidered after being blinded by the lights in the room. She couldn't pull herself off the floor either. She couldn't even string two coherent thoughts together.

"Stay on the floor. Your attacker shot you with sedatives, and you won't regain your strength for another thirty minutes or so. I didn't have the right drugs to get you back on your feet, so I made do with fuel oil. Do you need to inhale some more?"

Jackie managed to sit upright. She massaged her temples and blinked several times in hopes of regaining her sight as quickly as possible. The man addressing her didn't sound like the same individual she had spoken with on the phone. This voice was younger, softer, not as deep.

"Where am I?" she mumbled.

"With friends in a safe place."

"I apologize. I didn't have time to give you the lowdown over the phone," said another man whose presence Jackie hadn't detected. "So I had to rely on your memory."

This man was definitely her mysterious caller. She was dealing with not one, but two strangers. Jackie opened her eyes and found she could see now. She looked at the round face of a man who appeared to be in his sixties, maybe older. His cheeks and forehead were lined with deep wrinkles. He was wearing black tweed pants, a wool turtleneck, and a thick dark jacket. Despite his portliness, he looked strong.

"The defective handcuff that allowed us to escape from the Consortium's facility in Belgium two years ago."

"Exactly. And we both know that the only person other than you and your husband who was aware of this glitch was Eytan."

A ding indicated a new text message.

"I'll leave you with the doc. We'll see each other later."

Rattled by the mention of Belgium and the Consortium, Jackie regained full use of her cognitive abilities. She jumped to her feet but wasn't able to balance herself and started to topple forward. She felt two strong arms wrap around her and lower her gently to the floor. The stranger and her surroundings were coming into sharp focus. At first Jackie thought she was in a jail cell because the room was so narrow—a nightmare for someone who was claustrophobic. A small cot with a thin mattress was pushed against the steel wall. A single light bulb surrounded by a metal cage gave off a harsh light. Large bolts ran along the walls and all around the door. The pieces of the puzzle were coming together. She knew for sure that she was at sea, probably on a fishing boat.

She brought her attention back to the man who was still holding her. He was tall with fairly broad shoulders. And she was blown away by his good looks: the symmetrical face, the strong jaw, and a smile that belonged in a toothpaste commercial. His eyes, moreover, twinkled with a hint of mischievousness. He could easily have played the leading role in a romantic comedy. He was the kind of doctor—if that was his profession—who could make a girl bang her head against the wall just so she'd have an excuse to make an appointment. Actually, she saw several of the very same features in this stranger that made her fall for Jeremy.

The man gave her a wink.

"I've got you," he assured her with a soothing voice. "Let's get better acquainted."

~ ~ ~

Jeremy surveyed the street, which was getting darker by the minute, while Eytan and Greg inspected their attacker's van behind the house. Nestled in her father's arms, Annie was sleeping peacefully.

He took in a chestful of fresh air and let his eyes wander over his neighbors' homes. Jackie and he had settled in this suburb for a variety of reasons. It gave them a real taste of small town life but was a reasonable distance from Manhattan. They hardly ever went into the city, though. For the most part, they were satisfied with the county fairs, the summer band concerts, the opportunities to fish, the numerous bicycle trails in the area's parks, the high school football games, and the holiday light festivals.

Too bad there was no Big Trouble Festival. Jeremy figured he could organize the whole thing himself. "In one night, I've been held hostage by a geek," he muttered. "My house has been invaded by ninjas, and a Mossad assassin has shown up to take me to only God knows where."

He sighed and held his daughter a little tighter.

Mr. Adams, his old British neighbor, was walking down the street. The tall man looked like Prince Philip, the duke of Edinburgh. His Welsh corgi was with him. Jeremy pledged to invite the retiree over for tea once his issues were sorted out. But with his luck, the man was probably an MI6 agent ready to pounce on him with a pair of sugar tongs.

The bookseller was wondering whether he'd ever be able to lead a normal life again when he felt Eytan's hand on his shoulder. Startled, he turned to face his friend.

"You ready? We're leaving," the Kidon agent whispered.

He took one last look at his white house, which still needed some touch-ups, and noticed the green plastic garden table he hadn't had time to put away.

"Lead the way," he replied, surprised to hear a touch of excitement in his voice.

Fifteen minutes later, Greg was behind the wheel of their van, repeatedly glancing in the rearview mirror as he drove. Eytan was in the passenger seat, and Jeremy was in the back, with Annie sleeping peacefully in her car seat.

Their reunion was nothing like the hundreds of scenarios Jeremy had envisioned. He had seen them sipping beers in his backyard on a hot summer night. He'd listen to the stories told by the eighty-year-old man in a thirty-year-old body. They'd amuse themselves with witty banter and then confide their plans for the future. They'd talk well into the wee hours of the night, like blood brothers. Because over the course of the time they had spent together, that's exactly how Jeremy had come to see Eytan—as family.

But this stupid secret-agent business had messed up his fantasies, and Jeremy knew he had to face facts. Eytan's life didn't allow him to make any courtesy visits, and emotional heart-to-hearts were never—and would never be—his thing. If Eytan was there, it was because of a crisis. While Jeremy didn't understand what was going on yet, he knew for sure that it was a big deal. He judged it wise to save his questions for later.

Eytan spent the first minutes of the trip glued to his phone, shooting off one text after another. Once he had put the device away, he turned to Jeremy and shelled out a few veiled explanations.

"So Greg is a Kidon agent? An operative who specializes in kidnaps and assassination?" Jeremy was aghast.

Greg nodded.

"I didn't know how the Consortium would react after our European road trip," Eytan said. "So I had to keep an eye on you and Jackie."

"Damn Greg, I didn't see that one coming."

Judging by the driver's smile, Jeremy had paid him a compliment.

"You know we don't go around wearing badges," Eytan said. "The more unlikely we look, the better."

"Yeah, that makes sense. And you took care of the men charged with killing me and Annie?"

"Yep. Four commandos and one driver. Their bodies are stockpiled behind you."

"Gross! You know I have a baby back here," Jeremy exclaimed as he turned around and saw the huge mound covered with blankets. "Did these guys have anything to do with Bleiberg? Did you really have to kill them?"

"I don't know who they were taking orders from," Eytan said. "I only know that they were military guys, and they were no angels. I had to eliminate them. By the way, you'll have to redo the wallpaper in Annie's bedroom."

"Great," Jeremy grumbled. He turned his attention to the road."Hey, is it just me, or are we heading to the beach?"

"Very observant," Greg teased as he parked on the side of the road.

"Screw you," Jeremy replied.

"Save your lover's spat for later." Eytan intervened with an authority that immediately ended the interaction. "Our new ride awaits us."

Jeremy unbuckled Annie and got out of the van with her. He glanced around, taking in the lighthouse and the sound of the waves.

Greg shot off in the direction of a pontoon and disappeared in the darkness. Eytan leaned against the hood of the van. He took a cigar out of his jacket and stuck it between his teeth.

"I'm glad we have this chance to catch up," he told Jeremy as he lit a match.

He took a long drag of his cigar and gave his signature smile, which Jeremy had thought he might never see again. The bastard loved to put on a good show.

"Me too. But listen, buddy, I've got about a million questions for you."

Eytan snorted and let out one of his his goofy laughs.

"I promise to answer each and every one of them when the time comes. But we have to act fast, so just go with the flow and button up. Got it?"

"Got it."

"A friend of mine will take you to a fishing boat where you'll be reunited with Jackie.

"You're not coming?" Jeremy felt his anxiety rise.

"I am, but first I have some cleanup to do." The giant pointed to the van. "A half hour, tops."

"Well, this mission is bringing out your typical game face, I see."

"It's more than a typical mission, Jeremy."

"Oh really? What is it then?"

The giant took another drag of his cigar.

"This is war."

CHAPTER 8

With his attaché case in hand, Titus Bramble hurried down the hallways of the Pentagon. Soldiers crossing his path gave respectful salutes, but Titus continued on without acknowledging a single one. His position didn't merit this kind of greeting, but practically everyone knew about his glorious past in the military and treated him as one of their own. On any ordinary day, he would have returned their salutes, but this wasn't an ordinary day.

The head of the paramilitary operations branch of the CIA's Special Activities Division did not appreciate impromptu meetings. An obsessive-compulsive planner, he hated being caught unprepared. The meeting he was racing rather ungracefully toward had been hastily called by the highest command. No one had had the decency to give him the agenda or a list of attendees. This displeased the former Marine, whose feats in battle were written in blood deep in the jungles of Vietnam and South America.

In those days, Titus had a thick neck and a solid build, both of which had only grown tougher over the years. His body bore many scars, including an intimidating one on his face delivered by a Viet Cong bayonet. It started on his forehead and ran down his right cheek, but by some miracle, his eye had been spared. The North Vietnamese warrior had paid for it with a knife to the heart. Titus had long ago traded in his camouflage for expensive tailor-made suits. And these days he used his dagger to stab an entirely different breed in the back—those who lacked political savvy. New battlefield, new strategy, same philosophy: kill or be killed. That's where he found his drive to stay one step ahead.

The man gave the aide-de-camp who met him outside the conference room a cold look. The snot-nosed brat looked well-groomed and in good shape, probably thanks to Pilates.

He wore his uniform with the arrogance of someone whose only experience of war was viewing satellite images on a giant screen while seated in a comfortable chair. A power-hungry good-for-nothing with a cushy job, Titus thought as the boy extended a hesitant hand and introduced himself.

"Lieutenant Thomasson. Everyone's waiting. Please follow me."

"Negative," Titus replied, not budging an inch. "First give me the names and positions of each person in that room."

"I don't have orders to do that."

"You've just been given the order. Now respond."

"But, uh... Well, there's a general from the Marine Corps, an envoy from the White House, and two other men. I don't know any of their names. I've just been asked to..."

"That's enough," Titus interrupted. "Open the door." He needed to know just who those men were.

The lieutenant did a half-turn on his left foot and flashed a white badge with an American eagle past a sensor, which turned green. He opened the door and stepped aside."I won't be attending the..."

Before the man could finish, Titus had marched into the room, determined to impose his authority. The door closed behind him.

"Bramble, we were afraid you'd forgotten how to get around in the Pentagon. We've been waiting for you." The man rose from his chair at the end of the rectangular table.

"Lamont," Titus replied.

Travis Lamont walked over to the CIA representative. They shook hands, and Titus relaxed a bit. This was the White House envoy Thomasson had mentioned. He had survived both Republican and Democratic administrations. In fact, this portly fiftyish man in a tight gray suit had been a top advisor to three presidents. Despite his balding head and ill-fitting clothes, which made him look unkempt, Lamont was a savvy and prominent technology expert. He had a significant voice in the nation's major decisions when it came to field operations. Titus and he had known each other for quite some time and had worked together on several projects, with no backstabbing thus far.

"Please, have a seat."

"Why was I not informed of the agenda ahead of time?" Titus scowled.

"You know how DC works. Everything's decided at the last minute. Sit. We're about to begin," Lamont urged as he returned to his place at the table, where three other men were seated.

Titus took a chair next to Lamont, placed his attaché case on the table, and pulled out a tablet in a brown leather sleeve.

"Now that everyone's here, I'll make the introductions," Lamont continued. "Across from us is General Bennington from the Marines Corps. On our right are Jonathon Cavendish, president of H-Plus Dynamics, and his assistant... Let's see..." Lamont shuffled through his notes. "Ah, here it is: Fergus Hennessy."

Titus examined the men at the table.

First, General Bennington: approximately his own age, similar build, gray buzz cut, green eyes, strong jaw. Clearly self-confident, versed in the system. If it weren't for the missing scar, he could have been a look-alike. He had a brown dossier in front of him.

Next, Cavendish. He was in a stylish, well-made suit— maybe Armani. Thirty to thirty-five years old, thin, bony face, crooked nose. He appeared to be tall, but he didn't seem to be long on personality. Titus thought he might be a British expat. He had never heard of H-Plus Dynamics. They were probably one of the military's fortunate suppliers. Their CEOs were frequently seen with generals on the golf course and at fund-raisers for various pet projects. Suppliers were required to submit bids for the large national defense contracts, but the schmoozing never hurt.

Last, the assistant: a short man, about five-foot-two, maybe forty to forty-five, healthy-looking, piercing black eyes, square jaw. The subordinate appeared to be more at ease than his boss. He was certainly more quick-witted. Fergus: Scottish or of Scottish descent.

"What's the meeting's objective?" Titus asked.

"Direct, as usual," Lamont teased. "We've asked you here because we've encountered a problem that requires your assistance, and..."

"What problem?" Titus interrupted.

"This one," General Bennington replied.

He slid the dossier toward Titus with such force, it almost hit him. Titus opened the file and found two photographs. He examined both of them. The first one was a three-quarter view from behind of a bald tank-like figure in a green army jacket. The second one, taken from above, was of the same guy, this time wearing a T-shirt. Titus could see him from the front in this photo. He was chatting with a black man in athletic gear.

"If these photos are from the army's tech department, it's time to hire a real photographer," he said dryly. "How does this concern me?"

The general was wearing a tense smile and fidgeting. The two civilians weren't saying anything. Lamont intervened.

"The two photographs were taken thirty years apart. Our facial recognition program is bullet-proof. It's the same individual in both of these images, but his looks haven't changed in three decades."

"So why are you interested in this particular person? What does he have to do with the military?"

"This man is an Israeli agent named Eytan Morgenstern."

"Doesn't ring any bells. Could there be a glitch in the system?"

"There's no glitch," the general said. "And you should know more about these photos than anyone else, Bramble, because they came from one of *your* units."

The main players in the room exchanged glances. A long silence set in, too long for Titus's liking.

"Let's be clear, about this. No one is blaming the CIA for anything." Lamont was trying to be conciliatory.

"What would we be accused of?"

"Of withholding information that's imperative for national security." Bennington said. "I should point out that we haven't had access to the entire file, just these images."

Was Bennington really questioning the CIA's competence and even its loyalty?

"I demand an apology and an explanation," Titus barked. "How did you get your hands on these photographs? And what are civilians doing at this meeting?"

"Let's calm down. Clearly, the general wasn't thinking before he spoke," Lamont said, giving Bennington a severe look. "I didn't ask you here to put you or anyone else on trial. You see, we're developing a special military project that our friends in the Marines will spearhead. These gentlemen from H-Plus Dynamics are undertaking the research, and Morgenstern could play a vital role in said program." He turned to Cavendish. "Jonathan, could you please tell us a bit more?"

A seemingly indifferent observer to this point, Cavendish straightened in his chair and cleared his throat.

"Our company is conducting studies in hopes of improving the physical performance of the nation's fighting forces," he began cautiously. "If what we've seen in the photos provided by the general is true, if this Israeli agent, indeed, does not age, our project would benefit greatly if we could conduct medical exams on him."

As an experienced public speaker—an important quality for someone in his position—Titus knew all about talking without actually saying anything, and he recognized it immediately in Cavendish's explanation.

"Well that didn't clarify things at all," he said.

"There's nothing else to tell you," Lamont said. "We need this Morgenstern and for that, we need your help."

"All you had to do was ask," Titus said. "If he's a Mossad agent, that will complicate the interception. We're not on the best of terms with Israel. I'll see what I can do, but it may take some time."

"Well there you go," Lamont responded. He was sounding cheerier. "It always works out when all the cards are on the table."

"You do understand that I'll also be looking into how you acquired those photos," Titus said.

"Go right ahead," Bennington responded. "There was really no intrigue. Information circulates all the time. Aren't we on the same team here?"

Titus would need to keep an eye on that man.

"Gentlemen, seeing as we've reached an understanding, I would like to end the meeting," Titus said as he returned the unused tablet to his briefcase.

He stood up, as did the four others. He shook the hands of the two corporate pawns and the nasty general and headed toward the door of the conference room. Lamont joined him and opened it with the help of his badge. He extended his hand. Although Titus was feeling anxious and irritated, he thought it wise to accept the gesture.

"Find this guy, and bring him to us alive," Lamont said. "Time is of the essence. This is a crucial project. I'm not joking. If we don't get results on your end, we'll have to take more aggressive measures."

Typical Lamont—friendly, but making maximum use of his authority. The underlying threat was clear. Without unconditional collaboration, Titus could expect an early retirement—without the cushy pension.

"You can count on me," he promised.

Titus Bramble hurried out.

~ ~ ~

Fifteen minutes later, after a debriefing session, Jonathan Cavendish and Fergus Hennessy arrived at the limo that was waiting for them. The chauffeur got out and rushed to open the door.

Hennessy held out his heavy briefcase to Cavendish, who took it immediately.

"How was I, sir?" the latter asked anxiously.

"You lack confidence, but that will come with experience," Hennessy replied as he lit a cigarette.

"You've started up again?" Cavendish asked.

"Yes," Hennessy replied. "Electronic cigarettes didn't cut it. One day I'll quit."

"What do you think the CIA will do?"

"I have no idea, and I couldn't care less. Mr. Morg and I have a little affair to settle, and setting America's most elite intelligence agency on him gives me a great deal of pleasure. Plus this little cat-and-mouse game will work to our advantage. Two birds, one stone." He smiled as he threw his cigarette out the window of the limo.

CHAPTER 9

Jeremy was doing his best to keep Annie dry and warm as the motorboat sped toward a faint light offshore, spraying water all the way. The baby and he had boarded the nautical vessel a few minutes earlier, along with Greg and an older man with a husky voice and craggy face. The older man, who had introduced himself as Eli, was steering the boat.

They soon glimpsed a fishing trawler. Reaching it, Eli maneuvered the motorboat next to the larger vessel. Greg was the first to climb aboard via a rope ladder attached to the rail. He held his arms out to Jeremy, who, after a moment of hesitation, entrusted him with Annie so he could hoist himself onto the deck.

Without wasting any time, the man named Eli stepped on the gas and headed back toward the shore.

"Hand her back!" Jeremy ordered.

Greg complied. Holding babies probably wasn't Greg's thing anyway, Jeremy figured.

"Sorry about what I did earlier, but I was just following orders," Greg said.

"I get it, but now that you bring it up..."

Jeremy shifted his daughter to his left arm. He pulled back his right arm and delivered a punch to Greg's jaw.

"Now we're even," Jeremy said.

"I guess I deserved that," Greg said, rubbing his jaw. "But don't try it again. Come on. Let's go inside. Your baby girl must be getting cold."

"Mess with me any more, and I will be trying that again—trying it and nailing it. I still don't trust you a hundred percent. So you go first. I'll follow."

They headed toward the cockpit and descended into the crew's quarters. The two men followed a passageway with heavy metal doors on both sides before ending up in a small canteen room.

Jackie was there, sitting at a table with a steaming cup of coffee. She was giggling like a schoolgirl at jokes delivered by some dude who looked like he was straight off the pages of *GQ*, the kind of guy whose hair was perfectly styled before he rolled out of bed in the morning. Jeremy bet he had a year-round tan, not from tanning booths, but from spending his winters in the Caribbean. He was sitting down, so Jeremy couldn't see exactly how tall he was, but he looked lean and lanky. Guys weren't Jeremy's thing, but he had to admit the man looked sexy in his jeans and black sweater. And no man that hot needed to be shooting the breeze with the woman he loved.

Jackie turned toward the door. When she saw her husband and daughter, she shot up and rushed to them. She gave Jeremy a tender kiss and swept Annie into her arms.

GQ boy stood up and held out a hand. "Dr. Avi Lafner."

And a doctor to boot, Jeremy thought. He had hoped the man couldn't read or write.

"Jeremy Corbin." No handshake.

"I know! Eytan's told me so much about you," Avi replied.

He actually seemed a little star-struck. Why was that? Maybe the guy wasn't so bad, after all.

"We made the necessary preparations for your little girl. I've brought formula and baby food, plus plenty of toys. We even have a travel crib for her."

"Thanks, Avi," Jackie said, smiling.

She pulled a lock of hair behind her ear, a gesture that seemed entirely too flirtatious as far as Jeremy was concerned.

"I'll give you some time to yourselves while we wait for Eli to come back with Eytan. The baby's probably hungry, and you two have some catching up to do." The doctor and Greg left.

"Alone at last," Jeremy declared as soon as the two men disappeared. "So, Mrs. Walls-Corbin, it looks like I haven't been sorely missed!"

"Oh my, you're jealous."

"Me? Who would I be jealous of?"

Jackie let out a little laugh and started tending to the baby. She changed her diaper and pulled a bottle out of the bag Avi had left.

"What's Greg doing here?" she asked, giving Annie her bottle.

"Let's get Annie settled, and we can fill each other in."

After Jackie had fed Annie and put her in the travel crib, they sat down at the table, coffee mugs in hand. They spent the next fifteen minutes recounting the events of their respective evenings. The attack at the sheriff's department, the crazy basement hostage situation—no detail was spared. They spent several minutes discussing Greg's surprise identity. One thing was certain. The Walls-Corbin family was in serious trouble, and neither one of them had any idea what it was.

"Here," Jeremy said, handing his wife the bag Eytan had packed for them. "Eytan said you have to get into street clothes."

Jackie took out a pair of jeans, a gray crew-neck sweater, and a pair of boots with flat heels. She put on a wool hat and completed her metamorphosis by slipping on a black bomber jacket.

Avi returned, followed by Eli and Greg. Eytan came in last. He had to duck to pass through the doorway. Jeremy was hoping they would now get an explanation.

"The two of you good?" he asked.

Jackie and Jeremy nodded.

"Perfect. I'll introduce you to everyone. Eli Karman is my case officer at Mossad."

"Was," the man corrected.

A flash of irritation flickered on Eytan's face.

"Avi Lafner is—*was*—a physician for our division."

"Chief," GQ cut in. "Chief physician."

"As for Greg, he was responsible for ensuring your safety once you moved to New Jersey. Jeremy, you might have noticed that I chose my geekiest agent."

"Unlike my two friends here, I have no corrections to make," the geek said with a grin.

"Nice to meet everyone," Jeremy replied. "But uh, we think we need a little more info. Right, honey?"

"Yeah, that would be nice."

"Of course," the Kidon agent said. "It's a long story."

CHAPTER 10

Heavy dark clouds hung over the city. A bad storm seemed imminent, but a little rain had never rattled the queen's subjects. They were known for their grace under fire. Some seventy years earlier, these people had seen German bombers spew iron and steel. The British Empire had bravely resisted the fascist horde stampeding across Europe. And in the end, the Brits had been victorious.

Leaning on the railing of his apartment balcony, a cup of tea in hand, Eytan was feeling ashamed of his sentimental thoughts. Despite his constant struggle to change with the times, he was like most other former soldiers who gave in to the siren call of a bygone era. It was difficult for him to look at this city without seeing the demolished buildings and the allied forces marching through the streets. At times he even thought he could hear the whistle of V-2 rockets launched from across the channel. That's why he avoided London whenever possible. And so this little place on the Thames served only as a *pied-à-terre* on his rare visits to England.

Eytan admittedly had a weakness for chic hotels, but he preferred to hide out in this minimally decorated apartment when he was in London. And if bitter memories struck harder in this place than elsewhere, so be it.

The first drops plopped against the railing. The drops soon became a shower. Eytan closed his eyes, thrust his head back, and breathed. There was nothing like cold water to snap him out of his morbid reverie and bring him back to the present.

He finished his tea in one gulp, went back into the apartment, and walked over to the table, where a pile of papers was sitting. The papers were the culmination of a six-month tracking mission. A tricky mission, but one that had paid off. Without Avi Lafner's help and his many contacts in the medical world, none of this would have been possible. After many weeks of cross-referencing and hours on the phone, the physician had finally found the eagerly awaited address.

Eytan took his cargo jacket off the back of the chair and looked at his pistol.

"No need," he thought. "I'd rather do this with bare hands."

As he left the apartment, Eytan was whistling Supertramp: "It's Raining Again."

On this day, his target would have something much more unpleasant than water raining down on him.

~ ~ ~

With his forehead glued to the taxi window, Ian Jenkins could almost glimpse the end of the tunnel. After six months of recovery, one that had been much harder than expected, he'd soon enjoy full use of his leg. During his ligament reconstruction (not surprising, given the nature of the injury), they'd had to clean up his bullet-shattered kneecap and replace a destroyed meniscus.

As CEO of a start-up IT-service company specializing in logistics, the young man had learned the importance of patience, which previously hadn't meant much to him. He'd come from a posh British family that boasted a long line of entrepreneurs and politicians. With his intelligence, perfect academic record, and natural poise, Ian had assumed that his career would be smooth sailing. Then the Consortium hired him, and his ego grew tenfold. The organization's primary goal was to influence the evolution of the human race and bring order to a chaotic world. And they were interested in *him*!

That was, of course, until his disastrous mission in Prague. When briefed by Cypher—the pseudonym for the secret society's leader—he had been led to believe that the task would be a walk in the park. Ian was to reach an agreement with an agent of the Israeli forces whose mission was tracking and killing war criminals. The terms of the arrangement were simple. In exchange for the agent's collaboration, the Consortium would release a captive who happened to be one of the agent's closest companions. Ian had been given bodyguards and the assurance that the agent would be unarmed. Needless to say, the bodyguards didn't lift a finger, and the agent had come packed with more weapons than two dozen vendors at a gun show.

Money had eased some of the unpleasantness of his injuries, but it hadn't erased his newfound fear. The incident had put him in the crosshairs of the bald six-foot-five killer. And if that weren't enough, his new friends had thrown him under the bus.

Despite the pain inflicted by the bullet fired in the broken-down warehouse, Ian had picked up snippets of conversation between his attacker and the master of the Consortium. Cypher had mentioned the young Englishman's arrogance and the need to teach him a lesson. The star student had gotten the message loud and clear. That was the thing about a kneecapping. It had an uncanny way of inspiring Zen-like reflection. Ian now had a wiser take on caution, humility, and his own vulnerability.

All he had to figure out was how to take revenge while keeping a low profile. How could he move on without making waves? He hadn't heard from the Consortium. And God only knew what had happened to the giant psychopath.

Ian Jenkins was reflecting on that very thought as he headed to his last physical therapy session, a milestone he had been looking forward to for months. The clouds above the buildings he was passing told him that it would soon be raining. Because his joint pain flared with the humidity, he was weighing the idea of leaving England for a dry, sunny country.

"We're here, sir. That'll be twenty-three pounds," the cabby informed him.

Ian took his wallet out of his leather jacket and gave the driver thirty pounds. Not bothering to wait for his change, he pulled the door handle and climbed out.

He tried to place as little weight on his bad leg as possible, but it still made a cracking sound that reminded him of a twig snapping. It wasn't painful, but he was always afraid that his leg would give out.

Ian entered the exclusive Chelsea-based club. He went down a hallway and entered a room next to the fitness area. He stripped to his blue boxers with green polka dots and carefully put his clothes on hangers. He left the changing quarters and walked into the adjacent room, where he lay down on a massage table. He could no longer stand the sight of the thing, the very symbol of his painful therapy sessions.

Once settled on his stomach, Ian nestled his head in the face port for the very last time. He closed his eyes as he awaited the physical therapist. He was feeling something close to bliss. This final session would validate all his hard work and bring an end to the worst chapter of his career.

Someone grabbed both of his calves. Ian flinched and opened his eyes. "You startled me," he said, staring at the gray linoleum floor. I didn't hear you come in.

The therapist grunted and touched the back of Ian's knees. He kneaded Ian's thigh muscles and ligaments and then grabbed his ankle and rolled it around, testing its movement and flexibility.

"The knee looks good, but as for everything else, I'm afraid you're not out of the woods yet, my poor friend."

He knew that voice. Fuck, not *him*...

Ian tried to turn around, but the giant held his head firmly in the face port. "Did you really think I messed you up for the simple pleasure of seeing you humiliated?"

"That wasn't your plan?" Ian managed to say. He was shaking now.

"By putting you in an OR, I knew I'd have an opportunity—a small one—to track you down," the giant clarified. "Getting admitted to a German clinic under a false name, while clever, was not enough to keep me from finding you. You can imagine how many orthopedic surgeries are performed every day across the entire European continent. A friend once told me that the secret to good health was smoking, drinking, and, most of all, no physical exercise. Trust me, after all those files we had to sift through, I believe it!"

"You checked every single file related to my type of operation in all of Europe?" Ian asked, his head still stuck in the face port. He was as amazed as he was terrified.

"Persistence is in my blood. You'd have figured that out for yourself eventually, but I don't like to leave anything to chance."

The giant finally released the downward pressure on his victim's head, only to grab him by the hair and force him to sit up. He pulled him off the table and dragged him to a corner of the room.

"Here we go. This will be perfect," the giant declared as he propped Ian against a wall. He squatted next to Ian and looked him in the eye. Then he wrapped his arm around his neck.

"What are you going to do to me?" Ian croaked, struggling to breathe.

"Relax," the killer said as he took out his cell phone.

He nestled his huge head against Ian's and held the device in front of them.

"Say cheese," he ordered, flashing a grin. "You know, I hate cell phones sometimes. Such a nuisance when you're trying to get something done. But I have to confess, I'm really getting into selfies. I might even create a Facebook page. What do you think?"

The giant examined the photo and showed it to Ian. He looked like a happy camper. Ian looked freaked out. Then the operative released his captive and watched as Ian tried to catch his breath.

"Now we're buddies—or is that friends?" the giant announced as soon as Ian was breathing normally. "But I won't be tagging you right away. You understand."

Then, just as quickly as he had let go, the killer shoved Ian against the wall and took him by the throat again. He raised Ian off the ground by the neck.

"I guess I should fill you in on what's happening, since you still look clueless. From what I know about the Consortium, they like to keep an eye on their people. As of today, you're my mole. As soon as Cypher contacts you, I need to know. If you don't do what I ask, I'll be sending this photo to your boss before I even Tweet it or share it—whatever. I think the big chief of your secret society would get the wrong idea—or maybe the right idea—about our little pact. And that wouldn't be so good for you, considering my talk with Cypher in Prague. He wasn't so happy with you, if I remember correctly."

In keeping with his grab-and-release strategy, the giant freed Ian but stayed within arm's reach. Another round of gasping for air followed.

"How do you know he'll contact me? I haven't heard from anyone at the Consortium since Prague." Eytan could see Ian steeling himself for another choke hold.   "Cypher may have been unhappy with you, but he'll use you again. If he learns about our pact, you could try to tell him what happened here, but he's not the kind of man who's easily convinced, and he doesn't like taking risks. He'll make you disappear in no time. And if you ever double-cross me, I'll take a little longer making you disappear. You and I will have some fun first. Got it?"

Ian took a moment to evaluate his situation. His new pal hadn't given him much in the way of options. His idyllic career as an up-and-comer in an elite secret society had been smashed. Considering his vulnerable position, Ian opted for the better of two unappealing alternatives.

"Got it," he mumbled.

"I knew you were a smart man," the giant said.

He took out a second phone and gave it to his temporary ally. The latter took it, clearly still on the defensive.

"If you need me, use this. It's a burner. I'm counting on you," the giant said, leaving as stealthily as he had come.

Ian slid to the floor. Tears rolled down his cheeks, but they were quickly chased away by the relief of having once again survived a hellish encounter. Reminded of the pain he had suffered in Prague, he was perfectly fine with the relatively mild panic attack he was now experiencing. He focused on calming his breathing. He stood up and braced himself on the massage table before heading back to the changing room. Buttoning his shirt proved to be a difficult task, as his fingers seemed to have a mind of their own. Before he could finish, the phone left by his attacker rang. He jumped, looked at it, and took the call.

"Yes?"

"Jenkins, I forgot to tell you..."

"What?" Ian said, feeling his blood pressure rise again.

"Nice boxers."

CHAPTER 11

MEANWHILE, IN A SURBURB OF TEL AVIV

The man sneaked down the hall, trying not to alert the security guard slouched in his chair at the front desk on the other side of the clinic lobby. The place was deserted this late at night. Absolute discretion was required for his plan to succeed. Like ripping off an adhesive strip, the execution would be quick and precise, but not painless. Definitely not painless.

The catlike shadow glanced at the guard. He was watching a movie on his laptop, his legs propped on the desk. Focusing on the visitors' benches, the man tiptoed toward his victim.

"Tonight's your last night," he whispered when he reached his target. "I didn't want it to come to this, but you're a stubborn son of bitch, and you've given me no choice. You've been trying to poison me for months. You must have known that if I survived, I'd take my sweet revenge."

Tightening his grip on the Philips screwdriver, the man felt a wave of pleasure surge through his body. It was time.

Just as he was poised to act, he felt a vibration in the pocket of his white lab coat. Cursing, he fumbled for the cell phone. Too late. The ringing had already filled the lobby. He let go of the screwdriver, and it fell to the floor with a loud clack.

The night guard sprang from his chair and looked in the direction of the noise.

The intruder knew he had to act fast.

"Is there a problem, doctor?" the guard asked.

"Nope," Avi Lafner replied, casually leaning against the coffee machine, which he had hoped to cripple just enough to get it sent to the junkyard. "I was getting a coffee when my phone rang."

"I'd lay off that java. It's nasty," the guard said, sitting down again without noticing the screwdriver.

My point exactly, the doctor thought as he brought the phone to his ear.

"Damn, Eli, why are you calling me so late?" he yelled at the caller.

"Yes, Avi, it's good to hear your voice, too," Eli Karman replied dryly.

"Sorry," Avi said, taking a deep breath. "I was in the middle of doing something. What do you need?"

"Would it be a problem if I came by the clinic now? My results are in, and..."

"No, not at all. I still have a few files to finish. I'll wait for you."

Avi ended the call and bent down to retrieve his weapon. He tapped it menacingly against the machine.

"You got lucky tonight. But your time will come."

~ ~ ~

Thirty minutes later, the two men were in an exam room with their backs to each other. Eli was buttoning his shirt, while Avi was going over his friend's results. They confirmed what Avi had suspected when he listened to the man's lungs.

"So?" Eli asked, turning around with no worry written on his face.

"Please, just do me one favor and stop smoking," Avi said, opening the door to the hallway. "And I don't mean a year from now. I mean now."

"Or else?"

"Or else you'll worsen your emphysema, which already makes you exhausted after climbing three steps. I'll give you a prescription for something that'll alleviate the symptoms, especially your fatigue. But the damage done to your respiratory system is irreversible."

"At least it's not cancer," Eli sighed, leaving the room with Avi.

"It's not cancer *yet*," Avi stressed with a sober look. "Let's go to my office. I'll write up that prescription. Don't try to fool yourself, Eli. Your youth isn't coming back."

"I'm too old for such delusions."

They walked down the hallway to Avi's office. The doctor apologized for his rudeness on the phone. To cheer up his friend, he told him about his ongoing war with the coffee machine.

"You're going to wind up in a lot of trouble with your supervisors," Eli warned. "Our dear colleagues in the agency aren't known for their sense of humor."

"Do you realize how little I care? In the past few years I've come across more psychos working for the intelligence agency and the army than a single psychiatrist sees in his entire career. So instead of letting their craziness stress me out, I distract myself with harmless little fantasies. If they happen to piss off our almighty bosses, then I'll run to the private sector faster than you can say venti-nonfat-extra-foam-caramel-macchiato. And anyway, you're in no position to talk about ruffling feathers, my friend. You and Eytan are the grand marshals of the Stirring-Up-Shit Parade. Your last adventure as a captive is the most recent evidence of that."

"I'll give you that one. By the way, it's best to stay quiet about my unpleasant episode with the Consortium. The same goes for my health status. Oh, and speaking of Eytan, he called me before he got on his flight. He asked me to thank you for your investigation."

"Did he finally catch that guy whose leg he wrecked? He'd better have. I went through a lot of hell to locate him."

"Eytan always finds what he's looking for."

"Stop. You get me all excited when you talk like the Terminator."

"You're hopeless."

"Just trying to have a little fun."

Eli gave Avi a serious look. "So how are you these days?"

"Oh, I'm okay. But I have to admit I'm getting fed up with this place. You and Eytan go on all those cool missions, and the only intrigue I engage in is sabotaging a vending machine. Yes, now you know. I'm jealous."

"I haven't actually been in the field for quite a while, Avi."

"You're right about that, Eli. How long has it been? Twenty years?"

"Nineteen, to be precise."

"Do you miss it?"

"More every day."

CHAPTER 12

Five buildings made up the office park. The only touch of color offsetting the white concrete-block structures was the red trim around the narrow windows. The greenish-brown trees along the streetscape, however, did help to soften the overall effect.

Despite its drab appearance and a serious shortage of parking space, the complex in the quiet Tel Aviv suburb was prized real estate. Small companies and professionals in a variety of fields had claimed all the square footage. Here, entrepreneurs and attorneys schmoozed with engineers, graphic designers, and logistics experts.

In the shade of an olive tree, Eli was smoking a cigarillo and amusing himself by watching the flow of clients, suppliers, and employees. These people were going about their daily business, unaware that many of the companies in these buildings were fronts. Behind the doors of the bogus firms, the Kidon conducted its most-secret meetings.

The Mossad organization's headquarters were in Herzliya, fifteen minutes north of the city center. It was here that intelligence information was gathered, processed, and analyzed. But for obvious reasons of discretion and anonymity, those running Kidon wanted meetings with their operational agents to take place in another location. This office park was a natural choice: secrets were often hidden in plain sight.

A noisy motorcycle pulled into the parking lot, scattering the birds perched in the nearby trees. The biker did a full tour of the lot in search of a free space. No dice. The vehicle and its massive rider headed toward Eli, who could never understand the machine's appeal. He watched as the giant pulled onto the grass, parked, and flipped down the kickstand. He dismounted and took off his black helmet.

"Parking's always a bitch at this place," Eytan said.

"Why do you insist on coming here on that thing?" Eli asked. "You know it's impossible to find a space."

"Blame my eternal optimism."

"You should take the bus, like me. It's better for the environment, and you don't have to deal with angry drivers."

"After five hours on a plane, I was hoping you'd spare me another spiel about saving the planet, Eli."

"Well someone needs to educate you. If not me, then who?"

"Hey now, I've been nice enough to avoid bringing up certain embarrassing moments from your childhood, but I could get mean," Eytan threatened with a grin.

Eli was used to this gentle sparring with the man who was his father figure and like a son at the same time. How could this unbelievable relationship feel so natural? As a sickly seven-year-old orphan, Eli had been put on an Israel-bound ship in 1953. Fate had thrown him together with the exceptional colossus. A gregarious kid named Frank had met Eytan on the ship, and one thing had led to another. Eytan had wound up in the room below deck with all the orphans and their overworked nurses. Eli would always remember the moment he laid eyes on Eytan. He had grabbed the man's hand. Eytan had looked down on him, and his face had softened. "So, little Eli, how about we go for a quiet stroll, just the two of us?" Of course, he would go on that stroll. Their bond was forged.

In the years that followed, Eytan was frequently absent. He was off taking care of business, as he put it. But he made sure that Eli had a father's love and an education at the very best schools. When he was thirteen, old enough to understand, Eytan told him about his past—his deportation as a child, the exceptional physical traits acquired against his will, and his lifelong mission to find, stop, and eliminate war criminals.

Eytan had wanted Eli to have a simple, worry-free upbringing. He had given Eli the life that had been stolen from him. But as the sickly child became healthy and entered adolescence, he made it known that Eytan's plans for him weren't his own. He was devoted to his adoptive father, and he wanted to be just like him. After serving in the Israel Defense Forces, Eli joined the Mossad.

For some thirty years, Eli and Eytan scoured the planet together. But as Eytan became even stronger and more effective at his job, Eli succumbed to the effects of aging. Eventually he was forced to face facts and hand in his weapon. And so his fight took another form. He began coordinating the missions of his father-friend-mentor under the assumed title of Mossad's keeper of the archives.

Eli had found time for a marriage. He and his wife had divorced, but not before having a baby girl. The daughter, Rose, was an adult now and living in Boston. She had recently given birth to a child of her own. Fatherhood had marked a decisive turning point in Eli's relationship with Eytan. The protected had become the protector.

"Eli," Eytan said, "we should go in now, or else we'll be late."

"You're right," Eli replied, relieved to be shaken from his reflection. "It wasn't too hard to leave your little island in Ireland?"

"Nah, it's all good," Eytan said as they headed toward Building No. 5. He shortened his strides so Eli could keep up. "I used my vacation to make some repairs on the house. At this rate, that shanty might be a comfortable place to live someday. You should visit."

"Any news from your London informant?"

"Still no word. I'm laying the foundation for taking out the Consortium and our little friend Cypher. But Rome wasn't built in a day. We need to be patient."

"And God knows you're good at that," Eli said as they entered the building.

"Sometimes," Eytan corrected. "But not always."

~ ~ ~

Thirty minutes later, the two men were waiting in the lobby of a law office where not a single attorney had ever set foot. Slouched in a chair that was much too low for him, Eytan crossed and uncrossed his legs, trying to get comfortable. He could see Eli watching in amusement. He finally got up and walked over to the window. Eying the cars searching for a parking space was as good a way as any to pass the time. And here he had thought they were going to be late. Finally, a door opened.

"What are you doing here?" Eytan heard Eli ask.

Eytan turned around and wound up face-to-face with Avi Lafner. He was wearing faded jeans, sneakers, and a red-and-white striped rugby polo.

"I was summoned," the latter replied, He seemed equally surprised.

"You look like you're going on a picnic in those clothes," Eytan said.

"And you've got a lot of chutzpah to dress like *that*..."

"Touché."

"So okay, what are the two of you doing here?"

"We thought we'd be getting a new mission," Eli said. "Let me see what I can find out." He left the office.

He came back a few minutes later with a good-looking woman who appeared to be some sort of administrative assistant. Her long legs caught Avi's eye. But she seemed to have eyes only for Eytan.

"Please follow me," she said. "You're expected."

She led the way, followed by Eli, Avi, and Eytan. Avi hadn't taken his eyes off the young woman's shapely calves, and Eytan elbowed him playfully. The woman knocked on the door of a conference room and ushered the men inside.

Eli flinched when he saw who was waiting for them. "This isn't a meeting," he whispered.

Avi turned his attention away from their female escort, who was going out the door. "Oh really?" he asked. "I don't mean any disrespect, but what else could it be?".

Eytan felt the blood rush to his face. He was furious. "Eli's right. It isn't a meeting. It's a trial."

CHAPTER 13

Eytan's assessment gained traction with each introduction. Three masterminds of Israeli intelligence were sitting side-by-side at a brown melamine table. Their faces were cold and expressionless. Eli recognized two of them from debriefing sessions years earlier. The third man was no small fry. Chief Geopolitical Specialist Simon Attali was in charge of coordinating the intelligence of various clandestine agencies and services. The thirtyish man with dark hair and olive skin had a lean physique and hard-to-read eyes. As an administrator in the shadows, he kept track of intricate networks that gave him intelligence on anything and everything. His knack for staying two steps ahead of the most informed politicians was highly valued. He was powerful and dangerous.

Eli and Avi, glancing warily at Eytan, pulled out chairs at the table. Eytan remained on his feet and leaned nonchalantly against a wall, his hands clasped behind his back and his eyes glued to a plasma screen.

"Agent Morg, please take a seat," Attali insisted.

"I can't," Eytan responded. Attali looked taken aback.

"And why is that?"

"Your tiny chairs would collapse under my weight."

Avi chuckled, and Attali seemed to lighten up a bit.

"Now that some of us are in a more relaxed mood, let's begin. So, Karman, do you have anything to tell us?"

"I don't believe so," Eli replied. "We haven't been informed of the purpose of this meeting."

Attali turned to Eytan. "Morg, does anything come to mind?"

The Kidon agent shrugged. "Ya got me."

That did the trick.

"Okay, I gave you all a chance," Attali said.

Eytan heard a click, and a photograph appeared on the plasma screen. He felt a chill run down his spine when he saw the image. It was Eli with his hands tied behind his back and a mask covering his eyes.

"Does this jog your memory?" Attali asked, a smile on his lips.

The room was silent.

"No worries. Let's continue."

More clicks, and a series of photographs appeared on the screen. In the first one, four Israeli soldiers were sprawled on a tile floor, drenched in their own blood. In the second image, an unconscious woman with red hair was lying on a gurney.

"Since you have nothing to contribute, and this investigation has already wasted months of our time, I'll do a quick recap. Shortly before all of this, Eli Karman was scheduled to fly to Boston. He never got there. It seems that he was taken hostage by some unidentified kidnappers. At that same time, Morgenstern was on a mission to return a prisoner—the very same woman who had killed four of our soldiers in front of Dr. Lafner. Then, for unknown reasons, Morgenstern freed this killer with complete disregard for our protocol and without informing the chain of command. But that's not all," Attali continued as he removed a document from his briefcase. "According to a confidential message from the Czech Republic, there was a raid on one of its army camps the following day. One soldier was killed, and more than thirty were wounded. I have here the testimony of a survivor who described the incident in detail. She mentions, and I quote, 'a fully armed titan with a shaved head' who appeared to be bent on blowing up said camp without giving anyone a chance to escape. Naturally, I immediately thought of..."

Simon Attali stopped and looked at Eytan, who didn't respond.

"I'll explain," Eli intervened.

"Too late," Attali replied, his voice raised. "You had your chance. It's over. The fact that you've used Mossad resources to conduct a personal vendetta is one thing. But fucking with international relations is completely unacceptable." Attali pounded his fist on the table. "You can bet your sweet asses there'll be consequences."

"Wait, let them at least..." Avi was trying. Attali shot him down.

"Dr. Lafner, this is how you answered my administrative assistant's call. I loved it so much I had to write it down: 'You've reached the Golda Meir Veterinary Clinic.' Hilarious! And after examining an IDF soldier, you suggested that he be committed to a psychiatric ward. You also wrote, 'The patient presents numerous intellectual deficiencies indicating a serious learning disorder. Re-enrollment in a primary-school program is advised. And, he's a prick.'"

"I remember that jackass," Avi responded, shooting a glance at Eytan. "He was the worst!"

Eytan grinned at his ally.

"That jackass is a respected general and has the ear of several influential politicians."

"It's not my fault you recruit so many whack jobs."

"That we can agree on, but it's never too late to fix the mistakes. Karman, we're ordering you to retire. Lafner, I strongly encourage you to go into private practice, preferably abroad."

Clearly outraged, Avi and Eli rose from their chairs and started arguing. But the judge remained firm.

"Morg, you're being transferred to a special operations unit that's infiltrating Hezbollah."

"What?" Eli stormed.

"The World War II criminals who are still alive are too old to get out of bed. From here on out, Morg's talents will be better served on other fronts."

"May I remind you," Eli shouted, "that Winston Churchill and David Ben-Gurion personally commissioned Eytan? He is the only Israeli agent who's allowed to determine his own assignments, and he is permitted to refuse any missions."

"They agreed to that in secret well more than half a century ago. The world has changed. Agent Morgenstern is a big boy. He can tell us what he thinks himself."

As everyone looked on, Eytan opened his jacket and carefully removed his gun from its holster. He unloaded the magazine and put the gun on the table.

"So you've made your choice," Attali said, his lips pursed. "I'm suspending your accreditations on the spot, and your employment will end as of today. There are a few papers that you'll have to sign."

Attali gave his two colleagues a nod and told them he would join them shortly. Without a word, the two men got up and left the room, closing the door behind them.

"All right then," Attali said as soon as they were gone. He turned to Eli, Eytan, and Avi. "My associates will relay what has just been said here to the ministry. Now that you three have officially been fired, retired, and asked to leave, we can tackle the terms of your new mission in peace."

CHAPTER 14

Simon Attali was an expert in the art of deception, but Eytan was nobody's fool. The agent had to give Attali his props. The man had thrown him off his game. He suspected that Eli was even more shocked. And Avi, who had so little experience in this sphere, had to be struggling to wrap his head around the elaborate masquerade.

"What is the meaning of this farce?" Eli asked, stepping up as spokesman for the group.

"Sit down, Karman," Attali ordered. "Lafner, one word from you, even the slightest hint of a joke, and I will make your punishment effective immediately. As for you, Morg, take back your little plaything. You'll need it."

Avi mimed zipping his lips. Eli sat down in his chair, and Eytan reclaimed his gun.

"To give you this next assignment, one that chiefly concerns you, Agent Morgenstern, I had to sever your official ties with our agency and, more important, with our government. But let's start at the beginning."

Attali turned back to the plasma screen. Eytan, Eli, and Avi followed suit.

"Here we are," he said as two photographs appeared side by side. "On the left, we have Morg in 1975. This photo was taken by a surveillance camera at Langley Air Force Base during a training program with the Americans. On the right is Morg photographed in Switzerland more recently by a certain..."

"Jacqueline Walls," Eytan sighed. He threw his head back, closed his eyes, and rubbed his neck.

"Exactly. An anonymous and experienced source passed along some information about a little CIA genius who'd been having fun correlating database photos and ended up stumbling across a few long-forgotten files. It was an innocent search, and bam! The Holy Grail. Can you imagine his surprise when he discovered two photos taken decades apart of a man who looked as young in the second photo as he was in the first?"

"The Americans didn't know about Eytan?" Avi asked.

"Until now, they've thought Eytan Morg was a code name used for several of our agents over the years. At this point they believe he's a single person."

"I can see a few reasons for concern," Eli said.

"The worst-case scenario would be Eytan getting kidnapped by a foreign party and being used as a guinea pig again. I can see by the look on your face, Eytan, that you also see that possibility. You would never let yourself get captured without putting up a good fight, but we don't want to let that happen. There's one thing that's complicating the whole matter, though."

"Go on," Eytan ordered. He could feel his muscles tensing.

"According to my source, it's not the CIA that's after you. They're a single link in a complex chain that extends to the highest levels of power. The problem is, I don't know anything about this chain. It's up to you three to identify the links and, if possible, break them."

Avi cracked a child-like smile and raised his hand.

"Lafner, this isn't English class," Attali said. "You can speak when you want."

"I didn't want to test my luck. How do you expect me to help? This isn't exactly my area of expertise."

"Glad you brought that up," Attali said. "Our source has told us that the people interested in Eytan are connected to some medical project that the military is spearheading. I'm counting on you, as a physician, to help us find out what the Americans are up to."

"I have a question too," Eytan said. "How did you get that account from the Czechs?"

"That's another puzzling question in this whole affair. What I said earlier wasn't true. We actually haven't spent months on this investigation. I simply found a file on my desk with all the information, which leads me to believe that you have upset some powerful people."

Eli gave Eytan a look that was full of meaning. "Cypher," he said quietly.

The giant nodded in agreement.

"Put that on the back burner for the time being," Attali said. "We'll deal with it, but right now we have to focus on our main goal."

"What's first on the agenda?" Eytan asked.

"According to my informant, there are plans in the works to capture Jacqueline Walls and her husband, Jeremy Corbin. It's supposed to go down within the next seventy-two hours. Those two appear to be our opponents' primary means of getting at you. Karman, you'll coordinate everything on site. Lafner, you'll be our scientific conscience. Agent Morgenstern, do whatever it takes to stop the kidnappers. I believe that's right up your alley."

"I have some experience in that department."

"Keep in mind that your photo has been sent to the US immigration service. You run the risk of being nabbed if you enter the country by plane."

"I'll fly to eastern Canada and cross on foot. There are plenty of wooded areas where I won't be spotted."

"You'd better bundle up. The weather there is especially bad this time of year," Attali warned.

"You really think snow and ice can stop me?"

Attali grinned. "I don't think an avalanche could stop you. So gentlemen, you are officially flying under the radar now. From this point on, the agency is no longer protecting you. Exfiltration is not a possibility. Should you be captured, you will not be our concern. The only authorized contact will be via our cryptophones. Morg, what are you doing?"

Eytan was tapping away on his cell phone.

"I've had an agent, Greg Nadjar, watching Jackie and Jeremy for the past two years. I'm giving him the order to step up his surveillance until I get there."

"Yet another discreet initiative on your part. At least this one happens to be useful. All right, I'm activating my Pentagon and White House connections. The ball's in your court."

Eli and Avi got up.

"Go ahead," Eytan said. "I want to have another word with our friend."

Eli and Avi obeyed without asking any questions.

"Whatever happens, Eytan, don't get caught," Attali said once they were alone.

"Don't worry, I won't create any international incidents."

"It's not diplomacy that I'm worried about," Attali said. He stared at the Kidon agent until Eytan acknowledged his nonverbal message. This man did not want him to return to the hell he had experienced as a child. Eytan nodded, silently telling Attali that he would do whatever it took to avoid being captured.

He left the building and spotted his friends in the parking lot. They were already in the middle of a heated exchange over their flight to the United States. Ignoring them, Eytan headed for his motorcycle. This caught their attention, and they ran to meet him. They caught up just as he was putting on his helmet.

"We have to figure out how we're going to work together on this," Eli said. He was visibly annoyed with the doctor, whose sarcasm was beginning to grate on him.

"Hold up," Eytan said. "I know we've been ordered to collaborate, but I don't want either of you coming with me."

"So what am I supposed to do?" Avi protested. "If I don't do what they want, I'll be fired. And I know I make jokes about the clinic, but private practice isn't really my thing. Do you want to push me into a job that consists of wiping kids' noses and writing scrips for antibiotics?

"You can do better than that," Eytan replied, unfazed.

Avi looked at Eli, clearly pleading for help. In response, Eli gave Eytan's motorcycle a furious kick. It crashed to the ground.

"You're not going without us," Eli shouted.

Eytan bent down and picked up the motorcycle. As soon as it was upright, Eli forced it down again, smashing the rearview mirror. Still showing no emotion, Eytan made yet another attempt to bring his cycle upright. He was mumbling, but Eli could hear what he was saying: "There's no way you'll be put in harm's way because of me."

"You've got a lot of nerve," Eli yelled. The man was known for his grace under fire, but Eytan could see that he had been pushed too far. Eli grabbed the giant's combat jacket and pulled him close. "I'm going with you."

"Too many people have already died because of my mistakes, Eli, and I won't let you become one of them. Certainly not you."

"We are not just *people!* You raised me. And *him,*" Eli yelled as he pointed to Avi, "he's your friend, just like Jacqueline and Jeremy. I've always listened to you, even when you've told me it was time to retire. But I'm the one who's making the decisions today. You want to fight? Fine. I'm coming with you, and if Avi wants to come with us, well, he's old enough to make that decision for himself."

The Kidon agent was beginning to weaken.

"I know what you're dwelling on, Eytan. Loving others is not a flaw. It's a driving force, the driving force that gives our lives meaning. You're the one who taught me that."

Eli was out of breath and on the verge of tears.

The giant surrendered. "Fine. You can both come. But I'm warning you, it's not going to be easy."

CHAPTER 15

The boat was pitching slowly on the calm sea. The single light bulb in the room was swaying gently with the swells. Sitting at the table while nibbling sandwiches and sipping sodas, Jacqueline and Jeremy were glued to Eytan's every word. The Kidon agent was explaining Greg's surveillance assignment and their mission to take out those charged with kidnapping the Walls-Corbin family. Every so often, Eli and Avi would add a comment.

"When did you all arrive in the US?" Jeremy asked.

"Eli and I flew into JFK last night," Avi replied.

"But I had to fly into Canada and cross the border on foot," Eytan said. A snowstorm slowed me down, and I didn't arrive until this evening, barely in time to stop the commandos who broke into your house. Meanwhile, Eli was picking up Jackie and bringing her here."

"This was all my fault," Jackie said. "If I hadn't taken that picture of you in Switzerland, we wouldn't be here."

She looked at her hands for a moment and continued. "Do you really think it was the CIA that tried to kidnap us? Isn't that strange? The agency doesn't do domestic intervention."

"I can explain that one," Eli said. "We don't think your former employer is at the heart of this operation. The directions may be coming from the White House."

"Wow! And what did you do with the commandos?"

Eytan slipped two fingers into a pocket of his jacket and took out a small black puck packed with explosives. It was identical to the one used in the Zurich hotel room to blow up the bodies of three Consortium members Jackie had killed.

"No prisoners," he said coldly. No pity, no regret.

An uncomfortable silence settled in. When Eytan felt his cell phone vibrate, he got up and left the canteen to take the call. When he returned, he heard Jeremy asking where Greg was.

"Who do you think is steering the boat?" Jackie answered. Her answer was harsh, and Eytan could see the embarrassed look on Jeremy's face. She quickly apologized. "I didn't mean to snap at you. I just feel so guilty for..."

"Taking that picture? There's no way you could have known," Eli said. "Years ago, people took pictures for their own pleasure. These days, it's all about having the images seen by anyone and everyone. Cell phones and surveillance cameras, plus the Internet and social networks make it possible. Take a selfie right now, and it could be seen by the world in a matter of minutes. What happened with that photo of Eytan was almost inevitable. Anyone could have taken it."

"He's right," Jeremy agreed as he checked on Annie, who was still sleeping peacefully.

Eytan decided to get back to business. "We're headed for New York," he said. "Our anonymous informant would like to meet me tomorrow, early afternoon. The kidnapping attempt has apparently encouraged him to tell us more."

"This informant, is he your contact in Tel Aviv?" Jeremy asked. Eytan could see that he was confused.

"No," Avi answered. "This informant is the guy giving intel to Simon Attali. It's complicated."

"The invitation could easily be a trick," Eli warned.

"I hope it is," Eytan whispered in his ear, careful not to let anyone else hear.

"What about us?" Jackie asked.

"You have a choice," Eytan sighed. "Either you go with your little girl to a discreet location under Greg's protection. Or you come with us."

"So basically, in the first scenario, we'd be waiting safely on the sidelines while you all take care of this shitty situation. And in the second scenario, we'd be jumping right into the ring. Is that it?"

Eli sat down next to Jackie before Eytan had the chance to respond.

"In the event that there's a fight, we could use your skills, Jacqueline. And if you're close to us, we'll be able to protect you. But it's completely up to you, and we'll respect your decision either way."

"Is it okay if we take a few minutes to think it over?" she asked.

"Meet us in the cockpit in five minutes," Eytan said. "In the meantime, boys, we need to come up with a strategy."

With the others gone, Jeremy and Jackie walked over to the portable crib. They held each other as they gazed at their baby girl, untethered by the troubles of the adult world.

"He did say five minutes, right?" Jeremy asked.

Jackie took a deep breath, squeezed her husband a bit tighter, and laid her head on his shoulder.

"That gives us some time to say good-bye," she whispered.

After savoring every last second with Annie, they rejoined the secret agents in the cockpit. Greg was steering the boat like a master mariner. Eli and Eytan were shouldering fully packed military bags, which, despite their great difference in build, gave the odd impression that they were siblings. Avi, meanwhile, looked like a tourist with his little wheeled suitcase. The three of them were bent over a hastily drawn map spread across a metal table usually used for consulting sea charts.

Greg cracked a smile and saluted the couple. Eli and Avi gave them a nod. Eytan stayed focused and unfazed.

"Jackie, for you I've set aside an automatic, some bullets, and a holster."

"You knew our response before you even asked the question," she joked.

"I prepared for the worst."

CHAPTER 16

Water trickled down the cinder-block walls that bore vague traces of beige paint.

The military guard seemed oblivious to the decrepit surroundings. Neville was walking behind him, his eyes on the floor, which was full of puddles. His primary concern was protecting his leather shoes and the bottoms of his trousers.

The two men descended a flight of steps and entered a large corridor lit by five ceiling fixtures. The lights barely illuminated the dilapidated tiles, the rusted bars on the cells, and the white wooden benches.

The place reeked of mold and despair.

"How many prisoners do you have here?" Neville asked.

"Just one, sir," Sergeant Howard said without looking at the visitor. "This place is reserved for resistant personalities."

The stubby man had a triangular face and a thick neck. His little brown eyes didn't show any signs of intelligence, but they did reveal an unbridled passion for rules.

Men who can't be broken win battles, Neville thought.

Before he could make a cutting remark, his escort halted, pivoted brusquely, and stood straight as an arrow in front of a cell. The guy looked like he showered with starch every morning.

Neville reflected on the utter absurdity of these military rituals. When did a perfectly executed salute ever win a war?

"Attention!" the sergeant cried out.

"In your dreams," a deep voice answered.

Howard pulled out his nightstick and brought his arm back, ready to give the bars a good whack.

"Thank you, Sergeant," Neville intervened.

The order, sudden and authoritative, dissuaded the prison guard from completing his swing.

"You may leave. I'll find my way back on my own."

Sergeant Howard hesitated a moment, but faced with Neville's determined look, he returned the nightstick to his belt.

"Of course, sir," he muttered before making a crisp about-face and marching away.

The man in the cell spoke again.

"I'd ask my lovely secretary to bring you a cup of tea, but I'm afraid she just stepped out."

The young man moved into the light. He was of average height and was wearing faded green cotton pants and black combat boots, no laces. His oversized cargo jacket, which was missing all its buttons, was draped over a gray T-shirt that couldn't conceal his bulging pectoral muscles. The prisoner's strength was obvious. So were his rugged good looks: thick chestnut-brown hair, a strong forehead, prominent cheekbones, and a curved eagle-like nose. Despite his haggard face and a three-day-old beard that covered his proud jaw, the boy looked more like a Hollywood movie star than a soldier from the middle of nowhere and even less like a convict.

Neville understood that his looks couldn't begin to compare. Despite his height—six feet two—and his tailored suit, his face was too angular, and his soot-brown eyes were too tiny. But that didn't mean he lacked seductive power. Intelligence was his medium of entrapment. And Neville knew his power, as well as all the tricks.

Yet meeting this man behind bars, he felt every insecurity he had experienced as a child.

"Please, take a seat," the prisoner joked as he waved his arm toward one of the wooden benches.

Neville ran his finger over the wood. He was surprised to find that it was neither dirty nor wet, only eaten up by woodworms. He removed his trilby hat and sat down.

"You obviously know nothing about prisons," the captive said. "The only people treated to mold and muck in this place are the ones on this side of the bars."

He lifted his arms, wrapped his hands around the iron bars, and began doing pull-ups.

Neville watched him in silence for what felt like an eternity in the foul-smelling hellhole.

The man finally quit and let go of the bars. He ignored his visitor.

Neville broke the silence. "Stefan Starlin. Born in Birmingham on July 3, 1910. Mother, a seamstress, and father, a police officer. An accomplished athlete, you joined the army in 1930. Your superiors quickly noted your surprising ability to adapt and improvise. They also noted your arrogant nature and a need for recognition. Based on the many write-ups you received, I can easily deduce that your acts of insubordination have their roots in these little quirks of yours. During the retreat at Dunkirk, you broke every record—and regulation. You alone killed twenty-three German soldiers to cover for your fellow soldiers. And you continued to cover for them despite orders to join the retreat."

"The Germans had us surrounded. I wasn't about to leave any guys behind!" Starlin shouted, banging the bars with his open hands. "These were guys I had fought with. It was a matter of honor."

"Of course," Neville replied. "However, your superiors judged your decision harshly, and instead of heaping medals on you, they heaped you with blame."

"I don't care about medals."

"We have that in common."

Neville cleared his throat.

"They took you out of action and had you training new recruits. That was until last week, when you made your ultimate slipup. You killed a lieutenant at shooting practice. The fact that the two of you were constantly at each other certainly didn't help your case."

Starlin curled his lip and slipped into the dark recess of his cell. "Stop this little game of yours. State your name and position, sir, along with the exact purpose of your visit."

"One month from now, two at the most, you'll go on trial," Neville continued, ignoring Starlin's demand. "Considering the charges you're facing, I'd bet money that you'll be hanged."

"It was an accident!" Starlin protested. "I didn't mean to take the bastard out. Everyone knows that. If he wasn't a bloody daddy's boy, I wouldn't even be here!"

"Yes, of course. You're the victim of a horrible conspiracy. Such terrible injustice. Do you know what I think?"

Neville stood up and marched over to the cell. Now he was the one grabbing the bars.

"I think you're an out-of-control Polack who likes to stir up shit," he seethed.

"And you're a good-for-nothing asshole with his nose up in the air," Starlin cursed. He sprang from the darkness and grabbed the visitor by the collar. "If I weren't behind this cage, I'd..."

In a quick and coldly executed move, Neville slammed his elbows against the prisoner's wrists and broke his hold. Clearly stunned, Starlin pulled his hands back and held his wrists to his chest.

"I see your Polish origins are a touchy subject," Neville said as he smoothed his jacket.

He knew he had gotten to Starlin, but that wasn't much of a challenge. Starlin was one of those quick-to-anger guys. Neville walked back to the bench and sat down.

"You're cut out to be a sniper," he said. "Stick with that. You haven't mastered hand-to-hand combat."

"Most of my family lives in Poland, assuming they're not all dead. So are you going to tell me who you are and what you want from me?"

"All right, I know your time is precious. My name isn't as important as my position. You see, soldier Starlin, for the past two years, the government's war cabinet has been developing a secret organization called Special Operations Executive, SOE. When I say secret, I mean it's a secret from both our enemies and our allies. Most world leaders know nothing about it."

"Fascinating. What the hell does it have to do with me?"

Neville sighed and started again.

"My work consists of selecting and training candidates for this underground combat unit. First we set up coordinated resistance teams in occupied countries. Once dropped in by parachute, our agents will conduct sabotage and elimination missions. Obviously, the risk factor is high. I'm here to recruit you. In other words, my dear friend, I have the power to rescue you from your death sentence. If you take the assignment, however, it's probable that you'll die anyway."

"Fuck, I'm in! I'd rather die in combat than in this shit hole."

"I'm touched by your enthusiasm, but you'll require training before I allow you to jump into any mission. The training will correct your weaknesses and build on your strengths."

Starlin rubbed his wrists again. "Message received, loud and clear."

"No more slipups. Do everything you're told, no questions asked. I mean it: no questions asked. One false move, and you'll be back on death row. Have I made myself clear?"

"Crystal clear."

"If you prove to be half as talented as my subordinates claim you are, you'll be a top recruit."

With perfect timing, Sergeant Howard burst down the corridor. He stopped in front of Neville and stood at attention.

The man was born to do this, Neville thought. He gave the sergeant a nod.

"Colonel, your driver sent me to remind you of your meeting with the prime minister," Howard barked.

"Colonel?" Starlin inquired, stunned.

Neville stood up and put on his hat. "Colonel Neville Wladowski, at your service."

"Wladowski? You're Polish?"

"Yes, on my father's side," Neville confirmed as he gave the prisoner a wink. He suppressed a smile when he saw the stupefied look on Stefan Starlin's face. He turned around and walked back down the corridor.

"I'll see you tomorrow on the training field, soldier."

"Ah, so you'll be running my training sessions too?"

Neville had already vanished in the darkness.

"No, soldier. I'll be training along with you. I'll be at your side."

"Excuse me?" Starlin yelled. The man was completely confused.

"Of course," Neville replied. "We'll be parachuting into Poland together."

CHAPTER 17

The black Audi A6 came out of the Holland Tunnel. Jeremy hadn't been in Manhattan since the sale of his wildly expensive apartment next to the Guggenheim Museum. That was a lifetime ago, when he was willing to sacrifice even his dignity at the altar of the gods of finance.

Light was filtering over the tops of the West Street highrises that towered above the thick commuter traffic. Eytan could see that it would be a gray day. For the past two hours, he had been driving the first of two rental cars.

They hadn't gotten off to a smooth start. Jeremy had insisted that Jackie and he ride in his vehicle. Jackie was biting her nails and muttering second thoughts after handing Annie over to Greg, who had assured her that he had frequently fed, burped, and changed two nieces while telling them all about She-Hulk and Power Girl. Eli, meanwhile, had argued that he needed a core group of commandos to ride with Eytan, because they hadn't finished strategizing. Impatient to get going, Eytan had given in to Jeremy but regretted his decision as soon as the man started bombarding him with questions. He had spent most of the drive talking to Eli on his cell phone, leaving the former trader in the dark. Avi, meanwhile, seemed to be the only member of the group who couldn't care less. All he wanted was the decent cup of coffee that had been promised him when they reached New York.

They were to meet Simon Attali's informant on the High Line, an elevated railroad spur running along the Lower West Side that had been transformed into a pedestrian pathway lined with flowers and shrubbery. The meeting was set for two in the afternoon at Tenth Avenue and Seventeenth Street, close to the Chelsea Market.

Eytan was leading his team toward the Maritime, a boutique hotel with porthole-like windows. The building was around the corner from their meeting spot. The giant had booked three standard single rooms, one for himself and two for Eli and Avi, who still hadn't recovered from their jet lag, along with a double for Jackie and Jeremy, who were equally exhausted from everything they had been through.

They had seven hours until the meetup. Eytan decided to scope out the neighborhood while the others relaxed and grabbed some food. His teammates agreed, aware that they needed to be rested before confronting what was likely to be a dangerous situation.

At noon, the foursome reconvened at La Bottega Caffè on the ground floor. While the lobby and room décor were maritime down to the smallest detail, the restaurant was entirely different. A long dark-wood bar welcomed a host of clients. Even at midday, some were sipping martinis and Italian wines poured from bottles displayed in front of a large mirror. In the back, a chef was throwing enormous pizzas topped with ham and salami into an oven at a crazy speed.

Despite a quick nap, Jeremy had the feeling that he was floating in a thick haze. Jackie, on the other hand, looked refreshed and energized. He made out Eli and Avi and took his wife's hand as they worked their way over to the table. Avi was suspiciously eyeing a steaming cappuccino that his waitress—a smoldering and curvy Mediterranean-looking brunette—had just delivered.

"So it's not the cuppa joe you couldn't wait to wrap your hands around, is it?" Eli joked, looking at the menu.

"No, I guess I should have gone for the Caffè Americano. I need a bigger dose of caffeine."

"Slide that cappuccino over here," Jackie said. "It looks perfect to me."

Avi did as he was asked.

"You know how I am about my coffee," he said, staring at Jackie. "Think there might be a Starbucks around here?"

Jeremy didn't care about the doctor's coffee, but he did care about the man's chummy behavior with his wife. "Any word from Eytan?" he asked.

"Not yet," Eli replied. "But he's a perfectionist. He's probably going over every last nook and cranny in the neighborhood. Don't worry, Jeremy. He won't be long."

"You know him pretty well, don't you?" Jeremy asked.

"Better than anyone else, which doesn't say much, actually."

"What do you mean?"

"Eytan is a one big mystery, young man. I've hung around him for a long time now, and yet I've barely scratched the surface of his past. I'm sure you'd like to know all about his life, but I'm telling you, if you pry into his history, you'll hit a brick wall. I learned a long time ago that I needed to respect Eytan's privacy."

His answer wasn't the one Jeremy wanted to hear.

"Are you familiar with F. Scott Fitzgerald, Jeremy?"

"Of course."

"He wrote, 'Show me a hero and I will write you a tragedy,'" That's the best I can do to sum up Eytan."

The quote shamed Jeremy. Eytan had displayed unequaled heroism when Professor Bleiberg was holding them captive. Jeremy knew he had no business trying to snoop into the man's past. He apologized to the old Israeli, who gave him a look that was both gentle and fatherly.

"How about we order?" Jackie suggested.

"Good idea," Avi chimed in. "And on the subject of tragedy and heroism, I think I'll try ordering another coffee."

The foursome finished reading their menus and told the waitress what they wanted. When she arrived with the food, along with Avi's coffee, he frowned and took a sip. A smile lit his face when he put the mug back on the table.

"Mmm. Delicious!" he pronounced. "The best I've had in the US."

"Score one for the Yanks," Eli said, grinning. "Now let's enjoy ourselves. We've got some serious work ahead of us."

~ ~ ~

Returning from his scouting expedition, Eytan was pleased to see his protégés getting along so well.

"I take it that you all got some rest and had a good meal."

"Sit down and order," Jackie said. "It'll give us a chance to catch up."

"Thanks, but I already grabbed a sandwich. I hate being a killjoy, but it's almost time. Finish up, and meet me at our cars," he instructed before going back the way he had come.

Five minutes later, they were in their vehicles, heading toward a nearby side street.

After parking, Eytan asked Avi and Eli to be lookouts while he retrieved the bags from the trunks. He unzipped one of them and took out two small metal boxes. He gave a flesh-colored earpiece to each of them.

"They're headphones with an integrated communications system," he said as he placed one in his ear. "No loud talking needed. The microphone can pick up the vibrations in your vocal chords."

The team huddled, and like a star quarterback before a pivotal play, Eytan explained the game plan with poise and authority.

"Eli will blend in with the pedestrians and stay close to Jeremy. Avi will be behind the wheel of one car, and Jackie will be in the other vehicle. They'll keep the engines running in case we have to make a quick getaway. Jackie, you'll be positioned on the west side of the High Line, and Avi will be on the east side. I'll show you exactly where in a little bit. Jeremy, you'll be on foot."

"What about you? Where will you be?" Jeremy asked. "And how will you recognize our contact?"

"According to Simon Attali, we've already met. That's all I know. I'll be waiting on the roof of this building," he said, pointing to the apartment complex that spanned the side street. I'll be watching everyone from above. I'm expecting you to be as attentive as possible. Point out anything that looks suspicious. Paying attention to these details separates the suprisers from the surprisees. Any problem with our plan?"

There was no word of dissent.

"Great. Any questions?"

"Yeah, I've got one," Jackie said. "Jeremy has no training, so why are we throwing him into the middle of the ring?"

"The people who are after us will recognize you, Jeremy, and me. Avi and Eli are still off the radar. I'd like to keep that trick in my back pocket for as long as possible. Plus if it's a trap, better to let our enemies think we've walked right into it. Jeremy's the best choice for the job."

"But I'm better at hand-to-hand combat if it comes to that," the young woman objected.

"Yes, but you can drive. Jeremy can't, at least not since his car accident. Am I right?"

"Yeah, you're right on that score," Jeremy admitted. "I'm in no rush to get behind the wheel. But I'm pretty awesome at running and riding a bike."

"Sweet!" Avi cheered. It was hard to miss the sarcasm. "Learn how to swim, and you could enter a triathlon."

"Do me a favor, and cut the wisecracks," Jeremy said. "You're not the comedian you think you are."

"I beg your pardon. I'm the intellect's comedian."

"Which intellects have you been playing to? The ones you've anesthetized before surgeries at your clinic?"

Eli intervened before Avi could have a go at the bookseller. "Okay, let's be serious now. This mission is taking place in the middle of the city. The smallest mistake could cost us a life. Innocent bystanders are at risk too."

"He's right," Jackie agreed.

"Oh come on," Jeremy protested. "I'm just messing around."

"Recess is over, the two of you!" Eytan growled. "Make one more dumb joke, and I'll knock you out and stuff you in a trunk. I'm not kidding. This has to go down perfectly. Get to your posts, everybody." He shot Avi and Jeremy a dark glare, and both turned silent and sheepish.

Fifteen minutes later, they were all in position. From the top of the building, Eytan gave the starting signal.

"All right, friend, off you go," he whispered, looking through the scope of his rifle.

Hearing those words, Jeremy walked up the steps to the elevated park. Eytan watched and saw the change on his young colleague's face. Just seconds earlier, he had looked determined and brave. Now he looked like a mouse being tossed into a cage of ravenous snakes.

CHAPTER 18

Mesmerized by the panoramic view of the Big Apple, pedestrians meandered along the public pathway. The High Line, a linear park that ran from Gansevoort Street to West Thirty-fourth Street, was an oasis where concrete and greenery could coexist. It drew both New Yorkers and tourists.

Atop the apartment building, Eytan enjoyed a clear view of the elevated walkway, as well as the squeezed-together skyscrapers some distance away. A pleasant little chat and a wad of bills had persuaded a security guard to give him access. Eytan had posed as a paparazzi intent on photographing a celebrity who was cheating on her husband. The ploy had worked like a charm. All he had to do now was tend to a few final preparations.

On the walkway below, Jeremy slowly advanced past the white viburnum shrubs. His hands were stuffed inside the pockets of his black coat. Once upon a time he would have moved purposefully through the mix of runners, relaxed couples, and shoppers. But he was a different man now, and his reason for being there would have scared anyone.

Eytan could see that Jeremy was struggling hard to feign a relaxed expression, and he was struck with guilt. "Just breathe. I'm right here with you," he soothed.

"That's nice, but I wish I could see you," Jeremy mumbled.

"If it makes you feel any better, I promise to tell you lots of cool life stories when this is all over."

"Seriously?"

"Cross my heart."

"I won't forget that."

"You can count on me. From now on, I'm an open book."

"Ah, so now you're the geeky booklover, and I'm the spy."

Eytan smiled. "I guess so. Got anything newsworthy to report, Secret Agent Jeremy?"

"No, a group of kids with adults, some runners, a few old guys out for a stroll."

"Okay, keep your eyes peeled. Eli, what's happening at your end?"

"Nothing extraordinary," Eli replied as he walked into the Chelsea Market via a connecting bridge from the High Line. Some Japanese tourists taking pictures, a couple with two children, a legless guy in a wheelchair pushed by a man who's a Chris Waddle lookalike."

"I don't see anyone in a wheelchair," said Jeremy, who was about a hundred feet away. "Who's Chris Waddle?" He seemed to welcome the opportunity to get his mind off his worries.

"He was a British football player," Eli said. "Oh, I forgot. You Americans call it soccer. He was a great athlete and a good broadcaster. But he wasn't known for his sense of style."

"Never heard of him."

"Ah, I see them now," Eytan said. "The guy pushing the wheelchair has a big shoulder bag. Do you see it, Eli?"

"Do you think I'm rusty? Yes, I see it. It looks like a big gym bag. They're probably on their way to physical therapy. And anyway, they're heading toward the elevator that goes back down to the street."

"Yeah, they're getting into the elevator now. Jeremy, what time do you have?"

"My watch says 1:59. I hope our contact shows up on time. I can't wait to get out of here."

Eli broke in. "Look out! Three men in black suits and gray coats just entered the covered passageway."

"Give me a description," Eytan ordered as he propped his weapon on his shoulder.

"Tall, muscular, short hair, walking with intent. Each of them has a briefcase. They've stopped at the terrace."

"Are black suits the dress code for bad guys?" Jeremy's feeble attempt at humor couldn't hide his anxiety.

"Personally, I don't think it's a wise choice. But yeah, I see it a lot," Eytan said. "Eli, jump in at the first suspicious move."

"No problem, boss!" the Israeli responded.

Eytan spotted their man and gave the order. "Okay, the games have begun. Our client has arrived."

"Where is he?" Jeremy asked, looking all around.

"He's at the top of the staircase, to your right. Walk toward him slowly, and try not to make any sudden movements. Eli, if your three nitwits move an inch, let me know before tackling them."

"Message received," he replied.

"What does he look... Hold on, is it that tall guy with gray hair and a scary scar on his face?" Jeremy asked. "Don't they have plastic surgery for things like that?"

"It's Bramble," Eytan muttered. "I wouldn't have believed it if they had told me."

"Bramble? Titus Bramble?" repeated Jackie, who was parked on the side street, as instructed.

"You know him too?" Jeremy said.

"He's the head of the paramilitary operations branch of the CIA's Special Activities Division. He used to be part of an elite squad. The guy's a legend. Of course I know who he is."

"Tell me he's an okay guy, despite his creepy-ass face," Jeremy pleaded as he approached the man.

Bramble was in his fifties, but he still had an intimidating build. Eytan could see as much through the scope of his rifle. "If you disregard his obsession with sharp weapons and scalp-chopping, then yeah, he's an okay guy."

~ ~ ~

Jeremy gulped and squeaked a hello. He felt the man's stone-cold glare and feared his legs would give out.

He's okay. He's okay, Jeremy repeated silently, fighting to harness the power of positive thinking. Bramble continued to stare at him. Did the guy have X-ray vision or something?

"Corbin, where's Morg? He's the one I want to talk to," he boomed. The voice matched the build.

This Bramble guy wasn't okay.

"And he wants to talk to you," Jeremy muttered.

"Hand him the extra earpiece I gave you, and head back north toward Avi's car," Eytan instructed. "There's no point in staying out in the open any longer. Eli, anything new?"

"Red herring. The guys are lawyers. They look like they're on their lunch break. But I'll keep my eye on them."

Jeremy, following Eytan's instructions to avoid any sudden movements, slowly pulled the earpiece from his pocket and handed it to Bramble. The man put it in his ear. Jeremy edged away in the direction of the staircase. He was elated as he scrambled down the steps. He had survived.

~ ~ ~

"I imagine you've got your sniper focused on me."

"You got it, Bramble," Eytan lied as he scanned the other pedestrians through his sniper scope.

"I never thought we'd have the opportunity to speak again."

"And I never thought it would be you behind all of this."

"I had nothing to do with it. I did everything I could to cover your ass, but it's out of my hands now. That's why I contacted Attali."

"Spit it out. I don't have all day."

"Did you really think I'd set you up after everything we've been through? Semper Fidelis. Always faithful. Relax. I'm here alone."

"Well I'm not..."

"Of course, better safe than sorry," Bramble said as he walked over to the railing. "It's your MO."

"I'm losing patience, Titus, and my fingers are getting antsy."

"I've already lost a lot of men trying to protect you. The military is a hundred percent prepared to maintain its secret program, even if it means taking out government agents."

"And civilians. You know how much I hate it when civilians get hurt."

"I feel the same way about my men."

"Sorry to interrupt your testosterone-fueled conversation," Jeremy interrupted. "But I have a question for Eli and Eytan."

"What is it?" the latter asked.

"That guy in a wheelchair you spotted earlier, could you remind me what he looks like?"

"Unkempt, blue hat, long hair, pants that could use a wash. Why?"

"I'm on Tenth Avenue, and there's a guy walking in my direction who's giving me a mean look. He fits the description."

"That's impossible," Eli said. He was an amputee."

"Maybe someone should tell *him* that, because I can assure you he's got two legs now, and he's starting to run!"

"Go back up on the High Line, Jeremy! Get to Eli!" Eytan shouted. "Bramble, you bastard." His finger was on the trigger, ready to fire.

"Morg, it wasn't me! The program..."

Titus Bramble stumbled forward and collapsed against the railing. A geyser of blood gushed from his chest as he fell to the pavement. An orchestra of screams rose up. Serene just seconds ago, the park was now the picture of chaos. Onlookers scattered in all directions. Bolder bystanders took out their cell phones to call for help.

Eytan could see Jeremy frantically elbowing his way through the crush of people as he made a dash for the Chelsea Market. He was relieved when he saw the man giving chase lose Jeremy. Unable to get through the wall of pedestrians fleeing the High Line, he threw up his arms in frustration.

Eytan looked away from Jeremy's pursuer to find Eli. He spotted him squatting beside the three attorneys, who were sprawled on the ground. He saw Eli draw the gun that he had kept hidden under his jacket.

"What happened to Bramble, Eytan?" Jackie asked. He was amazed at her calmness, considering the peril her husband was in.

"Someone took him out. There's another sniper in the area," Eytan responded as he scanned the surroundings. "Change of plans. Eli, don't get involved, or else you'll be on the sniper's radar. Go see if Bramble is really dead, and, more important, get that earpiece. Jeremy, I can't cover you anymore, I'm looking for that fucking shooter. He must be acting alone. Run to the south."

"I'll get knocked out like a bunny rabbit!" the young man panted.

"If they've sent men to follow you on foot, it means they want you alive. Jackie, pick up Jeremy at the next exit. Avi, you wait for Eli. In three minutes tops, the area will be swarming with cops, so get a move on!"

Jeremy obeyed. He dashed down the green pathway at the speed of a middle-distance runner.

CHAPTER 19

Eytan hated group missions, especially ones in urban settings. The crowds—always unpredictable—the possibility of police interference, and traffic issues alone made planning almost pointless. Added to that was the reality that killing was always easier than protecting. Titus Bramble's gruesome end was resounding proof of that.

With one knee on the ground, Eytan went over his priorities as he got new information from his teammates and scanned the buildings for the likely location of the shooter. At the moment Bramble was killed, the CIA superstar was facing Eytan's location west of the High Line, with his back to the Hudson. Based on the direction the blood spurted and the way the victim's body moved on impact, Eytan concluded that the bullet was fired from a rooftop opposite his own position. Forcing the sniper out of hiding was becoming more crucial by the second. It was clear that he was watching the High Line mission play out and coaching his men on the ground as events unfolded—a strategy similar to the one the Kidon agent had set up that morning, a classic recon technique.

"All right, I'm parked at the bottom of the stairs on West Fourteenth Street," Jackie announced, anxious to see her husband appear.

"Bramble is dead," Eli said in turn. "But he..."

"If you've retrieved the device," Eytan interrupted, "meet back up with Avi, and both of you head toward Jackie as fast as you can. Jeremy, how are you holding up?"

"I'm not holding up!" the out-of-breath moving target yelled. "That asshole is gaining on me. If I take those fucking stairs, he'll catch up with me."

"Shit!" Jackie cursed. "Someone else is about to go up the stairs. He'll cut you off."

"You're just trying to cheer me up," Jeremy moaned.

"Are you sure he's one of the bad guys?" Eytan asked.

"A flash of light caught his attention. It was coming from atop a taller building about a quarter mile away on the other side of the High Line. He knew it was the sun hitting a rifle scope. Eytan was certain he had located the sniper who had succeeded in shooting Bramble with a single bullet despite the distance. In his entire career, Eytan had crossed paths with only two or three people capable of pulling off such a shot.

"Positive! Based on your description, it's definitely our man! I'll cut him off," Jackie growled.

"Jackie, no!" Eytan ordered. "I don't want you to be seen!"

"I don't fucking care!"

Because of Jackie's unexpected involvement, Eytan no longer had time to assess wind speed, attack angle, or the sniper's distance—factors that were necessary to execute a direct hit. He was further hindered by the height of the sniper's building and a parapet that protected him. Eytan could see only the top of his head. If he wanted to take the pressure off his friends, he had no choice. He had to sacrifice his own location and draw the attention in his direction, which meant using one of his back-pocket tricks sooner than he had planned.

He stood up to get a better view, took a breath, and pulled the trigger twice. His shots at the barrier surrounding the roof achieved the desired effect: his enemy was forced to hunker down, thereby losing his visual. Without pausing, Eytan pivoted toward the High Line and lowered his weapon. Down below, Jeremy was on the run. He had sped past another stairwell. Emerging from the steps was the man who had been in the wheelchair just a few minutes earlier. Seconds later, Jackie went rushing up the steps like a ball of fury.

The crowd at the southern end of the High Line was growing denser. Eytan's line of vision was blocked. He didn't dare to fire a shot for fear of hitting a bystander. But he was relieved to see Jeremy gain on his pursuer, thanks to his zigzagging. Had he been a weekend skier in his previous life as a trader? He hadn't said anything about it. Meanwhile, Jackie was capitalizing on her tiny size, weaving in and out like a cat. It wouldn't be long before she would swoop down on her prey.

"Eli, what's your status?" Eytan asked as he swiveled back toward the sniper.

"I'm in the car with Avi. We're going down Tenth Avenue toward the south side of the High Line.

"Permission to intervene granted."

"We're on it!" Eli replied.

Eytan focused on the sniper, who was looking back at him, standing upright as well, his weapon at his shoulder and aimed in the Kidon agent's direction.

"Finally," Eytan thought, satisfied.

It was impossible to fully make out the man's features, which were partially obscured by his weapon, but his blond buzz cut and confident posture confirmed the agent's hunch. This was a highly trained sniper fresh from the ranks of an elite squad. The fractions of a second Eytan had dedicated to analyzing Jeremy and Jackie's situation had given his opponent enough time to ready his aim. In this kind of faceoff, even the smallest mistake or the slightest delay could be fatal. Just one shot, a single bullet ripping through the air, and it would all be over.

The two men looked at each other for a brief moment, neither one moving. They were two fierce chess players, each determining his own moves while anticipating those of the opponent. Eytan knew his chances of hitting his bull's eye were small, almost impossible. But he had also calculated that the commando wanted him alive. The sniper would shoot to kill only as a last resort. That leveled the playing field.

The Kidon agent held his breath, aimed his weapon at the parapet, and fired all his ammo, closing in on his opponent shot after shot with a perfect balance of speed and precision. He had only one thought: keeping the guy from sending any more orders to the bastards chasing his teammate. The sniper was forced to take cover as the parapet crumbled under the gunfire. It wouldn't be long before Eytan's new game plan paid off.

"I'm gaining on my guy!" Jackie shouted. "Shit! What the fuck is he doing?"

"What's happening?" Eli asked.

"The two guys! They're veering off toward a staircase."

Ah, you've ordered them to withdraw, just as I hoped you would, Eytan said to himself. You're doing your fucking job, asshole.

"Honey, you can stop running now," Jackie yelled to Jeremy. "There's nothing to be scared of anymore. I'll go after them."

Breathless, Jeremy didn't need to be convinced.

"Negative! You're going to do what I say, Jacqueline," Eytan commanded as he kept up the pressure on his enemy. "Eli, new plan: go get Jeremy and Jackie. Use force if they refuse. Meet up with Avi in the Ford, and have him drive the three of you to her car. Then all four of you head north to Central Park: you and Jackie in one car and Jeremy and Avi in the other."

"Got it." Eli responded.

"Can you at least explain?" Jackie insisted, clearly pissed off and her eyes still glued to the two men as they went down the nearest stairwell.

"Now that I've given away my position, you're no longer a priority," Eytan replied calmly. "Plan B worked. The chief commando took his sweet time, but he finally directed his men toward their primary target. Me."

He didn't need to say the rest: they were going to play by his rules now.

CHAPTER 20

Alarmed by the increasing number of police cruisers speeding toward him, Avi was anxiously tapping the steering wheel. Having followed all the developments, he was praying that he wouldn't screw up his part of the mission: speeding off as soon as the trader-turned-bookseller and his hot wife were safe and sound inside the rented Ford. The doctor felt a wave a relief when he saw the couple appear at the end of the street. Eli slid into the front seat. He was wheezing badly. No surprise, considering the state of his lungs. The other two hopped in the back. Jeremy was dripping with sweat. Jackie was wearing an expression that couldn't be mistaken: Say one word to me, and I'll clock you. No problem. A dedicated womanizer, he had gotten that look before.

"Drop Jackie and me off at her car," Eli instructed, "And then head toward..."

"Central Park. Got it." Avi finished Eli's sentence as he pulled out.

"Are you really going to let Eytan fend for himself?" Jeremy asked.

"Welcome to my world," Eli growled. "He just cut off his communication device, so we have no choice but to stick to his plan. He knows what he's doing. The last thing he needs is us getting in his way, especially when some of us don't fully understand the concept of following orders. If he tells us to withdraw, we withdraw. Period."

In his rearview mirror, Avi watched as an angry Jackie curled up against the back door, arms crossed over her chest. Jeremy extended a hand to console her but pulled it back.

Avi quickly pulled up to the vehicle abandoned by Jackie and parked behind it. As she was about to get out of the sedan, she turned to Jeremy and gave him a passionate kiss.

Not a good sign, for sure.

~ ~ ~

Eytan dismantled his sniper rifle, carefully placing each piece in his cargo bag. His focus was no longer on the shooter, but on the goons that his opponent was sending his way. If they wanted to capture him, the best strategy would be to surround him. Two sets of stairs were the only access to the roof. The first set was inside the building. The second set was an exterior fire escape. Aside from a water tank, a typical fixture on New York rooftops, the Kidon agent had no means of cover. The sniper was most likely aware of this and had informed his accomplices. Nobody was more predictable than a military man. While this was reassuring, a question kept replaying in his head. How could Eli, a former agent with a sharp eye and proven experience, be duped by a fake cripple? This kind of mistake was understandable when someone was observing a scene through a sniper scope from afar. But from less than ten feet away?

He needed an answer to that question, but it could wait. The rooftop door opened, and three men emerged, stopping forty-some feet in front of him. They didn't look like the same guys from the High Line. Each one had his own distinct look. There was the chill runner type with curly brown hair, a well-groomed metrosexual, and a third guy who looked like he spent most of his afternoons lifting weights at the gym. In Manhattan, these guys could walk the streets relatively unnoticed. The only thing that really made them stand out was the killer glare in their eyes and the microphones hooked to their collars. Eytan knew the mikes were attached to earpieces.

Eytan, squatting as he placed the last magazine with the rest of the equipment, zipped the bag. He stood up, cocked his head, and opened dialogue.

"Well, boys, if no one says anything, we could be here all week."

"We're obligated to inform you of the terms of your surrender," the body-builder said.

"Ah, a negotiation. What a delicious surprise," Eytan said as he put a hand inside a pocket.

Taken aback, the men drew their guns. The barrels looked much larger than normal.

"Cool it, guys," Eytan said softly as he pulled out a cigar and matchbox. "I'm happy to listen to your bullshit, but let me enjoy the moment. A condemned prisoner is entitled to his last request, you know."

Without paying much attention to his opponents, whose erratic lip movements indicated they were consulting their superior, he lit the cigar, flung the used match on the ground, and took a long drag.

"All right, kids, what did Daddy say?"

"If you give up, your friends won't be bothered, and all you'll have to do is undergo a few simple medical examinations before being released," the one with the brown curly hair said.

"I'm onboard with the first part, but frankly a little troubled by the second bit."

"What do you mean?"

"I'm not a fan of needles. They make me nervous." Eytan could see the amused look on their faces. "No joke!"

"This is your last chance if you want to avoid any trouble."

"I see. I just have one question then."

"What is it?"

Eytan took one more puff before flicking his cigar to the ground.

"Who says I'm trying to avoid trouble, prick?"

~ ~ ~

Eli took the driver's seat and turned on the ignition without making eye contact with Jackie, who was sitting beside him. He crawled slowly to the end of a narrow street, followed by Avi and Jeremy in the Ford.

Several police cruisers went hurtling down Tenth Avenue, sirens blaring. Eli stopped to let them go by.

"How bad is your respiratory problem?" Jackie asked.

"Nice to see you've regained your powers of speech. It's pretty serious."

"I'm sorry," the young woman responded. "It must be especially upsetting for someone like you. You've had a physically demanding job."

"Just the unfortunate effects of getting older. I hope it's a very long time before you experience them," he said while waiting patiently for the right moment to make his turn.

"What would you have done if you had to run too?"

"I wouldn't have been able."

"That's all I needed to know," she said as she opened the car door and leaped out to Eli's astonishment. "I'm gonna rush to Eytan's position in case he's still there," she yelled as she sped off. "Leave the ride here. I might need it."

Eli got out too. He raised his arms in confusion and turned to an also-stunned Avi. The doctor looked at Jeremy.

"You've got a ballsy wife!"

"I don't like it when you talk about her that way."

~ ~ ~

Eytan whipped back his jacket panel to grab the Glock pistol inside his belt. But before he could wrap his fingers around the handle, he felt metal pierce his thigh, chest, and shoulder. He eyed the darts and coolly removed them one by one.

"Tranquilizers," he said before staggering, then falling to his knees.

The men recharged their weapons and approached the giant. They surrounded the Kidon agent, who was using all his strength to avoid face-planting. He kept his gaze on them despite his drooping eyelids, but they were growing heavier by the second.

"All right, we've got him, Sergeant. The second unit can retreat down the fire escape," the body-builder told the sniper.

"There was a second unit on the fire escape?" Eytan babbled.

"The Marines are professionals. You were trapped like a rat in a cage."

"True," the giant admitted, turning his head toward the fire escape, where he had placed two explosive pucks.

He shoved his hand into his pants pocket.

"But some rats are rabid," he spit as he pressed the detonator. A blast came in the next second, followed by the screech of shredded metal.

"What the...?"

The question went unfinished. Eytan whipped his right hand through the air and struck the body-builder in the leg, flipping him on his back. At the same time, he executed an uppercut to

the metrosexual's groin. The unlucky guy let out a shrill squeal
and collapsed in front of Eytan. The agent delivered a second
powerful blow to his perfectly coiffed head, leaving him with a
nose gushing blood. Before the last man standing could dodge
the giant, Eytan had grabbed him by the throat. The curly-
haired dude struggled to breathe. As the body-builder tried
to get up, Eytan used his free hand to draw his weapon, and
without even looking, lodged a bullet in his skull.

"I warned you, guys," he muttered as he lifted his prey off
the ground. "Needles make me nervous."

CHAPTER 21

As Jackie reassessed the events of the High Line, she began putting the puzzle pieces of Eytan's true intentions together. She didn't know if it was simple intuition or her years with the CIA. Either way, she was positive that Jeremy hadn't been used as bait, but rather as a decoy so Eytan could locate any opponents they hadn't sighted. She'd bet a million bucks that the agent had deliberately drawn his enemies to the roof. That way, he had control over where the fight would go down.

Although she was impressed by the genius of the plan, she beat herself up for taking so long to figure it out. As for his habit of using himself as a sacrifice—and disguising it behind a front of indifference—the Mossad agent would get a big talking-to.

For now, however, her objective was getting to him as quickly as possible. Jackie had practiced rigorous strength and conditioning exercises ever since she was a teenager, and she had above-average speed and agility, even after her pregnancy. Now was her opportunity to show off her skills.

Moments later, she had made it to the front of the building, at the top of which Eytan had set up camp. She ran to the alley to find the fire escape. Jackie stopped in her tracks. This alley was a graphic illustration of the paradox of urban life. In contrast to the pristine avenues where well-heeled residents lived, worked, dined, and shopped, this was a dark and desolate world. Trash containers overflowing with garbage lined the walls. They appeared to have been picked through. The smell of human urine filled the air. Abandoned sleeping bags, filthy blankets, and cardboard panels, the remnants of the homeless men and women who had spent the night in this place, littered the ground. While it didn't appear that any of them remained, two bloody and battered men were lying on the ground a few feet from the stairs, which were dangling down the side of the building. It looked like the men had taken a fall. They were groggy and staring at the sky. It was the ideal moment for a surprise attack.

~ ~ ~

Eytan resisted the temptation to crush the windpipe of the man whose neck he was gripping. He was spared for the moment, but Eytan had no compunction about settling this by leaving a trail of dead bodies. "War is horrible, but slavery is worse," Churchill had said. And Eytan would never again subject himself to enslavement, no matter the cost—the death of dozens, hundreds, or if it came to it, his own. That was bad news for anyone who wanted to capture him again. In an absurd world where some people understood only violence and cruelty, war was necessary to bring about peace. He had promised himself years earlier that if he had to resort to violence, it would be because he had hope. He hoped that one day violence would no longer be necessary. He would never give up on that ideal.

He put away his weapon and ripped the little microphone from his prey's throat, pulling out a flesh-colored wire and earpiece along with it.

"Don't be offended," Eytan said as he wiped the device against his jacket. "You look clean enough, but you never know. What's your sergeant's name?"

"I'm not telling you anything," the man wheezed.

"Spare me your heroic special-forces bullshit," Eytan said as he equipped himself with the earpiece. "I just killed one of your teammates in cold blood, bashed another one's skull in, and am now holding you in a rather compromising position. Your feet are dangling off the ground, and you're between me and your sniper boss, meaning he'll have to tear a hole through you to get to me. Just how far do you think I'll go to get what I want?"

Looking terrified, his hostage answered the question.

"Terry. Sergeant Tim Terry, Marines Corps."

"See, that wasn't so hard. All right, now you're going to be a good little captive and keep your mouth shut. I need to have a word with Daddy. Can you hear me, Sergeant Terry?" Keeping his gun aimed at the hostage's heart, Eytan lowered him to the ground.

"Loud and clear, Eytan Morgenstern," Terry said. "How is it that you're still standing after my men shot you with those sedatives?"

"Sedatives and other anesthetics have little effect on me, I'm afraid."

"That trait's not mentioned in your file. It must come in handy."

"Not when I'm getting a bullet pulled out of my flesh, trust me."

"How did you know we weren't going to kill you?"

"I'm often in the predicament of attracting unsavory admirers who lust after my body. I'm no good to them if I'm not alive. And the team that tried to kidnap Jacqueline Walls at the sheriff's department last night used sedatives. I didn't see why the strategy today would be any different."

"Makes sense."

"Doesn't it? So, I'm giving you the opportunity to abandon your mission without losing any more men."

"Negative. My orders are clear. You are to join the program."

"What program?"

"Come with me, and find out."

"I have a better idea. How about I don't listen to you and finish off your men."

"Don't waste your time. Those three are disposables," Terry said as he took a deep breath.

Eytan released his prisoner and rolled on his side just as a bullet penetrated the skull of the curly-haired jogger. A second shot executed the metrosexual, who had been writhing on the ground after getting punched in the head. The bullet definitively ended his suffering.

"Looks like it's time to play ball," Eytan announced as he somersaulted back toward his bag.

"I have to bring you back alive, but no one said anything about unharmed or in one piece," said Terry.

The Mossad agent leaped to his feet and ran toward the rooftop door, his only way down.

As he sped toward the door, the questions raced through his mind. Terry had called the men on the rooftop disposables. Did that mean the second team wasn't disposable? And if so, why? He turned around and ran back the other way, toward the side of the roof where the fire escape had been located. The second team would be somewhere in this vicinity.

Despite the bullets flying around him, he heard a voice down below: a woman screaming at the top of her lungs, "Eytan... If you're nearby, help me!"

Jacqueline clearly had serious issues with authority.

Without a moment's hesitation, he propelled himself forward and leaped off the roof.

~ ~ ~

TWO MINUTES EARLIER

Damn it. Here she was, cornered in another dirty alley, the same way she was in Zurich, when she first encountered the giant. Jackie was sick and tired of oafs preying on the weaker sex, even if, as in this case, weakness was a relative term.

Sure, a nitpicker would point out that she was the one who initiated the fight by kicking the first guy in the head before sending a right hook to the second guy's stomach. But according to the laws of physics, the two goons should have been conked out or at least down for the count. And yet the blows seemed to have doubled their desire to beat her up. She was now forced to twirl in all directions to dodge her opponents' attacks.

Jackie knew she had three things going for her. First, if the fight turned into a chase, the fake cripple appeared to be just a tad off his game. Meanwhile, the other guy, the one who had been behind the wheelchair, had an odd windmill-like swing—a technique that wasn't working for him. And she had a gun, while the two attackers didn't appear to be armed. But she hadn't been able to draw her weapon, because she was busy dodging and landing blows. And the two men worked well together. Without her realizing it, they had backed her against the wall. The fake gimp went in for a kick, which she narrowly dodged. Her attacker's foot smashed into the bricks, which crumbled under the blow. Cornered, Jackie called for help.

~ ~ ~

Ten feet before hitting the ground, Eytan grabbed the fire escape railing, which creaked under his weight and swung like a pendulum.

Startled by the noise from above, the men looked up. Before they had time to react, the Kidon agent steadied himself against the wall, and with every bit of strength in his legs, he thrust himself backward. He landed in a crouch next to Jackie.

"You don't have to yell," he chided as he stood up. "I'm here."

The two attackers bolted off.

"What's with that? They were ready to kill me two seconds ago, and as soon as you show up, they race off," Jackie said.

"They received orders to withdraw," Eytan yelled, giving them chase. "We need one of them, and in a condition to talk!"

The fake gimp picked up his pace, like an accelerating car about to reach cruising speed. He quickly outdistanced Eytan, who knew he wouldn't be able to catch up. The man's associate, however, was still fair game.

The Mossad agent lunged, and with the help of his impressive size and reach, grabbed the slowpoke's ankle. He brought him to the ground, caught hold of his hair, and smashed his face against the pavement. But with a limber chest swerve, the guy landed a backswing. A second swing, this time to the throat, sent the giant flying against a trash collector. Two garbage bags landed on Eytan's head as he crashed on the pavement. Although his head didn't hurt, his ribs did. The attacker rose from the ground, and to Eytan's surprise, he didn't take off. Instead, he began reporting to Sergeant Terry through his communication device, his eyes fixed on Jackie, who until now had been staring wide-eyed at the confrontation.

The man rushed toward Jackie. She dodged a right jab—just barely—then a left. The attempted punches, however, managed to destabilize her. The attacker pulled his arm back to land a hook. Eytan knew she couldn't avoid this one, but in the blink of an eye, she made a desperate move. She placed both hands on the man's wrist and followed his movement rather than countering it. With her firm hold, she jumped up, wrapped her legs around his outstretched arm, and secured her feet on his shoulder. Locked in place, she pulled with strength Eytan couldn't believe. No tendon or joint could resist such punishment—he was sure of it. He heard an awful cracking. Then ripped fabric. Jackie fell backward and wound up on the ground. Eytan could see by the look on her face that she had no comprehension of what had just happened.

Eytan hoisted himself up. His vision was blurry. His balance was shaky, and his side hurt so much, he was having a hard time breathing. He estimated that he had sustained two—no three—broken ribs. Once on his feet, he watched the man run off. Eytan felt too bad to chase him. He looked at Jackie. She was sprawled on the ground, frozen still. She was holding the sleeve of the man's jacket. And his entire arm was inside.

CHAPTER 22

A man and woman were taking comfort in the generous warmth of the blaze in their stone fireplace as they sat in front of a piping-hot tureen of soup. Cecilia picked up a wooden ladle and dipped it into the dish. She slowly stirred the few carrots and potatoes in the watery broth.

Bohdan watched with ravenous eyes. The uncustomary breakfast would be the highlight of his day and was, indeed, an indulgence in these times. Like a swarm of insatiable parasites, the occupying troops had forced farmers like Bohdan to turn over a substantial portion of their crops and livestock. According to the Wehrmacht, they were to use the meager resources they were left with to survive and grow more crops. Bohdan didn't doubt that they'd be looted all over again.

The hard yet honest tradition of working the land had become servitude. Bohdan felt not only defeated, but also enslaved.

Admittedly, everyone had little tricks for improving the situation, like burying small stashes in a nearby forest. They did it both to survive and to undermine the Germans' efforts.

Bohdan held out his bowl to Cecilia. She gave him a healthy portion but hardly filled her own bowl. As a girl, she had been blessed with a slender figure and a fair complexion. The lines that creased her face now didn't affect her beauty in Bohdan's eyes. In fact, he found her even lovelier than she had been on their wedding day. He never tired of the sight of her. He didn't tell her, though. He wasn't the kind of man who expressed emotion, partly because he couldn't find the words and partly because he would have been embarrassed.

They had been married for fifty years, and he still couldn't figure out why she had been attracted to a big schmuck like him. With her effortless charm, perfect upbringing, and strong will, she could have done much better. She could have married a college professor or a doctor. So why had she picked him, a simple farmer with hardly any education? Was she attracted to his huge build, his strong hands, and his mop of salt-and-pepper hair, which had been that color ever since he was a teenager? Granted, he did have an extraordinary work ethic. Tales about him—some of which were far-fetched—had circulated in the nearby villages.

According to one rumor, Bohdan had once hauled a cart filled to the brim with wood for several miles after his ox had gotten injured. A lie. The cart had only been a third full.

Some people claimed that Bohdan could do the work of ten farmers. He didn't deny that one. From the time he was a young man, he had been able to outperform several farmers combined. Even today he could outdo most strapping boys.

But Bohdan did consider himself a failure at one thing. He had never been able to say "I love you" to the two people who gave meaning to his life: his wife and his son, Josef. The boy, whose colossal size mirrored his father's, had enlisted in the Polish army and had climbed his way to lieutenant. The family had celebrated Josef's commission in the summer of 1939. That was his last visit to the farm. One month before the German forces invaded.

Since then, the couple hadn't heard from Josef, whose picture stood on their dresser. More than three years of silence. More than three years of waiting. But Bohdan never gave up hope of seeing his pride and joy walk through the door.

He refused to consider, even for a moment, the possibility that something had happened to their son. He ignored Cecylia whenever she mentioned her fears. He would dive into his work with even more earnestness. It distracted him from any worries.

On this morning, Bohdan looked at his wife with tenderness and gratitude, then plunged his spoon into his soup.

Two knocks on the window interrupted their feast. Cecylia was about to get up, but Bohdan stopped her with a hand gesture. He pushed back his chair and walked cautiously toward the window.

"Who's there?"

"The hungry," someone replied in a hushed but determined voice. The farmer relaxed, stepped over to the front door, and opened it a crack to find a man with long hair the color of sand and a matching beard. People called him the Tawny Bear—or just the Bear. He was wearing a snow-speckled brown parka. A German MP40 submachine gun was hoisted over his shoulder. In his hands was a white *czapka*.

Bohdan stared at him for a few moments. Despite the bulldog-like expression under the beard and the fearsome reputation, the old man could still recognize Janusz, Josef's childhood friend, now in his thirties, who had often joined them on their fishing trips.

"Hello, Mr. and Mrs. Jablonski," he said.

"Come in, Janusz," Bohdan replied, glancing over the man's shoulder to make sure he was alone.

"I don't have a lot of time."

"Don't worry," Bohdan said as he put on a thick coat, a gift from Josef. The Germans came by yesterday. They won't be back for a little while. The crates are ready. I'll go to the barn to get them."

He lit a small lantern, and as he closed the door behind him, an icy breath of winter air rushed into the small dining room. The flames in the fireplace flickered for a few seconds before rising again.

~ ~ ~

Cecylia pulled back a chair. "Have a seat," she said.

The man declined the invitation and remained standing. He had always been a gawky kid, Cecylia thought. Even if he was a hardened resistance fighter now, he still had some of that boyish awkwardness.

"Any news?" Janusz asked, pointing toward the framed black-and-white photo.

"Of course not," Cecylia answered, getting up from her chair. "Bohdan is still hanging onto the hope that Josef will come back one day. When he thinks I'm asleep, he plants himself in front of the dresser and talks to that photo for hours. Sometimes I see tears running down his cheeks. Can you believe it, Janusz? My Bohdan crying?"

Janusz walked over to Cecylia and put a hand on her shoulder. "You have to stay optimistic, Mrs. Jablonski. That's all we can do."

She took Janusz's hand and gave it a tender kiss. "Optimism is no longer appropriate," she replied. "The time for hatred has come. Can you do us a favor?"

"I don't have much to offer, but you know I'd do anything for the two of you."

"Be merciless," she begged. "Kill as many of them as possible. Do whatever it takes."

Janusz looked at his gun and cracked a predatory smile.

"You can count on me. I'm going to go join your husband. Wish me luck," he concluded as he put on his cap.

He walked out the door, and Cecylia felt a lump in her throat. Janusz hadn't said "see you soon." His life was too uncertain. But even though she thought her husband was foolish to cling to the illusion that their son was still alive, she wanted to believe there was a future, a future without bullets and hatred, without cruelty and submission. She secretly held onto that hope. But for that to happen, they had to endure—and resist.

Her eyes brimmed with tears. "Kill as many of them as possible."

~ ~ ~

The lantern hanging from a beam in the barn gave off a faint light as Bohdan toiled with growing frustration. He was pulling with all his might on an iron ring fixed to the hatch over his hiding place. This was where he stored extra food and sometimes weapons. But at the moment, the hatch was stubbornly insisting on staying shut. Bohdan exhaled a thick mist of warm air with every failed attempt.

"Hold on. Let me help," Janusz offered as soon as he entered the barn and saw the farmer struggling.

The two men grasped the metal ring and pulled at the same time. At last, the planks creaked, and the hatch opened to reveal a cellar.

Using a small ladder, Bohdan descended into the cave-like space. He reappeared a few moments later with a crate of carrots and potatoes. Janusz repositioned his gun and leaned over to take the crate. Bohdan went down again and came up with a second carton filled with more potatoes and carrots. This one also had a rare find: a piece of meat.

"That's strange," the farmer said. "I thought there were more vegetables."

"This is more than enough," Janusz said. "If everyone..."

He was brutally interrupted.

He felt the barrel of a gun against his back. His weapon was being yanked off his shoulder. The Bear cursed his lack of vigilance.

"Don't turn around," someone with a youthful voice ordered. "Put down the crate, and get on your knees. Hands on your head. And you, get out of there," he commanded Bohdan. "On your knees, and hands on your head."

Janusz and Bohdan complied.

Just as Janusz was steeling himself for the worst, he heard a commotion. It sounded like two wild animals locked in a ferocious battle. No longer feeling the weapon in his back, he dared to glance over his shoulder.

In the half-light of the barn, two men were rolling on the floor. One of them was wearing a German uniform. No, it was worse than that. As the man passed in and out of the circle of light cast by the lantern, Janusz was able to make out the SS insignia on the collar of his feldgrau. But his fears vanished when he recognized the man the German was locked in battle with. The SS officer was going down, and it would be painful.

Over the course of the two years he had spent fighting alongside Vassili, Janusz had learned that nobody could escape the Siberian. Nobody.

The fierce hand-to-hand combat was turning in the Siberian's favor. So far he had lost only his hat, and he had succeeded in pinning down his opponent. His blade was at the SS officer's neck. A split second later, however, the soldier managed to push the knife away.

Janusz spotted his machine gun on the floor, next to a Luger pistol. He retrieved his weapon and stood up.

Using superhuman strength, the German quickly overpowered Vassili and was now sitting on top of him. Even worse, the attacker was drawing the blade toward Vassili's jugular, and the latter was showing unexpected and worrisome signs of weakness.

Janusz rushed toward the action and slammed the butt of his weapon against the German's head. He face-planted on the floor.

The winded Siberian remained prostrate a few seconds before getting up. His square face, chapped by the wind and cold, showed his anger, frustration, and confusion. Wordlessly, he picked up his knife and put it back in his belt.

Bohdan was standing next to the enemy's motionless body.

"It's odd that he came alone," he said. "These guys never do."

"I know. Vassili?"

No answer.

"Vassili!" Janusz repeated.

The Siberian giant—the tallest member of Janusz's group—looked at the Bear with weary eyes.

"Secure the perimeter," Janusz ordered. "We're not leaving until we're sure there aren't any more of these goons out there."

Vassili nodded and left the barn.

"I've never seen him so shaken up before," Janusz muttered.

He watched as Bohdan turned over the unconscious German. The two men looked at each other in shock when they saw his face. His features were fine and youthful. His blond hair was so light, it was practically white. And it was too long for a branch of the army known for its strict regulations.

"I guess they're recruiting from the cradle these days," Bohdan jeered as he rummaged through the pockets of the dirt-and-dust-covered coat.

He took out a small notebook and military ID. He gave them to Janusz, who flipped through the contents.

"Horst Geller, lives in Hamburg, Schutzstaffel, assigned to Stutthof."

That's more than thirty miles away," Bohdan said. "What's he doing here?"

"Okay, we have a little problem," Janusz said. "The photo doesn't look anything like our Sleeping Beauty. His age doesn't match either. Horst Geller was born in 1913."

"This one here doesn't look a day older than sixteen."

Janusz readjusted his MP40 and slid the Luger into his belt. How had this kid managed to overpower Vassili? Why was he carrying another SS soldier's documents? And he had spoken perfect Polish without the trace of an accent. That was entirely unexpected.

Janusz planned to get answers to his questions.

Continuing his body search, Bohdan pulled back the boy's coat. He stopped when he spotted the forearm.

Janusz couldn't believe what he saw: a tattoo branded on the boy's skin.

One letter and six numbers that had sealed his fate.

Janusz was a gentile. He had never worn a tattoo. But like this boy, his fate had been sealed the day the German reign of terror reached into and snatched the land of his fathers.

CHAPTER 23

Leaning against the trash collector, Eytan was trying to calm Jackie as she sat on the ground with the detached limb. She was holding it as though it were a venomous snake that would bite her at any second. Yes, the severed limb was gross, but she looked so cute. Eytan couldn't help laughing.

"What the hell? I tore off his fucking arm!" she repeated over and over.

"Yeah, sort of," he said as he lit a Cuban.

He tried to inhale but reconsidered when the pain pierced his side.

Bad idea, he said to himself, tossing the cigar on the ground.

"What do you mean, *sort of*?" Jackie asked. Now she was waving her trophy in the air.

He walked unsteadily toward the young woman, picked up his cargo bag, and carefully knelt next to her.

"Come on, Jackie, how can you possibly think that you'd be capable of ripping off a grown man's arm? And look around you. There's no blood."

She scanned the scene and nodded. There wasn't a drop of blood on the ground or her clothes.

"But no shocker there." He started to push the sleeve off the arm. At the place where there should have been a shoulder joint, he found an electrode-studded suction cup. Sticking out of it were two thin silver tubes and several electrical wires. Eytan slid the sleeve all the way off the limb.

"It's a prosthetic, Jacqueline."

She closed her eyes and exhaled.

"And it's a prosthetic like no other I've ever seen" he said, examining the limb from all angles. "All right, get up. We shouldn't stick around. I'm going to put this thing in my bag. We can't go traipsing into the subway with it out in the open."

"Don't worry. I asked Eli to leave me the car before I ditched him," she said as she stood up. "How do you feel?"

"Like a china plate that's been stomped on by an elephant. But I'm used to it. A couple of bandages will do the trick. Avi will fix me up real nice. By the way, one of these days you'll have to explain why you suck at following instructions."

"Apparently, I had what they call a frictional relationship with my father. At least that's what the shrinks have told me," Jackie responded with an innocent smile. "Besides, you should be thanking me."

"And why is that, pray tell?" he asked, raising an eyebrow.

"I came to your rescue, didn't I?"

"Yes, and thanks to you, I had to jump off a building, I shattered my ribs, and we don't even have any hostages to show for it."

Jackie's cheeks turned red. "I was only trying to help."

The giant grumbled as he limped toward the main avenue. "That kind of help I can do without."

~ ~ ~

The painfully slow traffic made for an arduous drive north to Central Park. Eli, Avi, and Jeremy were stuck in their car. Nobody spoke. They were all waiting to hear a voice in their earpieces, which had been silent ever since they had left the High Line.

For his part, Eli was obsessing over the two wheelchair posers. He had made an egregious error in judgment, and he was furious with himself. Had he lost his observational skills? Meanwhile, sitting by himself in the back, Jeremy was biting his nails. Eli could guess what was on his mind: he had left his baby daughter in the hands of some guy who claimed the members of Metallica were musical geniuses, and his wife had jumped into the ring, determined to get herself killed.

The sound of static jolted Eli out of his despondent thoughts.

"How does this thing work? Ah, is it turned on? Boys, can you hear me?"

Three sighs greeted Jackie's melodious voice.

"Loud and clear, Jacqueline," Eli replied. "How's it going? And how's Eytan?"

"We're both fine. Eytan's just a little banged up. Avi, can you go buy something for mending injured ribs?"

"Gladly," Avi said. "Is it for you or him?"

"For him."

"How bad is it?"

"He says it's not serious."

"That means it *is* serious! I'll take care of it."

"Great. He suggests that we meet at this French restaurant at the corner of Madison and Eighty-Second Street. It's close to the Met. Jeremy will know how to get there. Until then, turn off your receivers. Eytan says we should save battery. See you in a bit. Oh, and honey?"

"Yes?" Jeremy replied.

"I love you."

"I love you too, but you'd better not put me through that again. Okay?"

"Of course I won't! Mwah..."

Their conversation ended, and a flurry of commotion replaced the silence that preceded the call. Avi had Eli stop at the first minimarket they spotted. They loaded their shopping baskets with enough supplies to fill a small pharmacy. As per the doctor's orders, Eli and Jeremy stocked up on sandwiches, bottled water, and soda. They paid for everything in cash before getting back in the car.

Ten minutes later, they parked with baffling ease. Avi was gloating, as Jeremy had warned him that finding a spot in this neighborhood would be impossible. The three men walked up to the small restaurant.

Its low-key exterior suggested a cozy dining room, and the blue, white, and red awning advertised the owner's origins, or at least the restaurant's brand of cuisine. Both assumptions were confirmed as soon as they walked in. Five tables covered with checked tablecloths were jammed together in the tiny space, while photographs of delectable French-inspired dishes adorned the walls. Avi was eyeing them longingly and bemoaning the snack he had downed just outside the minimarket.

"How do you possibley stay in shape?"Eli asked.

Avi responded by launching into a convoluted biochemical explanation peppered with obscure medical terms. Eli rolled his eyes and grinned at Jeremy.

"Bunch of morons," Avi muttered under his breath. Jeremy greeted the chef-owner, a pot-bellied gentleman with thinning hair. In heavily accented English, the owner invited them to sit at any table. The group noisily pulled out their chairs and unceremoniously plopped down as their host watched with visible disapproval. He tossed some menus on the table and disappeared into the kitchen.

Jackie and Eytan showed up a few minutes later. Jackie had a bounce in her step, but Eytan was lumbering. Jeremy rushed to his wife, who assured him that she was okay. Then Jeremy turned to Eytan, whose sagging posture and pained expression made him look more like an old retiree than an elite Mossad agent. Jeremy reached out to help him but was brushed off.

"Why'd you have us come here?" Avi inquired once the Kidon assassin was settled across from him. "The owner is as friendly as a tapeworm."

"Because I've been here many times, and I knew no other customers would be here during the day."

"It's pretty obvious why," Eli sighed as he examined the menu.

"At night, though, this place is packed," Eytan said. "The owner may not be the most charming guy in the world, but he's an excellent chef. And he has a much more important quality, in my opinion: Monsieur Lionel Datoist loves money."

The chef came back through the kitchen door. His sour face brightened when he spotted Eytan. They chatted a bit in French. Then, without warning, Datoist departed.

"All right, alone at last," Eytan said.

"I didn't catch all that," Jeremy said.

"Whenever I go to a new city, I look for one or two places to meet with people, other than the usual Mossad spots. I like to hang loose—you know that. I make friends with the owners of the places I choose, and I can count on privacy when I need it. Okay, let's get on with the debriefing, assuming no one objects."

"I'd like nothing better," Eli replied as he sent his menu gliding across the plastic tablecloth. "The past hour has raised more questions than answers. A thorough recap is in order, as well as a detailed report of what happened after Jacqueline's *departure*." He shot her a look dripping with disapproval.

"I'm sorry, Eli, but you would have never let me intervene. And of all of us, I was the only one who could help Eytan." Eli's face relaxed a bit.

"Water under the bridge," Eytan said. "Let's move on to more important things."

"Before filling us in," Avi interrupted, "shouldn't I have a look at your injuries?"

"After the recap. I'll be fine. So..."

"Okay, if you're into pain, that's cool with me," the doctor said, pretending to read his menu.

"One more snide remark, and you'll need bandages too. That's your last warning, Avi. So," the agent continued once all eyes were on him, "we know that a government organization is interested in me. They were even prepared to kidnap Jackie and Jeremy just to obtain information. We also know that the organization had ties with Titus Bramble from the CIA. He turned out to be our contact on the High Line. Bramble was a former Marine who crossed my path on several occasions in South America. At the time, I was chasing Nazi war criminals. Since some of them were working with the local juntas, the CIA provided me with backup. I don't believe for one second that Titus willingly set me up."

"He was followed. They used him to get to you," Eli surmised.

"Exactly. Before he died, he mentioned a program and the fact that the people in charge of it will go to any lengths to protect its secret."

"On that topic," Eli interrupted, "he..."

Eytan cut him off. "Eli, I'd liked to finish my thought. At this point I'm certain that the men sent to get us were members of a Marine commando unit led by a Sergeant Terry, a talented high-precision sniper. He made it very clear that while they didn't need me in one piece, they wanted me alive for the purposes of this mysterious program."

"If I may..."

"Give me one more second. I'm almost done. I eliminated a man on the roof and neutralized two others before Terry took them out himself. The two guys chasing Jeremy were trying to corner me when Jackie showed up, and we fought the two puppets together. And then the big surprise... Eli, could you reach my duffle bag for me? I'd rather not bend over right now."

Once he had the duffle in his lap, Eytan unzipped it and pulled out the artificial arm. He placed it on the table. Avi picked it up and examined it inch by inch.

"A highly advanced prosthetic," he said, still looking it over.

"That thing's crazy," Jeremy said. "It looks like something from *I, Robot*."

"It's one sweet piece of technology, for sure," Avi said.

The guy pushing the man in the wheelchair was carrying a long bag," Eytan said. "Considering the way we were chased, I have every reason to believe that a pair of sophisticated prosthetic legs were in that bag. Eli, what is it that you wanted to say?"

"It's about time. Before Bramble died, he gave me two names. General Bennington and H-Plus Dynamics. I have no idea what he was referring to, but I suspect it was relevant information, given the circumstances."

"What did you just say?" Avi asked

"That I suspect..."

"Not that part—the name of the company?"

"H-Plus Dynamics."

"H-Plus..." Avi was quiet for a few seconds. "Okay, now it all makes sense."

"Not to anyone else, it doesn't," Jackie said.

"Of course not. If you're not a doctor or a techie who's working in this specific area of medicine, you wouldn't have heard about mechatronics. But prosthetics such as this one—and legs that can enable an amputee to run like a cheetah—aren't the stuff of fantasy anymore."

"What are you talking about?" Eytan asked.

"I'm talking about transhumanism, Eytan."

CHAPTER 24

Avi was wrapping an ace bandage around Eytan to hold his injured ribs in place. The shirtless giant was sitting patiently in the middle of the restaurant, which the team still had exclusive use of. Jeremy and Jackie were focused on Eytan's physique and scars. And off to the side, Eli was sneaking a Spanish cigarillo.

"Transhumanism," Avi explained, "is, for lack of a better word, a *philosophical* movement that promotes human enhancement through the use of biotechnology and nanotechnology. Simply put, the idea is that the average man is now archaic, in terms of evolution. The most extreme advocates of these robotic limbs are in favor of chopping off perfectly healthy arms and legs and replacing them with better-performing high-tech prosthetics. More moderate transhumanists, as you can imagine, have ethical concerns. This is a hotly debated area of medical science, and much of the research is top-secret."

"So are most of these transhumanists whack jobs?" Jackie asked. She had almost reached out and touched an especially puffy wound on Eytan's side.

"Some are, yes. But many aren't. First, though, let's understand what we're talking about. From time immemorial, human beings have strived to enhance their performance. Transhumanism is just the latest wrinkle. Take sports, for example. Lots of athletes inject themselves with performance-enhancing drugs. Take EPO, which stimulates red blood-cell production. The effects, however, are temporary, and some scientists are working on a gene that would permanently enhance red blood-cell production."

"So much for hero-worshipping our athletes," Jeremy said.

"No kidding. Listen to this. Remember Yao Ming, the seven-foot-six Houston Rockets superstar? His conception and growth as a child were painstakingly manipulated by the Chinese government, whose aim was to turn out a world-class athlete."

"Now you're just messing with us."

"Not at all. Lots of articles have been written about it, even a book or two. The one I read was *Operation Yao Ming*. His parents, both of whom had played basketball, were specifically chosen by the Chinese government. His mother was six-two, and his father was six-ten. Yao weighed eleven pounds when he was born, and by the age of eight, he was already five-foot-five. Then he started getting injections of growth hormone. That's when he really took off. After starting his career as a teenager with the Shanghai Sharks, he came to America as the Rockets' top draft pick. He quickly became an international celebrity, a real money-making machine, and a way for China to promote itself."

"Wow, that's pretty scary. So if I'm following all this, Eytan would be the perfect incarnation of this so-called enhanced human."

"I'd say a prototype more than an incarnation. According to the criteria set by the movement's defenders, he isn't perfect. For many of them, immortality is the end goal. Eytan is not immortal. Of course, his life expectancy is exceptional, because he'll probably live to be a hundred and ten. His special quality is that he doesn't show any signs of aging, inside or out. I'd describe him as a highly skilled athlete with an above-average ability to recover and adapt. He's sort of a super-Olympian. Unfortunately, he has several limitations, including the need to inject himself with a serum that keeps his body from self-destructing."

"I'm sitting right here, you know," Eytan mumbled.

"We're well aware of that, you big oaf," Avi said as he finished wrapping the bandage.

"So what does H-Plus Dynamics have to do with transhumanism?" the Kidon agent asked as he grabbed his T-shirt.

"The transhumanist symbol is an 'H' and the plus sign. 'Dynamics' makes me think it's a specialized corporation. I might be wrong, but everything seems to match up with that."

"How do you know so much about all of this?" Jackie inquired.

"I work for the intelligence agency of a country that sees war as a constant threat. Every government dreams of building a better army, whether it's in terms of supplies or soldiers. The use of performance-enhancing substances is not exclusive to athletes. Soldiers have access to compounds that allow them to stay alert and resist the effects of cold, heat, and stress. Believe me, all means of gaining an upper hand are in play when it comes to war. Keeping up on the latest advances in biochemistry and medical technology is part of my job."

"Avi is right," Eli chimed in as he rejoined his friends. "Armies around the world spend tons of money on chemical and technological research. The advances they come up with aren't made public until they're obsolete for the military. So while medical reporters are busy writing stories about the latest prosthetics, newer and more improved ones are already being created, tested, and used. The arm we have here is proof of that. This isn't science fiction. It's clandestine science. Bramble mentioned some covert program. Eytan thinks the guys who attacked us were hardcore military men, and Avi just clearly and expertly explained the connection with transhumanism. There's no doubt in my mind that the US government is setting up some kind of special unit composed of enhanced fighters. And they're getting help from a corporation that deals with the latest advancements in prosthetics. But we still need to figure out why they want Eytan and find a way out of this mess."

Short and sweet, Jeremy thought. Avi and Eli seemed just as comfortable in their own fields as Eytan was with hand-to-hand combat. As individuals, they were incredible. But as a threesome, they were a force to be reckoned with. And you sure as hell wanted them on your side.

"I'm going to call Attali to bring him up to speed and see if he can tell us more about General Bennington," Eytan said.

He took out his cell phone and stepped away from the table, Eli at his side.

The others left the restaurant to give the duo some privacy. Jeremy needed a cigarette. Once outside, he offered one to the doctor, who made a crack about tobacco breath and declined. Jackie laughed. Jeremy growled and turned away. But he turned back around just as quickly. He wasn't going to let them out of his sight.

"And what do you think about all this?" he asked Avi.

"About what?"

"Human enhancement, superprosthetics, the full monty."

"I'm more in favor of human *healing*. I'm sure you know about Oscar Pistorius, the four-hundred-meter runner. Set aside, for the moment, what happened with his girlfriend, and just think of him as an athlete. Didn't it amaze you that a double amputee was competing in the Olympic semifinals of the four-hundred meter and that he made it all the way to the finals?"

"Well, yes."

"Point proven! We're in the midst of a revolution. Everyone who watched the Olympics can attest to that. Healing a human is one thing, and the devices we create to allow someone to overcome adversity have terrific merit. But messing with the human genome, mixing man and machine with ulterior motives that have nothing to do with healing, and deliberately tampering with the course of evolution... That's bad news, my friend."

Jeremy threw his cigarette to the ground and looked up at the sky.

"No question about it now. This little adventure has their name written all over it. Don't you agree, honey?"

"I was afraid of that," Jackie replied.

"Care to explain?" Avi said.

Jeremy started running back toward the door of the restaurant. "Don't move," he instructed Avi.

Eytan was just wrapping up his cell-phone conversation when Jeremy got inside.

"The Consortium," he yelled.

"Yeah, no shocker there. It's not exactly a cause for celebration, though," Eytan replied, his eyes glued to his cell as he entered another number.

"We just realized it ourselves, but I'm happy you've reached the same conclusion," Eli said. He gave the young man a friendly pat on the shoulder and walked outside to join Jackie and Avi.

Jeremy was speechless. Here he had thought he was onto something.

"Who are you calling?" he asked Eytan.

"An old friend, Ian Jenkins. Hello, Jenkins?" Eytan's voice resonated. "How's the knee holding up? And just curious, what boxers do you have on today? Stripes or polka dots?"

Getting a playful wink from Eytan, Jeremy decided a second cigarette was in order. He returned to the sidewalk with one thought running through his head: they'd gone bonkers.

CHAPTER 25

The discussion on the Madison Avenue sidewalk was flying faster than the yellow taxicabs ferrying harried businessmen and awestruck tourists. The three men and one woman in front of the little French restaurant were going on and on about doping, genetic mutation, prosthetics, and robotics and their military and police-force applications. Eli and Avi were answering Jeremy's many questions. This wasn't the sci-fi that filled the shelves of his store. It wasn't something out of Jules Verne. It was the real thing.

Avi weighed in. "You have to wonder whether Jules Verne was prophesying the future or if his works were a source of inspiration for inventors. It's even possible that he picked up on ideas floating in the collective subconscious. Other celebrated sci-fi writers have created machinery and devices that we're seeing in the real world today. Take Robert Heinlein's powered armor, which also goes by the name powered exoskeleton. The French Army has introduced Hercule, which allows a solder to easily carry more than 200 pounds. American engineers have designed a similar device called HULC. There's no doubt in my mind that mythology influences creative minds and excites the imagination. Science and fiction feed off one another to the point of becoming inseparable. Sometimes it's a positive thing, but more often than not, it's..."

Eytan emerged from the restaurant. "Well aren't you all looking serious. What did I miss?"

"Avi was sharing his philosophical views, while Jeremy was enlightening us with his geeky sci-fi information," Jackie teased. "Any updates at your end?"

Eytan nodded toward the door. "Let's go back in, and I'll tell you everything."

Jackie went in first, followed by Jeremy, Eli, Avi, and Eytan.

"So now the coffee-machine maniac is waxing philosophical?" Eytan asked.

"Diogenes lived in a ceramic jar," the doctor retorted without missing a beat. "The ambitions of great minds are not easily understood by the common folk."

He gently patted the giant's injured ribs. Eytan had already tensed up in anticipation.

"Let's go," Eytan grunted, "Or I guarantee you'll feel the wrath of the common folk."

Eytan swung his foot back, ready to kick his friend in the behind. Avi hurried to the table.

"So I just spoke with my friend Jenkins," Eytan said, getting back to business. "He's a member of the Consortium, but he's simultaneously collaborating with us."

"A member of the Consortium in cahoots with us?" Jackie asked.

"You have no idea how far you can get with a little kindness and a well-aimed bullet."

"I have a vague idea. Please, go on."

"I asked him if the name H-Plus Dynamics rang any bells, and he said it sounded familiar. He confirmed that this company does, indeed, belong to the Consortium, but he didn't really know what it does. He's going to get back to me with the address."

"He seems very cooperative for someone from the Consortium," Jeremy said.

"I was very considerate when I aimed the bullet," Eytan said, grinning.

"I'm sure you were. While we're on the subject of the Consortium, whatever happened to Elena, that bitch who killed my mom?"

"She's..."

Eytan stopped himself. He was experiencing an unusual feeling: embarrassment. How could he tell Jeremy that he and the genetically modified killer had grown close to each other, so close that he had helped her fake her death and free herself from the Consortium? Was Jeremy capable of understanding that Eytan had been able to move past his enmity and had even trusted her on a mission that had thrown them together? He had been caught up in rescuing Jeremy and Jackie and hadn't prepared himself for Jeremy's question. Just how wide was the gap between the agent's life and Jeremy's expectations? And above all, how could he deceive this goofy but terribly sweet boy who was more than ready to get involved in adventures that were way bigger than he was.

"She's dead," Eli intervened. Eytan silently thanked Eli for sparing him the discomfort of lying or burdening the young man with a truth that was impossible to accept. "Eytan killed her in front of me with two bullets to the chest."

Jeremy remained stone-faced. "Too bad that couldn't bring Mom back," he said.

Avi swooped in and changed the subject.

"Do you trust this Jenkins fellow?"

"No, but the fear I've instilled in him should make up for that little detail."

"And Attali, what does he think?" Avi asked.

"He's pulling together what he can find on Sergeant Terry, General Bennington, and H-Plus Dynamics. He should be calling back any minute now. By the way, he'd like to have a little examination done on our trophy."

"That's a good idea," the doctor said. "But there's no way we'll be able to get this thing out of the country and into the hands of a Mossad expert. And when I say expert, I mean a real genius in engineering, electronics, and what have you."

"Well, it just so happens that we know someone just like that right here in the US, right Eli?"

Eli turned to Eytan with shock written all over his face.

"Excuse me? You want to go see... No, no, no, not on your life!"

"We don't have a choice."

"You know very well how things end up every time we're together. It's always a disaster."

"Do you mind telling us what you're talking about?" Jackie asked.

Eytan and Eli launched into an answer at the same time. Eytan couldn't make himself understood because Eli was talking over him.

"One at a time!" Jackie ordered.

"A very old friend of ours holds a position at a university in Illinois. He excels in the fields that Avi mentioned. If there's anyone who can help us with this arm, it's *him*."

"He's unbearable." Eli was fuming.

"Maybe now isn't the best time to let our egos get in the way of what we need to do," Jackie told the men. "You both know this professor well?"

"He's my brother," Eli surrendered with a sigh. "Not my biological brother. My adopted brother. But don't ask me to explain right now. It's too complicated. All right, Eytan, I'll go. What's our next move?"

"You, Avi, and the prosthetic will leave for Chicago immediately. I'll wait here until I get an address for H-Plus Dynamics. When I find out where they're located, I'll pay them a little visit. I'll take Jeremy and Jackie with me. Jackie will cover me if I need help. Now that the little episode on the High Line is over, we're back on track. Our enemies have no idea where to find us. From here on out, we're the hunters. I intend to keep that advantage until the very end."

"And what is the very end?" Jeremy asked. He looked happier than a kid on Christmas morning. Eytan knew that Jeremy liked spending time with him, but to be this ecstatic over a few extra hours together? And with no idea of what awaited them during those hours? Okay. So be it.

"The systematic elimination of every honcho in this project. That's the end," Eytan declared. "It's the only possible way out of this fucking mess."

CHAPTER 26

The night was drawing to a close, and the first rays of sunshine were struggling to pierce the thick clouds that threatened to add to the blanket of snow. Today, like every other day of the rotten war, the members of this small band of fighters were cold and miserable. But they weren't hungry, thanks to Jablonski's generosity. There were many farmers who could not or would not feed the resistance fighters. Some farmers had nothing to share. Others feared retaliation—most often summary execution—from the occupying forces. A handful of Poles embraced Hitler's cause and saw nothing wrong with the mistreatment of Jews, intellectuals, and homosexuals. They were convinced that a powerful Poland would emerge from the war. Fortunately, these Poles were in the minority, and those who fought in the shadows received much-appreciated support from everyday heroes. In a state seized by insanity, freedom hung on acts of solidarity.

A natural-born leader, Janusz had always commanded respect from those around him. His role in this grim farce was made clear in the flames that ravaged Warsaw on the last night of the Luftwaffe bombings. The flames had engulfed the apartment where he lived with his wife and two sons. Only he had survived. On the night that he lost his family, he shed his identity as a simple peace-loving man. Hitler's troops wanted insane and savage warfare. And that was what they were getting from Janusz—a full share of it.

Over the following months, the construction foreman had turned into a merciless killer. He slaughtered the enemy at every opportunity. Two soldiers strolling on a deserted street, a careless driver who had gone off to piss in a dark alley. No game plan, no strategy, just a wild dive into the deep abyss. Janusz answered to no one. He simply killed.

Some resistance fighters vehemently disapproved of his renegade actions, which brought about disastrous consequences.

The Wehrmacht had reinforced its patrols, stepped up its raids, and retaliated against civilians. A few fighters even wanted to see him eliminated, although none of them would have pulled the trigger.

A more sensible branch of the Armia Krajowa had approached Janusz. They wanted him to sabotage the railway tracks used to transport provisions to German garrisons. It was a dangerous mission with practically no chance of success. Suicidal, in fact. If this man had to die, it was better to get something out of it. Janusz accepted the assignment, and before he knew it, he had pulled together a band of raging-mad rebels from all over Poland. From their very first outing, the eclectic team had proved to be an undeniably effective attack force. As individuals, these guys were unpredictable radicals. Collectively, they accomplished the unthinkable. With his crack unit, Janusz now had a sense of responsibility and organization. Their job was unchanged: killing the Germans. But oddly, Janusz's mental state was more balanced.

Tales of the feats achieved by the Tawny Bear and his band of men soon spread throughout the country.

From then on, he had fought for his men, the memory of his family, and the sovereignty of his country. Death had to wait a little longer.

The morning promised to be a busy one. During the night, they had secured the food they badly needed, but their restocking mission had also yielded a surprise in the form of a boy in an SS uniform. During their trek from the Jablonski farm to the campsite in the forest, Vassili hadn't spoken a word. The humiliating confrontation with the kid, whom he was now lugging on his massive shoulder, had completely silenced the usually quiet Siberian. Janusz was also reflecting on the scene he had witnessed. If he hadn't stepped in, there was no question that Vassili would have been defeated. And yet in any other barehanded fight no one could have matched the strength and speed of the Red Army deserter. Furthermore, what was the meaning of the tattoo on the boy's forearm?

"Food and a prisoner—twice the work for me," Karol complained as he stepped out from behind a large tree, rifle in hand.

"A meal and an opportunity to interrogate," Janusz sighed as he placed the crates of food on the thick coat of snow. Karol, the team's cook, began inspecting each food item.

"Let's eat," Janusz said. "We'll deal with our special guest later."

The campsite was in a rolling, difficult-to-traverse, and especially dense section of the forest. The bivouac was composed of four small wooden huts built against a hill. A fire, or rather a heap of skillfully maintained embers, and a table fashioned from a few tree limbs were the only semblances of comfort.

Vassili dumped the unconscious boy next to a tree. He hoisted him into a sitting position and grabbed some rope to tie him to the trunk. Vassili tested his knots. Three other men joined him.

"Who's that?" Marek, a young pyrotechnist from Lviv, asked as he emerged from one of the wooden huts, where he had been sleeping.

Pawel, a man in his fifties with a long nose, thinning hair, and an underbite, walked over to Vassili. "Where'd you find him?"

"Who cares!" responded Piotr, Vassili's Polish doppelgänger. "After he talks, we'll slit his throat. We'll be done with him."

"He sneaked up on us in the Jablonski barn," Janusz explained, studying the boy. The body was just too massive for a youth his age.

"He's in that SS uniform. But he doesn't look old enough to be an officer. He's a kid. We'll find out more after we fill our bellies. And until then, no one touches or speaks to him. Got that, Piotr?"

"Why are you singling me out?" the boxer protested.

"Because I want him to answer our questions. The last one we caught could barely spit out three words after you were done with him. I'm not letting that happen again. Once we're finished, he's all yours." Janusz walked away to join Karol, who was working on the fire.

Piotr scowled. He slammed his right fist into the palm of his left hand. Pawel gave Marek a playful jab, and Marek cracked a grin.

Fifteen minutes later, the six teammates were gathered around a large pot filled with something other than tasteless goo. A few of them made suggestive jokes about Karol's culinary talents. It was a shame, they said, that there were no women for Karol to seduce with his cooking at their woodsy campsite, populated exclusively by hairy men.

Karol adjusted his wire-rim glasses. The former University of Krakow professor was in his thirties and was as blind as a bat. For that reason, the Polish army wouldn't have him. Further, Karol had never handled a weapon before joining his brothers in the resistance. And yet Janusz considered him a prized member of the team. He was an extraordinary cook and could turn a box of root vegetables into a culinary treat. He could also quote from the world's greatest authors and keep the men entertained. These two qualities helped Janusz's men maintain a crumb of civilization. In addition, Karol spoke German so well, he could lead solo missions in the enemy's uniform. He wasn't a soldier's soldier. Nevertheless, Karol was a valiant man.

Sitting off to the side, Vassili was eating in silence and watching the tied-up kid for signs of life. The boy shook his head and opened his eyes, which immediately darted to the ropes. He rolled his shoulders a few times to test the ropes' strength. Vassili thrust his chin at Janusz. The group leader placed his mess tin on the ground, stood up, and waved to Karol to follow him. The others kept eating.

Janusz and Karol spoke a few hushed words and planted themselves in front of the prisoner, who was glaring at them. The college professor squatted next to the boy.

"Name and ID number," he said in German.

No response.

Janusz took a step closer and delivered a hard slap. The kid took it without batting an eye. He even cracked a nasty smile.

"If you don't talk, you'll suffer," Karol said, trying to hide his discomfort.

The response came at last. In Polish.

"My name is Eytan Morgenstern. Hit me as many times as you want. I'm not afraid of pain."

CHAPTER 27

Eli and Avi prepared to leave Manhattan for Illinois in the late afternoon. Eytan was still waiting to hear from Jenkins and Simon Attali. He needed to know more about the main players and find out where he would be headed. The good-byes outside the restaurant proved to be difficult. The members of the group—some of whom had been perfect strangers a day earlier—had grown close to each other.

Eli gave Jackie a hug. "That big-hearted brute will take good care of you and Jeremy," he whispered in her ear. "Swear to me you'll behave yourself. Don't do anything crazy. You've been loyal friends to Eytan, and he intends to send you home safe and sound when this is all over."

Eytan shook hands with the doctor and the man who had been both a son and a father to him, a man who was willing to throw everything into this match. They parted ways without saying a word. Eli, however, put his little finger in front of his lips and his thumb to his ear to mime a phone call. Eytan acknowledged the message with a nod.

Jeremy's face was drawn.

"I'm sure those two will have a squabble or two, but Avi and Eli have nothing to worry about," the giant said as he checked his silent cell phone yet again. "My pal Jenkins seems to be dawdling."

"Do you think he might have double-crossed you?" Jackie asked.

"I doubt that. It's a long story, but he's as afraid of his old pals as he is of me. And those guys don't show any mercy. I think he'll be extra careful not to cause any more problems for himself than he already has."

Jeremy rubbed his hands together. "Hey, since we have some time to kill, can I ask you about something that's been bothering me for almost two years now?"

"I promised you answers."

"Why did you let us think you were killed in the explosion at the BCI facility in Brussels?"

Eytan looked at the thick black clouds hovering over the skyscrapers. The wind seemed to be picking up, and the air had the smell of an approaching rainstorm.

"Crossing paths with me is never a good thing, Jeremy. It's a twist of fate that both baffles and saddens me. My friends and foes often share the same end."

"So you really thought you needed to keep us in the dark?"

"Jeremy," Eytan sighed, "are the worlds of a Mossad assassin and a nice New Jersey couple really compatible? Can you actually see me setting my Glock down on the table at Thanksgiving between the turkey and mashed potatoes? After reading all those books of yours, you've created a delusional picture of me. I've spent my life systematically assassinating war criminals. No matter the price. Don't kid yourself: if you and Jackie had been on the wrong side, I wouldn't have hesitated to take both of you out. Because of me, people have lost their husbands, wives, and children. I'm a killer, Jeremy. Not a hero."

Eytan shrugged and held out his arms, palms up. His two friends remained wordless for a moment before Jackie broke the wall of silence that separated them.

"The way you talk about yourself makes you sound like a garden-variety assassin, if there is such a thing. But if you really were the man you describe, why did you send us that Christmas message?"

"Because the man that I am sometimes dreams of being the man I wish I were."

Eytan's cell phone rang, and he was quick to answer. He cleared his throat and went back into the restaurant. Jackie and Jeremy followed.

"Eli Karman and Avi Lafner have left to examine the arm. I'm with Jacqueline and Jeremy Corbin. I'm putting you on speaker phone so I don't have to repeat everything."

Eytan pressed a button. Simon Attali's authoritative voice filled the room.

"I have some information on Sergeant Terry and General Bennington. We've traced Timothy Terry to a Marines Corps reconnaissance unit where he served as an elite shooter, as you've pointed out. The man had a remarkable career with more than commendable accomplishments. According to his file, he might have been the best shooter in the ranks."

"After what I saw, I can't say I disagree with that. But why are you talking about him in the past tense?"

"Tim Terry was killed in Iraq in 2003, along with three other members of his team. The bodies of his comrades were identified, but a few parts were all that remained of Terry. For some reason, though, those body parts were never submitted for DNA identification."

"And they would have needed a DNA sample to confirm his identity," Eytan concluded with a disappointed smile. "No body, no confirmation, aside from the one given by the Marines. Quite convenient when you're forming a zombie commando unit."

"What do mean by 'zombie commando unit'?" Jeremy asked.

"Mr. Corbin," Attali responded, "a zombie commando unit is a group of fighters who work in the shadows, cut off from their families and previous lives. On paper, they don't exist. It's believed that the Americans have been using them for special operations since the nineteen seventies: assassinations of political leaders and drug traffickers, coups d'états, and all sorts of other nasty tricks."

"If they're so secret, how did you have access to Terry's file?" Jeremy pressed.

"We work for Mossad, Mr. Corbin. We keep one eye on our enemies and the other on our allies. We're not nitwits."

"In 2010, a bunch of your agents managed to get themselves caught on surveillance cameras at a Dubai hotel where they had just executed a man," the bookseller let slip.

Eytan could see that Jeremy was already regretting the remark. Jeremy looked to his friend for help. Eytan just sighed. No one was perfect, even military assassins, special agents, and plain ordinary spies. Embarrassing errors were part of the job.

Attali cleared his throat before continuing. "Unfortunately, mistakes happen."

"Please excuse us," Eytan rushed in. "We've veered off-course." He gestured to Jeremy to zip his lip. "Could you expand your search to see if any other precision Marines fell off the radar around 2003?"

"I'm one step ahead, Morg. I've come up with ten Marines who stand out. They were listed as killed in action between 2003 and 2005, but there's reason to believe they're among the living. Each excelled in a specific field: shooting, close-range combat, long-distance running, sprinting. These were all high-performance athletes. And they were at the end of their enlistments when they were allegedly killed."

"The military has always been interested in athletes," Eytan said. "Avi Lafner saw the prosthetic arm that we acquired as a sign of the rise of the enhanced man. Do you think the US military could be creating a force composed of elite soldiers who've been disabled and then equipped with advanced technology?"

"It seems like a stretch at this point. But you're the ones who were attacked. So you are in the best position to venture a guess."

In his head, Eytan quickly reviewed the High Line confrontation.

"Tim Terry, if that's definitely the guy you're talking about, killed the two men I managed to corner up there. He called them disposables."

Jackie chimed in. "If I understand what you're telling us, soldiers who were believed to be dead were actually still alive but wounded. They were whisked away and jacked up with top-of-the-line prosthetics. Uncle Sam recycled these guys. But the second version was actually superior to the first." She stopped before delivering the KO punch. "That's the program that Bramble was talking about."

"It's only a hypothesis," Attali insisted. "Highly likely, but still a hypothesis. Eytan, were the men that Terry eliminated enhanced?"

"I didn't have time to check, and to be honest, I had no reason to check. Nothing seemed abnormal, at any rate. However, the two men we encountered on the High Line, were abnormal. The first one had an artificial arm, and the second was a double amputee who miraculously got his legs back and smashed a wall with a single kick."

"So our theory could very well be correct. But we still have to figure out why they are so interested in you, Morg. You're in perfect condition with two very healthy legs and a set of just-as-healthy arms. No need for repairs, as far as I know."

"I can confirm that, although they've taken a scrape or two over the years."

"Now for General Paul Bennington. He's had quite a career. He saw his first action in the US invasion of Panama. He served in Operation Desert Storm and was on the ground in Somalia. He rose through the ranks, finally becoming a general. Although he's seen his share of combat, he's better known for his political savvy. Just after 9/11, he was recruited to serve on a committee created by the George W. Bush administration. It was called Advanced Technology and Military Enforcement. In conjunction with that, he was named head of an operational command. What that command was doing appears to be top-secret. But it seems that our general made quite a few trips to Afghanistan and Iraq after he took over."

"So maybe he was enlisting men for his special unit?" Eytan conjectured. "Bennington is definitely a Marine, right?"

"I knew you'd be able to keep up."

"Sometimes I amaze even myself. So we've found our program leader. Where is he based?"

"Give me another couple of hours, and I'll let you know."

"I can't wait."

"Do what you think is best. And collect as much evidence as possible. I may need it to put pressure on our American friends."

"I'm sure we'll find something for you to feast on."

"I have faith in you. Now a final concern. I couldn't find anything on H-Plus Dynamics. Not a sliver of information, which isn't surprising."

Another call interrupted their conversation. It was Jenkins.

"Attali, I have to hang up. I should have more info very soon. Let me know as soon as you find out where Bennington is."

Without saying good-bye, Eytan switched over to Jenkins. "I thought you didn't like me anymore, buddy."

"It's ten thirty at night here, and it wasn't that easy to find this place," Jenkins said.

Jeremy and Jackie grinned. The man with the stuffy English accent was frightened and defensive. Eytan was keeping him on his toes.

"I don't give a shit about your little problems with time and geography. Spit it out."

"The company is located in Baltimore."

Eytan grabbed a pen and pad of paper with the restaurant's logo and wrote down the full address.

"I think we make a nice team, you and I," the agent said. "One last thing. Still no word from Cypher at your end?"

"No," the informant replied. Eytan ended the call.

"Cypher?" Jackie asked.

"It's the alias that the head of the Consortium goes by. I know next to nothing about the guy, but we don't need to worry about him right now. We've got more pressing things to worry about. Time to roll."

Less than two minutes later, the trio left the restaurant and slid into their rented Audi for the four-hour trip south. Simon Attali wanted evidence, and the Kidon agent had no doubt that he'd be getting more than he needed.

CHAPTER 28

What began as an interrogation became an awkward conversation. The young prisoner met each question with a curt response. After ten minutes of this, his origins were clear. He was Polish, Jewish in fact, and he and his family had been deported to the Warsaw Ghetto. The boy had then been sent to Stutthof. He refused to discuss his imprisonment or his escape. But the kid did speak freely about his weeks on the run, when he pillaged homes for food and clothing, slept in barns, and trudged through the snow-covered countryside all by himself. He explained that he had acquired the military getup by taking a dead guard's coat before fleeing Stutthof.

His tale, which obviously had a few holes, was less impressive to Janusz than the calm way he told it. Bound to a tree and at the mercy of a group of fierce killers, even the toughest man would have been wetting his pants. But the kid showed no sign of fear or worry. He hesitated only when Karol asked him how old he was.

"Sixteen," he replied after a few seconds. The professor gave his leader a nod, indicating that he wanted to speak with him in private.

"His story seems believable to me," Karol said.

"He's not telling us everything, but there's no arguing with that tattoo. And despite his physique, I don't believe he's sixteen. He's younger."

"We'll have to find people to hide him. If he's escaped from a labor camp..."

"They aren't *labor* camps!"

Karol didn't respond.

"All right," Janusz told Karol. "We'll protect him. But I was wondering..."

"What?"

"What I'm about to tell you cannot be repeated to the others," he warned.

"My lips are sealed."

"I saw that kid go head-to-head with Vassili. If I hadn't stepped in, he'd have beaten him to a pulp."

Karol looked stunned. "You're joking," he said. "Even Piotr is no match for Vassili."

"Exactly. There's something special about this boy. I want to keep him close."

"Wait, are you seriously considering recruiting him?" the professor whispered.

"Let's test him. What do we have to lose?"

"Janusz, he's just a child. He doesn't have any particular skills."

"He's a child who escaped the SS and survived on his own for several weeks. You don't think that proves he has skills? I think it does."

"Suppose he's not telling the truth."

"Why would he lie? And anyway, if we don't think he's good enough, we'll find a family that can hide him. We've got nothing to lose, I'm telling you."

"How do we know that he'd want to join us?"

"The easiest way to find out is to ask him, don't you think? And don't say anything to the Siberian. He's been in a shitty mood ever since the incident."

"I swear on my glasses," Karol joked.

They went back to the prisoner, who had kept both eyes on his captors while they were talking.

"Eytan, what were your plans before you ran into us?" Janusz asked.

"To survive," the kid replied.

"Survive? And what for?"

"To kill as many Germans as possible."

"I can help you make that happen if you can keep up with us."

"What do I have to do?"

"Prove yourself."

He pulled out a large hunting knife from a brown leather case attached to his belt and cut the ropes that bound Eytan to the tree. To Janusz's surprise, the boy stood up nimbly, using only his legs. The blow Janusz had inflicted just a few hours earlier seemed to be a distant memory. There wasn't even a bruise on the kid's face.

"There, you're free," Janusz declared. "If you want to leave, you can go. No one will stop you."

Once back on his feet, the boy's first instinct was to reach into his coat pocket. His search quickly grew frantic. For the first time, he was showing signs of worry, panic even.

"Where is my notebook?"

"It's safe," Janusz assured him. "Now come with us."

He turned around and started walking toward his men, who were waiting around the dwindling fire. He sat down on a rock and pointed to the block of wood next to him.

"Have a seat," he said without looking at Eytan.

Eytan complied silently. He crossed his large legs and discreetly inspected the strange faces before him.

"This is Eytan Morgenstern," Janusz told the team. "While his getup would have you believe otherwise, he's Polish. I have invited him to join us. Anyone object?"

Janusz could feel his crew's shock. Piotr opened his mouth but closed it just as fast, apparently unwilling to say what was on his mind. Pawel tilted his head to the side as he skeptically eyed the newbie.

"He's pretty young, isn't he? He doesn't even look like he's shaving yet." He was silent for a few seconds and then added, "But beggars can't be choosers. It's not like we happen upon a good fighter every day. If he's okay with you, he's okay with us."

The rest of the group grunted approval.

"Good, I knew I could count on you," Janusz replied. "Eytan, this man who has just agreed to accept you is Pawel. He's got the eye of an eagle, and there's no better shooter anywhere. He's saved our asses many times over.

To his right is Marek, a clockmaker from Lviv. He would have taken over his family's business if the Germans hadn't decided otherwise. Instead, he's with us."

"Now I'm the fire guy," Marek said, grinning. Although his hair was gray for the most part, he had youthful eyes with long lashes. In his day, he had turned the heads of many fine-looking girls.

"With the explosives he makes, he could teach a professional pyrotechnician a thing or two," Janusz said.

The team leader continued. "And this is Piotr. He's also from Warsaw, where he was a middle-weight boxer. He's our close-combat expert.

"Vassili, over there, doesn't need any introductions. You've already seen what he's capable of."

Vassili was the team's silent killer. Like Piotr, he had once been a boxer. The young talent had left the ring to go underground and had vowed not to return until every last German soldier was out of Poland. He was hardly twenty years old, but he already had a badly scarred face. His eyes, meanwhile, were so dark, they were almost black. In combat he slaughtered like a butcher.

"Gentlemen, I'm handing Eytan over to you. I would like each one of you to test our new recruit in your specific area of expertise, starting with Karol, who will introduce himself."

"What about you," Eytan interrupted. "Who are you?"

"I'm the leader," Janusz replied, smacking his hands against his thighs. "And the leader is now off to get some sleep."

He rose to his feet. "A good soldier knows how to conserve his energy," he said before leaving.

The tests began that morning. Karol evaluated Eytan's reading skills and general knowledge. After a meager lunch, he turned Eytan over to Piotr. The boxer spent two hours with the boy, who learned not only the moves, but also the taunts that could be used in the ring and in battle. In the late afternoon, Pawel was given permission to take the apprentice out for a shooting lesson. Vassili kept an eye on them—just in case.

They returned at nightfall. Eytan was worn out and asked if he could lie down in one of the huts. Rested and reenergized, Janusz called his men together around a late-night pot of vegetable stew. As Vassili sharpened his blade against a rock and Marek lapped up his meal like a dog, the way he always did, Janusz listened to their various accounts.

"He's a strange and contradictory fellow," Karol began, glaring at the slurping fire specialist. Marek returned the look with a contrite smile before picking up a spoon and eating quietly. Karol continued. "He has the basic knowledge of a ten-year-old. And yet he comprehends and speaks German, which he claims to have learned by listening to the guards in the camp, which surprises me. To be honest, I'm a bit hesitant."

Janusz allowed Piotr to speak next.

"He may not be brainy, but he's got fucking potential as a brawler. He has cat-like reflexes, and he catches on quickly. The little bastard has a strong punch, whether he's using his right arm or his left, and to top it off, he's fast. I can definitely do something with him."

Janusz turned to Pawel and asked for his assessment.

"I went over the basics of precision shooting with him. I had him take five shots at an improvised target, first from thirty feet, then a hundred, and finally 150. He was spot-on every time. I've never seen anything like it."

Janusz was pleased.

"That's not all," Pawel went on. "I wanted to show him how to slow his heartbeat to keep his arm still. It was a huge waste of time. His heart rate was thirty beats a minute—before, during, and immediately after his shot. It was crazy. Since he's also got excellent sight, all he'll need is a week of intensive training, and he'll be shooting better than me. I've never seen anything like it, I'm telling you."

The men looked at each other. Pawel wasn't the kind of guy who passed out praise. He was a perfectionist who was never satisfied with his own performance or anyone else's. Eytan had clearly made an impression on him. But Janusz wanted to hear one last—and very important—opinion before making his decision.

"Vassili?"

The bald Siberian, absorbed in the cleaning and sharpening of his hunting knife, looked up. He snorted, brought up a loogie, and sent it into the darkness. He nodded in approval, then went back to sharpening his tool.

"It's decided then. He's staying with us," the Bear concluded, looking from one brother to the next. "Tonight, Marek and I will do the first watch. Vassili and Piotr, you'll take the second watch. Everyone else, rest up. We've got plenty of work tomorrow."

There were no disturbances that night. The Germans rarely raided this forest. Nonetheless, Janusz insisted on keeping watch at all times. Those who wanted to stay alive had to remain vigilant. He spent part of his lookout leafing through Eytan's little notebook. It was filled, page after page, with indecipherable equations scribbled in blue ink. Certain passages were scratched out. Others were underlined in red, but none of them made any sense to Janusz. He had had some schooling, and he thought he might be holding the log of a chemist who had jotted down complex notes and formulas. Written on the cover was the number 302.

The Bear didn't intend to squeeze out the kid's secrets before he felt ready to divulge them. When his watch was over, he drifted off to sleep, hoping that in time he'd earn the trust of this strange boy and find out more about his mysterious past.

~ ~ ~

At dawn, Janusz and Karol set up Eytan's daily training regimen. Like every other fighter in the unit, he would commit to an area of expertise. But first he'd have to acquire the basics of each member's skill set in order to strengthen any weaknesses. The schedule would remain unchanged until their next mission. Eytan would begin with two hours of higher-level schooling and end the morning with Piotr. After lunch, Pawel would go shooting with him. Finally, Janusz would coach him in team combat. Fearing a visceral reaction from Vassili, Janusz decided against throwing the former Red Army solder and the boy together—at least until Vassili said otherwise. Marek and his explosive toys would also be kept off the schedule. Janusz wanted to wait awhile for that.

Janusz approached the hut where Eytan was sleeping, figuring he would have to shake him from his slumber. A thin ray of sunlight broke through the darkness as Janusz opened the door. He was horrified when bloodcurdling screams erupted. Curled in a ball, his head between his knees, the kid looked terrified. Janusz collected himself and squatted next to the boy. He struggled to grab Eytan's thrashing arms.

"Eytan! Eytan!" Janusz shouted, finally managing to calm the boy.

The kid lifted his head slowly. Despite his massive physique, the boy had the terrified eyes of a child. Janusz felt a knot in his throat. He was overwhelmed with a feeling he thought he'd never experience again, one that had been buried in the ruins of his past. A father's instinct. He wrapped the kid in his arms and, without getting any resistance from Eytan, held him close. While Janusz didn't know it yet, this scene would become a morning ritual.

"*Ich bin der Patient 302*," Eytan panted as he stuck out his forearm, his fist squeezed tight.

Janusz looked at the tattoo and saw 302 in the row of numbers. His face went white.

"You want to kill as many as possible?" he whispered, gently sweeping his fingers though Eytan's hair. "We'll teach you."

CHAPTER 29

The thirteen-hour trip from Manhattan to Chicago was rough. Avi and Eli, who were taking I-80 for most of the trip, had to drive through the night—this after the events in the Big Apple. And they still hadn't gotten over their flight from Israel.

The doctor had suggested that they switch off behind the wheel every three hours. That way, they'd each amass a whopping six hours of sleep, just enough to get through the day in Chicago. They snacked on the food they had purchased in New York, thereby avoiding any unnecessary stops. While their reasons differed, both men were eager to get this part of the mission behind them. Eli was dreading his reunion with his brother, whose ADHD behavior was still formidable, even though he was now an old man. Frank also had a knack for belittling people. In fact, he hadn't lost any time when Eli called him before leaving Manhattan.

Avi, meanwhile, had confessed that he was worried about the distance separating them from Eytan, Jackie, and Jeremy. Nearly thirty hours on the road (there and back), plus however much time they needed to spend in Illinois. That amounted to well more than a day for those crazy kids to get into all kinds of trouble. And if something happened, Eli and Avi wouldn't be there to help. Granted, they hadn't done a whole lot of rescuing thus far—Eytan could stand perfectly well on his own two feet. But the doctor said he felt more attached to his team than ever and hated being so far away. The last time they had been in touch with Eytan was the night before, when the giant had relayed the information provided by Attali and Jenkins. The Kidon agent also informed them of the planned trip to Baltimore, where they would visit the H-Plus Dynamics headquarters. So basically, nothing reassuring...

It was around six o'clock in the morning when Eli and the doctor finally made out the shimmering Chicago skyline.

They crossed the city, heading in the direction of Hyde Park, where Chicago University was located. The closer they came to the campus, the more Eli's anxiety rose.

"If you keep grinding your teeth like that, you'll crack a molar," Avi said. "Is your brother really that bad?"

"He's worse," Eli replied.

"Well then, this should be fun."

The sun was hovering on the horizon when they pulled into a deserted campus parking lot on the main quad. With their mechanical arm safely tucked in a brown paper bag, they braved the bitter cold and made their way toward the building where their appointment was scheduled. Eli was as nervous as ever, but Avi was admiring the place, with its English Gothic façades that looked like those at a prestigious British university. The stone buildings and contemporary glass and steel structures designed by American architects were juxtaposed in a way that gave the institution a majestic balance of nostalgia and modernity. It all looked quite inviting. Eli, however, would have declined, had he been given the option.

Eli became even more rigid when he spotted the older gentleman waiting for them. Tall and slim, the man was wearing faded jeans, a tight black turtleneck sweater, and a leather bomber jacket. He had a square face with a prominent jaw and smooth skin with hardly any wrinkles. Oddly, the mop of white hair that hung over his forehead made him look especially intimidating. Adding to the impression was his puckish grin and mischievous eyes.

The professor rushed toward them with surprising agility and took Eli in his arms. "Buddy!" he cried. Eli, feeling almost suffocated, pulled himself out of the man's grasp.

"Frank, this is Avi Lafner. Avi, this is Frank Meyer."

"Dr. Frank Meyer," the latter corrected. "I didn't suffer through years of blood, sweat, and tears to earn an array of degrees for nothing! You have no idea how happy I am to see you. It's been what... Two years?"

"Two years and three months to be exact," Eli muttered.

"Still a stickler for details, aren't you, kid?" Frank said as he walked up the steps to the building where his office was located.

"Come on, let's have a look at this technological wonder you brought with you. How's Eytan?"

"Stop calling me kid," Eli fumed. "At our age, it's ridiculous. Eytan's fine. He says hello. He couldn't join us. He's off on another mission at the moment."

"He's off on another mission at the moment," Frank repeated in a theatrical tone. "I love how secret agents talk!" He turned to Avi. "Do you also play around with grenades and machine guns?"

"Never! I'm a doctor," Avi said.

"Ah, a scientist. All right, let's go!"

Frank pushed open the main door and hurried his two visitors into the hushed halls of the building.

"Is he always this excited?" Avi whispered to Eli as they tried to keep up with the professor.

"Oh, believe me, he's just warming up. In an hour, you'll see him at his peak."

Once on the second floor, they walked down a wood-paneled hallway, where each door had a plaque bearing the name of a distinguished professor. Frank Meyer took a key out of his pocket, opened the door to his office, and ushered his guests in.

"I'm beyond the age that most professors retire, but the university hasn't given me the boot yet. I'm certainly not ready to leave this place."

Frank's large office was cluttered with books stacked three and four feet high. Eli couldn't help but wonder how he kept them from toppling over. Blackboards were filled with chemical formulas scribbled in white chalk. Papers were strewn all over the professor's desk, and an obsolete IBM monitor suggested that he was still working his way through the twentieth century. From a high shelf, a dozen oddly placed model airplanes watched over the pigsty.

"Sorry about the mess. It may not look like it, but I actually do know where everything is." He carefully picked up the pile of papers on his desk and dropped them on the floor.

His task completed, he sat down in his chair and put on a pair of glasses. Still standing, Eli took the prosthetic out of the bag and placed it on the desk. Frank let out an admiring whistle when he laid eyes on the object. He picked up the arm to examine it, letting out "not bad" and "hmm" every now and then as he went over each and every inch. After five minutes of this, he put it back on his desk and picked up his telephone.

"I took the liberty of calling on some of my best students to give us a hand, so to speak. Eli, don't just stand there like a deer caught in the headlights. Have a seat. You too, doctor." He pointed to two chairs on the other side of his desk. "Just move those papers to the floor." Turning back to the phone, he spoke into the receiver. "Yeah, it's Meyer. Come up to my office right away. I have a fun surprise for you."

No more than sixty seconds later, three young men, all of them out of breath, came galloping into the office. They were wearing white lab coats and eyeglasses with thick lenses. The very personification of bookworms, Eli thought.

"I want a detailed analysis of this thingamajig ASAP," Frank instructed. "Start with the layer of software activating the nervous-muscular senses. The purely mechanical function is not a priority. Okay morons, hop to it!"

The three students scurried off as quickly as they arrived.

"You didn't have to speak to them like that," Eli said.

"Chicago University has produced nearly ninety Nobel laureates. And one of them, Barack Obama, was twice elected president. If we're not hard on them, they'll consider themselves geniuses before they've proved themselves. So I try to keep their egos in check. Your little gadget is quite fascinating. Where'd you find it?"

Eli recounted the events of the prior few days, starting with the meeting with Simon Attali and ending with the confrontation in Manhattan. He described the man in the wheelchair and his attendant. He also told Frank how Jackie had acquired the artificial arm.

"If I understand correctly, and I believe I do, the Marines are equipping amputees with highly developed prosthetics, which wouldn't necessarily be a problem if they weren't interested in Eytan. Is that the gist?"

"That's the gist," Avi said. "The alleged program appears to have something to do with transhumanism. But that doesn't tell us why the military wants Eytan. I thought they were interested in the way he doesn't age, but that seems to be too easy an assumption."

"Yes, it is a bit easy. However, you are partially correct."

"We're just dying to hear your words of wisdom," Eli said.

"Do you see how upset he is that I'm the smarter one?" Frank said as he walked over to one of the blackboards. "I'll draw it out for you. That way it'll be easier to understand."

He erased the traces of his research with a rag and drew a human form.

"From a purely mechanical standpoint, there's nothing revolutionary about the arm you've brought to me. This kind of medical technology has been around for a while. For example, in targeted muscle reinnervation, developed right here in Chicago, severed nerves are redirected to allow an amputee to control his artificial limb. It works along these lines. Normally, your brain sends electrical signals down your spine and through the peripheral nerves to the muscles that control your limbs. If you lose an arm or a leg, the nerves still carry the commands generated by the brain, but they can't get to the place they're intended to go. In TMR, the nerves are redirected to a healthy muscle elsewhere in the body. A surgeon might attach the nerves that controlled an arm to your chest. When you try to move your amputated arm, the signal will cause your chest muscle to contract. Then electrodes can be attached to your chest to provide signals to a prosthetic arm. So just by thinking, you can control the prosthetic device. It's the same principle with a prosthetic leg.

"Although we'll have to wait to hear what my students have to say about the arm you've brought me, its technology appears to be much more sophisticated than what most specialists in the field have been able to accomplish so far. I'm wondering if this arm is the next step—if it has the capability to carry the signal in both directions: from the brain to the limb and also from the limb to the brain."

"So what does that mean?" Eli asked.

Frank sighed.

"It means, dimwit, that human beings could take a big leap forward from an evolutionary standpoint. At its very simplest, someone wearing one of these arms could detect hot and cold.

But let's think of the military applications. Soldiers gain experience in training and combat. At the same time, however, they're getting older and less efficient. If you hook them up with artificial limbs, which are immune to the type of aging that humans experience, you'll increase their longevity. Plus you can continually upgrade the equipment. Over time, you'll end up with a fighting force of seasoned veterans with super-powered arms and legs. But the thing is, the brains and central nervous systems of these seasoned vets will deteriorate through the natural process of aging. Therefore, to fully exploit the prosthetics, the military needs skilled subjects with superior physical abilities."

"Okay, so if your soldiers don't show any signs of deteriorating, they'll remain efficient longer," Avi said.

"Which means they'll be more profitable. It takes a lot of money and time to train someone for combat. So now you understand why they want Eytan. It's his nervous system they're interested in. These days, we can make technological advancements much more quickly than we can modify the genome. And there are too many ethical barriers related to genetic manipulation. In the case of prosthetics, all you have to do is tell the public how beneficial they are for the millions of disabled people out there, and the whole world will give you a standing ovation. Never mind that they cost a fortune, and only the very wealthy can afford them."

Frank turned back to the blackboard and wrote "proved" in capital letters.

"You know your stuff. I feel like such an idiot in comparison," Avi said, plainly impressed.

"That's how most people feel," Frank said. "But I've managed to stay down-to-earth, wouldn't you say, Eli?"

Eli tried hard not to snigger.

"Now if you don't have any other questions," Frank continued, "I'll go ahead and prepare the doses for Eli to take back to our favorite bald giant.

"What doses?" Avi asked.

"His serum," Frank said.

"You're the one who makes it for him?"

"Under top-secret conditions. I use my best students, and each one prepares just a single ingredient. That way, no one knows the end result. Then I measure the ingredients and mix them to make the serum. All right, I'm off. Wait for me here. I won't be long."

Frank Meyer left the office. While Eli was relieved for the few minutes of respite from his overbearing sibling, Avi was clearly impressed with the man.

"Your brother is quite a character. You are polar opposites."

"Quite a character, indeed. And it makes sense that we're so different. Frank and I happened to be on the same ship after the war, when we were being transported from England to Israel. We were orphans. Eytan took us under his wing, and Frank and I practically grew up together. I dedicated my life to Eytan by pursuing a military career. Frank did the same, but he went into science. He wanted to be a fighter pilot, but couldn't because of his poor eyesight."

"So that's why Frank's in charge of making the serum. You're a one-of-a-kind family. That's all I can say."

Eli's jacket started vibrating. He took out his phone and answered the call.

"Eytan?"

"Hi Eli, it's Jackie. Eytan's behind the wheel. We've completed the Baltimore mission. We're heading toward Fort Wayne now. We have big news."

"We do too. Everything went well at your end?"

"Yes. Well, kind of."

"What do you mean *kind of*? Did Eytan get hurt again?"

"No, this time we had trouble with Jeremy," she replied.

Eli picked up some embarrassment in her voice. "Be more precise. You're making me anxious. Is Jeremy okay?"

"He's okay, I think."

"You think? Where is he? Let me talk to him."

"I'm sorry, Eli. No can do. He's in the trunk."

CHAPTER 30

The men passed the matchbox around, and each of them lit a cigarette. The captain slipped the matches back in the pocket of his jacket. The five soldiers smoked to take their minds off the bitter cold. The captain complained about the weather almost as much as he complained about women. And the subject of women often filled their conversations—ribald stories were a favorite, and the captain let them have at it. On this day, one of the men was bragging about seeing a young elementary school teacher being raped by a bunch of Luftwaffe pilots in Krakow.

"The best part was that it took place in the middle of a downtown café in front of a crowd of like-minded privates," he said.

The men stopped laughing and elbowing each other. The light-hearted vibe vanished, and an awkward silence fell on the group.

Sheltered from the snow by a large evergreen, Karol watched and listened. He felt the simultaneous urge to throw up and put a bullet between the eyes of that asshole, who was still laughing. The professor took some comfort in the other men's silence, which he took for disapproval.

Captain Reinke led his small Wehrmacht garrison with an iron fist and refused to tolerate any violence against civilians. He was an old-school officer who was tough but fair. Those who lived in villages under his authority considered themselves lucky. Younger, less-seasoned commanders could be very hard on civilians. Even Janusz was inclined to let Reinke be, at least for the time being, even though some of the other men wanted to eliminate him. Janusz was convinced that a replacement would lack Reinke's moral compass.

Reinke gave the man a tongue lashing before sending him to the hut next to the elementary school that had been turned into a barracks. The shamed private obeyed without protest.

They're not all monsters, Karol thought. But his musings would have to wait. He had to focus on the night's objective.

Spotlights on metal supports illuminated three buildings situated in a U shape. The Germans had put up the lights immediately after taking over the place. Surrounded by a six-foot metal fence, the school playground now served as a lot for the troop's trucks. At that very moment, two of the trucks were parked next to each other between the fence and the covered pavilion under which Reinke and the four other soldiers were conversing.

Immediately after Karol raised his arm, two shadows dashed out from the edge of the woods a hundred feet behind him. The professor watched as they flew by. Even crouched, Vassili and Eytan soared ahead with astounding speed, like two ghosts hovering above the snow. They reached the fence in the blink of an eye and nimbly climbed over it.

Once over the fence, they headed toward the trucks and ducked behind one of them. From there, they looked back at Karol, who dropped his arm. Vassili stood up first and carefully lifted the hood of the truck. Eytan rummaged through his shoulder satchel and took out a tin. He opened it and scooped up a dark substance, which he smeared on the engine's oil filter.

They quickly executed the same maneuver on the second truck. The Germans were still chatting, unaware of the two saboteurs. With their crime completed, the duo returned to the forest, with Karol following behind.

A safe distance into the woods, the three men met up with the others. Pawel and Janusz had been covering them—Pawel in a tree with a rifle and Janusz on the ground with a machine gun.

"Nice work, guys. First nighttime mission completed," Janusz said.

"Karol, what did we put in their engines?" Eytan asked.

"Carborundum. It'll clog up the pistons, causing the engine to overheat and the head gasket to explode. The truck will hemorrhage oil until it stops completely. That will keep our dear Reinke quite busy during his next drive," the scholar boasted.

"Is this really how wars are won?"

"You might see this as a minor setback, but all these small acts of sabotage add up and will eventually create big problems, especially since this is an army that depends on logistics. Trust me, this will take a toll on troop morale."

"Nicely put," Pawel said. "Plus it's fun. Right?"

"When you talked to me about my first mission, I imagined something different," Eytan said.

"If the devil is in the details, then we're the demons who haunt the Wehrmacht. The Polish people will rise up one day. That moment has yet to come, but it's fast approaching. Anyway, don't worry. By sunrise you'll have your share of action."

"Karol's right," Janusz agreed, putting his hand on Eytan's shoulder. "Our next mission is a more serious one. We'll be intercepting a convoy of weapons."

He looked at the feathery clouds obscuring the full moon. With a whistle, he ordered his men to move out. Vassili led the group, holding back the tree branches when necessary. Following behind were Eytan, Karol, Pawel, and the Bear, bringing up the rear. They marched steadily for half an hour, despite the snow, which weighed down their boots and slowed their stride.

The Siberian stopped in his tracks and raised his fist. The row of men did the same, their senses heightened. Then they heard a familiar voice coming from the underbrush.

"You're as discreet as a herd of cattle," Piotr mocked, emerging from his hiding spot. He brushed off his parka.

"And you, you're so well hidden, we almost stampeded right over you," Pawel taunted back.

"Tell me that the convoy hasn't passed through yet and that you've brought the bag," Janusz demanded.

"Who do you think I am?" Piotr replied. He tossed a bulky army duffle to Karol, who was nearly thrown to the ground by its weight.

"The Germans are more precise than one of Marek's detonators," Piotr said, spitting on the snow. "Those bastards should be here soon."

"Their timeliness will screw them over tonight," Pawel jeered as he made sure for the tenth time that his rifle was loaded.

"Keep your jokes for the campsite," the Bear said. He pushed aside some bushes to scan the main forest road. "You all know the plan. Now get to your positions!"

Pawel and Vassili crossed to the other side of the road. The shooter climbed a tree overlooking the road and got into position.

Piotr armed himself with his new machine gun, which he had swiped from a German officer during their last attack, and crouched behind a tree with Eytan. He looked at the kid's fearless face. In the two months since Eytan had joined the Armia Krajowa, he had undergone an incredible growth spurt, and every one of his teammates had been forced to dig through his measly stash of personal items to find clothes that would fit him.

Janusz was positioned about forty feet in front of them. He readied his machine gun before lying down on the ground.

Karol pulled a Wehrmacht soldier's uniform from the duffle that Piotr had brought. Pants, jacket, shirt, boots—all the standard items were there. Shivering in the cold, he put on the outfit and stuffed his own clothes into the bag. He then planted himself in the middle of the road.

"We used to run a rope across the road to stop the motorcyclist at the front of the convoy," Piotr whispered to Eytan. "But the Fritz have gotten more careful. They drive slower when it's dark. So we're trying something new tonight."

"Wouldn't it be better to put me or Vassili on the road instead of Karol?" Eytan asked. "We're better at close combat than him."

"That's true, but Karol can act German better than anyone else. How do you think we know so much about the way they transport their troops and ammo?"

"I never thought about it. So you mean when Karol disappears..."

"He goes off to blend in with the Krauts and comes back with pockets full of information. Did you really think he was just in our unit to teach you math, reading, and phil-whatever-it's-called?"

"Philosophy." Eytan corrected him with a mocking smile.

"Yeah, whatever," Piotr said before spitting out a loogie. Eytan could tell he was annoyed. "We all have our jobs here."

"What's mine?"

"Hard to say. You're good at everything, even boxing, you little shit." He faked a round of jabs to the kid's chest, which Eytan pretended to block. "You gotta tell me how you stay so calm. The first time we attacked the Fritz, I pissed my pants. It's no big deal if you're scared."

"Scared?" Eytan repeated. "I'm not scared."

"No kidding."

"Fear is only a fuzzy memory for me. Nah, I'm just restless."

The sound of distant engines interrupted their chat. A motorcycle headlight lit up the road, followed by the much stronger beams of a truck, then a second, and a third. The procession was rolling along slowly. Karol, meanwhile, was lying on the ground with his arms outstretched.

The motorcyclist slowed down about sixty feet from Karol and then came to a complete halt, as did the rest of his convoy. He dismounted and approached the prostrate Karol, his machine gun at the ready. At the same time, someone inside the closest truck lifted the rear flap, and two men, also armed, emerged. They joined the motorcyclist.

The motorcyclist yelled something abusive at Karol twice. Still lying on the ground, he turned his head toward his comrades in the bushes.

Eytan, the only one who could speak perfect German, resisted the temptation to translate the conversation. He settled for giving a thumbs-up to assure Piotr that things were going smoothly.

As evidence, one of the soldiers put down his weapon and held out his hand to help Karol off the ground.

That was when the grim staccato sounds of Janusz's machine gun erupted. The bullets studded the truck's tarp in sync with the cries of shock and pain from the men inside.

The three Germans tending to Karol spun around to face the convoy. Karol, in turn, grabbed his pistol and fired a bullet into each of their skulls.

The panicked soldier behind the wheel of the first truck started pulling away, but a perfectly aimed bullet delivered by Pawel soared through the windshield—shattering it—and continued until it hit the poor guy between the eyes. A second shot nailed the soldier in the passenger seat. The crazed vehicle was now rolling toward Karol, but the professor managed to leap out of the way. He dived into the forest and hit a tree. Before they had time to react, the entire team in the second truck was taken out.

The machine gun stopped spitting bullets, and Janusz rushed to reload his weapon. Five survivors took advantage of the pause to jump out of the third truck and flee into the forest.

Two of the soldiers headed in Vassili and Pawel's direction. The others were close to Eytan and Piotr, who leaped up to give them chase. But Eytan soon lost Piotr. After weeks of training with Vassili, the Siberian forester, Eytan now moved through the woods as naturally as a wolf. Piotr, the stocky boxer, couldn't keep up with his huge strides. Eytan was weaving in and out of the branches all by himself.

The three soldiers, meanwhile, were staying together, apparently unaware that their only chance of surviving was to split up.

Piotr, who was familiar with the forest terrain, managed to catch up quickly. He could see the Germans, but not Eytan. He ran even faster. Once he was close enough to the enemy, he hoisted his machine gun into shooting position. But just as he was about to start firing, he caught a movement to the right of his targets. A shadow emerged out of nowhere and pounced on the Germans, grabbing one of them by the hips. The figure raised the man in the air and threw him to the ground.

Piotr spotted the reflection of the moonlight on the steel blade of the knife as Eytan plunged it into the throat of the soldier sprawled on the ground. The man let out a gurgling cry. Piotr crept closer to find Eytan sitting atop his victim. There was an insane glimmer in the boy's blue eyes and a wicked smile on his face. Eytan pulled the knife out and plunged it into the soldier's guts, twisting as he bore down.

Shocked, Piotr did nothing for a few seconds. Then he snapped out of it and took aim at the other two men. But

Eytan was in the way, and a bullet to either of them would have hit the boy. This gave the surviving soldiers the opportunity they needed to catch their breath and run off. They were now scampering like bunnies in different directions. One darted deeper into the woods, and the other veered in the opposite direction, back toward the main road.

"Eytan, stop!" Piotr commanded several times as the boy ran after the second soldier.

The order had no effect on him.

"Then have at it, you little shit!" he shouted. Eytan was determined to chase after the prey.

Even from afar, Piotr could make out the trembling soldier as he looked left and right in search of the unleashed predator. The hunter was tormenting the hunted, switching up his pace so at times he was fifteen feet behind and in the blink of an eye only a few steps away.

Stop messing around, Piotr thought anxiously. Kill him already!

Eytan reached the road, and now Piotr saw him whispering something in the soldier's ear as he strangled him. The boxer couldn't make out what he was saying. By the time he had quietly caught up, increasingly mistrustful of the boy, Eytan was jabbing his knife through the terrified soldier's neck. Blood gushed from his mouth, and his body convulsed from head to toe. Eytan held the dying man against his chest, as if to taste his enemy's demise. He released his hold, and the body fell to the ground.

Piotr felt a shiver shoot up his spine as Eytan turned in his direction. Eytan's fierce glare rivaled that of his blade. Their eyes remained locked.

"Come on," Piotr said after sensing that the fire in his student's eyes had cooled down. "Let's go find the others."

They rejoined their unit in silence. Pawel was lugging a crate that he had unloaded from one of the ambushed trucks. "You took your sweet old time," he said. "Vassili finished off our guys. Are yours dead?"

Piotr, more somber than ever, ignored his comrade and approached Janusz, who had another crate loaded with plundered goods.

"I didn't hear any gunfire," the Bear said. "Did everything go all right?"

"Two are dead. One managed to escape."

"Shit. Well, considering what we've managed to get here, things could've been worse."

"How's the supply?" Piotr asked.

"Rifles, pistols, ammo. Christmas came early this year," Karol said. He sounded giddy, but he toned it down when he saw that Piotr was upset. "What's the problem?"

"I need to have a chat with both of you. You and the Bear," he said as he nodded in Eytan's direction.

Janusz and Karol glanced at the boy, who was looking at himself in the side-view mirror of the last truck in the convoy. He was holding a lock of his long blond hair against his cheek.

"When we get back," Janusz suggested. "For now, come help us hide this stash."

Half an hour later, the time it took to conceal their treasure in the forest, Janusz set fire to the trucks, along with the bodies they had crammed inside.

Exhausted, they started back toward the camp and arrived with the first rays of the sun. Marek was sitting on a tree stump, occupied with some kind of clock mechanism.

"So?" he asked. "Everything go as planned? Did the kid pass his initiation?"

"You could say that," Piotr spit out, throwing his bag to the ground.

Eytan grabbed an empty mess tin and used it to collect several handfuls of snow before storming into his sleeping hut. He slammed the door behind him.

Vassili put down the weapons he had been lugging over his shoulder and crouched in front of the fire. Simmering above it was a pot of stew prepared by Marek. The clockmaker-pyrotechnic served the Siberian.

Piotr took Janusz and Karol aside and recounted the gruesome episode he had witnessed.

"He looked like a crazed person, like he was possessed. He didn't listen to a word I said. The only thing he was after was blood—I saw it in his eyes. He even messed around with one of the guys before stabbing him in the throat!"

"I was exactly like him after my wife and kids were murdered," Janusz sighed.

"It's his fault one of the soldiers got away," Piotr insisted. "If he doesn't listen to us, if he ignores our instructions, he'll put us all in danger."

Using only his eyes, Janusz gave Karol an order. The latter left the group and headed toward the hut. He carefully nudged open the door and was shocked to find Eytan shearing off his hair.

"What are you doing?"

"I'm shaving my head," Eytan replied through clenched teeth. "I'm not blond."

"I don't mean to make you angry, but you're as blond as Goldilocks," the professor joked.

"I wasn't blond before," Eytan corrected.

"I'd ask before what, but I know you won't say anything, so I won't press. But I will ask one thing: why do you think we're fighting?"

"To get revenge," Eytan spat as he continued to chop off his hair.

"Interesting," Karol said. "And once we've satisfied our vengeance, once the Allies show up and the Wehrmacht retreats, what will we do then? Are we going to destroy the Germans on their own turf?"

Eytan seemed taken aback, baffled by his professor's logic. "I don't know."

"Okay, after what you did tonight, you have some idea. You want to slit women's throats and tear out children's guts?"

"Of course not."

"Good answer. Okay then, what will you do when the object of your hatred is gone? What will Janusz and Pawel do? Marek and Piotr? Vassili? Or me?"

The teenager thought for a second, but didn't respond.

"I'll tell you what's driving us, kid. We're fighting out of love. For the love of our country, our history, our friends and family—living and dead. We're fighting for the right to live. We're fighting for dignity and humanity. If you don't understand that, Eytan, you don't belong with us. No one will stop you if you decide to live like a savage beast, always on the hunt, blindly stabbing anything in your path. Obviously, you'll end up getting yourself killed, and your presence on this earth, the talents you possess and have demonstrated over the past few weeks will make no difference."

The boy hung his head and sighed.

"And above all, Eytan, we're fighting for a dream. A dream that I would like to see you cherish, as well."

"What's that?"

"Freedom."

CHAPTER 31

For the past hour, Eytan had kept his eyes glued to the entrance of a large building overlooking Baltimore's harbor. The revolving door of the tall structure was churning out white-collar workers who could finally fill their lungs with fresh air after spending a long day in the belly of a half-glass, half-steel beast. While many people who knew nothing about surveillance assumed that stakeouts were tedious, Eytan reveled in this moment of peace and quiet after four long hours on the road, during which Jackie and Jeremy had drilled him with questions.

The two were shy at first, but they quickly overcame their awkwardness and began quizzing him. Eytan did his best to fend off any questions that were too painful to answer, especially those about his life before he and his family were deported to the Warsaw Ghetto, and his brother, Roman, was murdered by the Germans.

Eytan preferred to talk about his little house on the Irish island, his life-saving retreat far removed from violence and the ordinary stresses of the world. It was the one place he could be alone and indulge his passion for painting. It blew Jeremy's mind to picture Eytan in front of an easel with a palette on his lap and a paintbrush in his hand. Brainwashed by the movies, the fantasy-story enthusiast had fostered the illusion that this mystery man couldn't possibly have anything in common with mere mortals.

Eytan and Jackie, the former special agent, had spent several minutes trying to make the bookseller understand that the better part of the work involved long stakeouts when nothing happened.

"Patience is the most basic skill in this line of work," Eytan said. "I went through a lot of training to master it."

"Actually, I was wondering," Jackie began. "Well, I'm not really sure how to put this..."

"Let 'er rip. I can handle it. I promised you answers, and no questions are off limits," Eytan insisted.

"Well then: how much did Bleiberg's treatments—if I dare to call them that—influence the way you are today, and how much of it is your own doing?"

"In his quest to create the master race, Bleiberg provided me with certain advantages, especially in terms of vision and cardiovascular strength. But other than that, I'm not so different from any other man. For decades, I've had to train every single day. The qualities that make me unique, in addition to my vision and strength, are my versatility and endurance. While most people are highly skilled in just one or two areas, I have the ability to master many more. And as far as endurance goes, I could never sprint as fast as Usain Bolt, but I'd outlast him in a marathon. And I can't punch as hard as Tyson could in his prime, but I can bounce back from a heavyweight's blows better than a champion fighter."

"You mean you don't have any superpowers," Jeremy said, sounding like a disappointed kid after discovering the truth about Santa Claus.

"You've got to stop reading so many comic books," Eytan said. "You're confusing reality with make believe."

Jackie snickered.

"Fine, make fun of me," Jeremy whined.

"I don't age. I heal faster than you do, and I can go several days without sleep. Those are my superpowers. But without my serum, I'll die—which you'd agree is a pretty big draw-back. Actually, what Bleiberg and the Nazis passed on to me is an unstoppable drive."

Eytan told them about Janusz, Karol, Vassili, and the other members of his Armia Krajowa unit. He described each of his friends, all of whom had been sucked into the chaos of a horrific war. These exceptional men, like so many others, had risen up against a savage world by repeating a single word: freedom.

The Kidon agent didn't have time to tell the entire story during their drive to Baltimore, but he was happy all the same. He rarely had the opportunity to talk about the Bear, the wise professor, the soft-spoken Siberian, or Piotr, Pawel, or Marek. To make up for the harsh sting of their absence, Eytan hoped to preserve the memory of these men, unfairly forgotten by the history books.

For the time being, however, he needed to put aside his nostalgia and focus on what he had to do on this cool Baltimore evening. Because Eytan required some undisturbed time to prepare for the attack, which he hoped to execute in the middle of the night, he had given the Corbins a few hours off. Before reconvening at one in the morning, they would be able to share a nice meal and see how Annie was doing. Eytan would have joined them for dinner, as he loved discovering new foods whenever he traveled (compensation for his deprived youth), but he figured the couple needed some privacy.

After assessing the twenty floors of the building, he made a list of every possible variable.

Entering the building would be a cinch, as it was kept open all night, and access to the main lobby was not off-limits. Penetrating the H-Plus Dynamics offices, on the other hand, would be a bit more challenging. Considering the extremely sensitive equipment the company fabricated for the military, as well as its connection to the Consortium, the place would be fortified with highly sophisticated security measures. At the least, there would be surveillance cameras, multiple alarm systems, and round-the-clock guards.

And because he didn't have enough time, Eytan couldn't plan a discreet entrance. He didn't know the building's floor plan, nor would he be able to confidently identify an H-Plus Dynamics employee with whom he could conspire. Stealing a company ID or dummying up a fake one were out of the question, as well.

On top of all that, he was obsessing over the possibility that innocent workers might get hurt. It was quite possible that H-Plus Dynamics was an accomplice in the commando missions in New Jersey and New York and was operating outside the scope of the law. But it was also quite possible that the company's workers had no knowledge of their employer's involvement with the mysterious Consortium. After all, what was the harm in producing prosthetic limbs?

Given the circumstances, Eytan couldn't opt for a subtle approach. The frontal attack appeared to be the only way— except his principles prevented him from resorting to a senseless attack on innocent bystanders.

Kidnapping Adolf Eichmann was a breeze compared to this, he thought as his plan finally became clear.

The agent glanced at his watch. Lost in thought, he had failed to notice how late it was. It was already time to meet up with Jeremy and Jackie. He looked up and saw Jackie's petite form under the streetlights. Jeremy, looming a foot taller, was walking alongside her like a protective shadow. These two had their faults, like lack of discipline and questionable humor, but they certainly knew the importance of being on time.

"Since we didn't know what you liked, we brought you a couple of Baltimore specialties: crab cakes and Bergers cookies," Jackie said as she handed Eytan the bag. "There's some Old Bay seasoning for the crab cakes, too." The bag also held bottles of water and cans of soda.

"Thanks. I'm not picky, but I don't mind sampling the local food when I'm visiting a city," Eytan replied, smiling at the sweet little face all red from the cold.

He grabbed a crab cake and devoured it without paying any attention to what he was eating.

Jeremy rubbed his gloved hands together and stamped his feet. White mist escaped from his mouth with every word. It quickly evaporated in the air.

"So, what's up?" he asked. "Those guys from the Marines aren't protecting the place because of what you've put them through in the past two days?"

"They have no reason to do so. They have no idea that we're aware of this company's existence. No one's waiting for us, and that's exactly why we've got the upper hand, for now, at least. And if I were you, I wouldn't refer to our enemies so lightly."

"Relax. I'm just having a little fun before we get serious," the bookseller protested. "Did you figure out a strategy?"

"Yes," Eytan said. "We can't go in there without setting off the alarms, so we need to create a diversion."

"Why do I have the feeling that this isn't going to be pretty?" Jackie said.

"You have no idea how right you are," the special agent confirmed as he took out two explosive pucks from his jacket pocket.

"Are you going to blow up the building?" the young woman asked, clearly worried.

"Not the *whole* building. Our goal is to get inside, not destroy the place. All right, kids," he said with a sinister smile. "Have you seen *The Towering Inferno*?"

CHAPTER 32

The neighborhood was swarming with police cruisers and fire trucks. Drawn to the building by the wailing sirens and flashing lights, curious bystanders from nearby night spots were viewing the scene from behind hastily installed security barriers. All eyes were on the pillars of smoke escaping from the second floor, where Eytan had thrown explosives after propelling himself up the wall. The bystanders soon heard the thumping of helicopter blades. The aircraft was circling above them in search of any new fires.

Complying with Eytan's instructions, Jeremy mingled in the crowd. As he wormed his way into their conversations, he spread the rumor that the fire was no accident. The television reporters were already saying something about an attack. They had appeared in a matter of minutes with their satellite-equipped trucks. And the reporters had no trouble finding people to interview. Almost all of the bystanders, it seemed, were eager to give their versions of the events.

His mission accomplished, Jeremy left the mob and walked to the next street, where Jackie and Eytan were waiting. The giant was puffing a cigar while his relaxed pocket-sized partner was sipping root beer from a can.

"Man, they ate that shit up," Jeremy said. "It's almost scary, how easy it was."

"Combine one huge lie with a population's biggest fears... It works every time. Remember when Colin Powell held up that fake vial of anthrax at the UN? The administration used the anthrax hoax to rationalize invading Iraq. Admittedly, there were a few other lies—like Iraq was responsible for 9/11, but that's a whole other story."

"If you're trying to prove that we're all idiots, you've won," Jackie said. "All right, it's my turn to take the stage."

Jackie pecked her husband on the lips and gave Eytan a little wink. Her determined face masked any hesitation. As she ran off at full speed, she retraced Jeremy's steps to the chaotic scene in front of the building. She observed the firefighters as they pulled out their equipment. She counted at least fifty, some of whom were already harnessed and beginning to file into the main lobby. She felt a wave a guilt sweep over her. Jackie wasn't proud of what she was about to do, but the ends justified the means. Like Jeremy, who had immediately jumped onboard, she considered Eytan's scheme more brilliant than reprehensible.

Jackie searched for the perfect target. She elbowed her way through the crowd yelling, "Police!" She finally spotted the best candidate. The officer was tall, overweight, and about thirty. She stuck her deputy sheriff's badge in his face. Legitimate value in Baltimore: zero. Chances of getting caught if he examined her badge carefully: maximum.

"Sheriff's office," she shouted with as much authority as she could muster. She slipped her badge back in her pocket as quickly as she had whipped it out. "We were called here as backups to question the witnesses. One of them has given me information that I need to relay to the firefighters. I have to get over to them. Now!"

The officer stepped aside to let Jackie pass. She thanked the man with a charming smile and ran toward the firefighters. She had her eyes set on three guys who were leaning against a truck—waiting for instructions, most likely. She got ready to perform again.

"Gentlemen, a man in the crowd is claiming that there's another fire in a nearby building. I need you to check on that."

"I'm sorry, ma'am," one of the men said, removing his helmet. "We can't leave our post without our captain's orders."

"And where is your captain?" Jackie asked. "This is an emergency."

"I don't see him out here. He must be inside, directing the men."

"There's no time to wait for him to come back!" she fumed. "We have to step up."

They looked at each other inquisitively. The firefighter who had taken off his helmet finally gave in. "I guess we can take a look," he said. "But we're not stepping in unless we're given orders."

"Great. Come on, I'll take full responsibility. Let's go!"

The men pulled on their oxygen tanks and went to tell a colleague that they were checking out a report of another fire. They ran off to catch up with an already sprinting Jackie.

She led the men to an adjacent street and then swerved toward a dark and narrow alley. Jeremy met them there. He was rocking nervously, and his hands were shaking.

"That's him, the guy who spotted the blaze," Jackie shouted, nodding toward Jeremy.

As soon as the first firefighter got up close, Jeremy began pouring out a stream of nonsensical information about an explosion and a shower of flames. After calming the agitated witness, the firefighter told Jackie and him to stay back as a precautionary measure. They bolted down a small street in the direction of the building Jeremy had pointed out.

"Those guys definitely live up to their courageous reputation. I can't believe the way they run headlong into danger," Jeremy said.

"I get why we had to set them up, but I still feel pretty bad," Jackie confessed.

"Yeah, that makes two of us."

Thirty seconds and a series of muffled cries later, Eytan emerged from the small street and walked up to the couple.

"We've got our gear," he said.

"I hope you went easy on them," Jeremy said, still showing his guilty feelings.

"I did. Okay, you'll have all the time in the world to feel guilty once this is done, and I'll be doing the same. But for now, go get changed."

Five minutes later, three firefighters plunged into the crowd, oxygen masks over their faces and visors covering their eyes. The police let them through. Eytan, Jackie, and Jeremy entered the building.

CHAPTER 33

Converted into a command post, the building's main lobby was the scene of a highly unusual confrontation between the firefighters and police officers. The firefighters wanted to start evacuating the building's occupants immediately, although there weren't many at this hour, and start putting out the blaze. The police officers, fearful that this might be a terrorist attack, wanted to contact the mayor, the bomb squad, and Homeland Security before giving the go-ahead. Meanwhile, the public relations manager for the owners of the building was trying to keep everything and everyone quiet. Several minutes and profanities later, the firefighters won out. They started up the stairs to evacuate the occupants of the building and put out the blaze.

The team quickly shut off the fire alarms, as everyone knew there was a blaze, and the blare was distracting. But the truce and the relative silence were short-lived. The arguing picked up again when the city officials showed up and started throwing their weight around.

"Proud of yourself?" Jackie asked Eytan as they walked past the command post. He couldn't miss the disapproval in her voice.

"Not my finest moment, but I'll get over it," he replied distractedly, taking note of four men talking with higher-ups.

The small Uzi that peeped out from under the navy blue jacket on one of the men was hardly a police officer's typical weapon.

Pensive yet determined, the giant moved toward the closest stairwell and turned on his flashlight.

"Do you know what floor their offices are on?" Jeremy asked. Eytan could tell he wasn't looking forward to climbing several floors with thirty pounds of equipment on his back. Jackie, however, didn't seem too bothered by the prospect.

"No clue, kids," Eytan said. "We'll have to check each floor."

"How do you know you didn't set fire to H-Plus Dynamics?"

"I don't know, but considering the number of companies in this building, that would be real crappy luck."

"Great plan you have there."

"Who do you think I am, Jeremy?" the agent said, annoyed with his teammate's naivety. "I was just pulling your leg. While you were getting dinner, I slipped into the lobby and looked at the directory. A company called HPD is on the twelfth floor."

"The twelfth floor?" Jeremy moaned. "Can we at least toss these tanks? They weigh a ton!"

"Definitely not. We don't want to attract any unwanted attention. Now stop complaining, and save your breath. As a bonus, that'll give us all a nice break from your blabbering."

~ ~ ~

The trio walked up the stairs, the glow of Eytan's flashlight showing the way. Thus began a grueling trek for the bookseller. By the fourth floor, his calf muscles were throbbing. By the sixth, they were cramping. By the eighth, he was feeling a sharp stitch in his side. Panting like a dog, he stopped in his tracks while his companions kept up their steady climb.

"Can you guys... just slow down?"

The Kidon agent said nothing and continued his ascent. Jackie, however, stopped and turned back to her husband. He smiled at her, relieved to know that he could count on her loving support.

"How long have I been telling you to quit smoking?" she yelled before catching up with Eytan.

"Fucking wedding vows," he muttered as he resumed his climb.

When he reached the final level, his lungs on fire and his entire body in pain, Eytan and Jackie dashed all his hopes of getting a few seconds of rest. They waved at him to join them in the main hallway. They were standing next to two elevators, which faced gray doors that the agent hurried to examine. He surveyed their surface and frame and gently rapped the surrounding wall.

"Typical," he sighed.

"Is it reinforced?" Jackie asked.

"Yes, but it's stupid, because the perimeter isn't... He gave the adjacent wall a powerful kick. It caved with the blow.

"And is that typical?" she asked.

"For some American construction, yes. Take off your tanks."

"With pleasure!" Jeremy said, removing his harness. His teammates did the same.

Eytan grabbed one of the heavy oxygen canisters and used it to batter the drywall. It soon gave way. Eytan shoved aside the debris to get into the offices and handed an earpiece to each teammate.

"Now it's your turn to play. Look for files, briefcases, a safe, anything. I'll stay here and watch your backs in case anyone decides to pay us a visit. If there's an emergency, call me."

"One second," Jeremy said. "How do we know the offices are empty?"

"I don't see any security guards waiting around to get their mustaches barbequed by the fire. But if someone spots you, find somewhere to hide, and Jackie will take care of it."

"Are you messing with me again?"

"I wouldn't dream of it."

"So what is it that we hope to find in the files, briefcases, or safe?" Jackie asked.

"We're interested in legal documents, administrative papers, protocols, bank records, balance sheets, anything that seems relevant. Jeremy, this is why I brought you along. I'm not familiar with this kind of data, but considering your old job on Wall Street, I figured it would be right up your alley. From this point forward, you're the head of operations, and Jackie is your second-in-command. We need proof of any H-Plus Dynamics collaboration with the US military or some kind of connection with the Consortium."

"Well, let's hope they still have some information on paper, because with the power outage, we can kiss the computers good-bye," Jeremy said as Jackie stepped over the rubble.

"Plus we don't have any passwords or the time and the skills to crack the system, even if we did have power," Eytan replied.

"That's true," Jeremy said. "Talk about pressure."

"Just do your best, and everything will be fine. Whatever you come up with will be a huge help."

With a nod, Jeremy turned on his flashlight and entered the offices behind his wife, determined not to let down those counting on him.

~ ~ ~

Meanwhile, Eytan attached the three oxygen tanks to each other, using the harnesses, and kept an eye on the stairwell. The firefighters were creating quite a commotion as they battled the blaze on the second floor and inspected the floors above it. Eytan suspected the building was also crawling with federal agents looking for signs of terrorist involvement.

"There's a good chance our search will be cut short," Eytan informed his teammates.

"I need a couple more minutes," Jeremy replied via his communication device. "I have some accounting records, and I think I'm holding something that will make you very happy. Jackie's in the CEO's office, a Mr. Jonathan Cavendish. Honey, have you found anything?"

"Nothing special, but I... Oh, shit!" the young woman shouted a second before Eytan heard something banging. "There, I busted the lock on a cabinet. I'll grab what I can and get out of here."

"Negative. Stay inside and keep looking. We have guests," Eytan said, spotting the beams of four flashlights dancing on the walls. "Some people are coming up the stairwell. I'll stop them. Wait for my signal before taking off. Keep your radios on silent for now."

He placed the oxygen tanks against the elevator doors, stuck an explosive puck on one of them, and tried a few arm stretches to see how much movement his injured side could take. The pain was tolerable and would give him enough range for what he thought he might have to do. If his assumptions were correct, he wouldn't be confronting firefighters. He guessed that the men were members of the H-Plus Dynamics security team. Eytan took out his serrated blade and planted himself against the wall adjacent to the stairwell.

The first man entered the hallway, a small Uzi in his right hand and a flashlight in his left. He walked right by without noticing the still-as-a-statue giant. A colleague armed with the same equipment followed. They quickly discovered the crude opening in the wall.

At that moment, Eytan grabbed the second guy by the hair, pulled him backward, and deftly slipped the knife across his throat. The maneuver released a stream of blood. Making gurgling sounds, the man slid to the floor. Before the first man realized what was happening, the knife had pierced his back with diabolical precision. It struck him right through the heart, between the sixth and seventh ribs. Eytan withdrew his weapon from the lifeless body, turned toward the stairwell, where the back-ups were waiting, and threw his knife. It whipped through the air and landed in the newcomer's chest. Standing in firing position, the guy was deprived of the pleasure of pulling his trigger. His shirt turned red in an instant. A swift kick sent him soaring backward, knocking down the fourth stooge behind him. This one crashed into the wall and lost hold of his pistol. Without giving him the chance to pull himself together, Eytan closed the gap that separated him from his third victim, retrieving his knife from the corpse on the way, and planted it firmly in the heart of his final opponent.

"Threat neutralized. You can come back now," the agent announced as he wiped the bloody blade on the navy blue jacket of one of the dead men.

"Already?" Jackie said. She sounded shocked. "There must not have been..."

Accompanied by Jeremy, whose arms were weighed down with files and briefcases, she came rushing out of the offices. The blood drained from her face when she saw Eytan stockpiling the corpses in the hallway next to the oxygen tanks. Jackie finished her sentence before going silent. "...a lot of them."

"Eytan..." Jeremy said softly, putting his hand on his terrified wife's shoulder. The giant couldn't miss the despair in his tone.

"I spotted them when we walked into the lobby. It was them or us," Eytan said, finishing his task. "Hide as much as you can under your bunker gear. We're leaving. I'll go first in case we have any more unwelcome visitors."

Jackie followed his lead, as did Jeremy, who took one last look at the corpses.

Eytan was well aware that his friends were shocked by what he had just done, but he didn't have time to dwell on it. More pressing things—like getting out of the building with all of their papers—were on his mind.

The descent proved to be much easier than the climb. Eytan, Jackie, and Jeremy didn't cross paths with a single soul until the fifth floor, when they encountered firefighters coming up the stairwell. The firefighters had just asked the three for a report when Eytan slipped a hand into his pants pocket and pressed the button on his detonator. An explosion shook the building.

"Bomb!" Jackie cried out.

"We need to get out of here. Now!" Jeremy yelled. "Go, go, go!"

The firefighters, along with Eytan, Jeremy, and Jackie, barreled down the stairs. Arriving in the deserted lobby, they ran out of the building under a hailstorm of glass and paper. Outside, the crowd was dashing for cover, and the police officers were straining to maintain order.

The trio ducked around the building and into a dead-end street. They changed out of their uniforms and threw them into a trash collector before heading back to the main street, where their vehicle was parked.

"We did it," Jackie exclaimed as a fresh line of police cars flew by. Her cheeks had regained some of their color.

"It won't be long before the directors of the Consortium figure out what happened," Eytan said, sliding behind the wheel of their car.

He turned on his cell phone, which he had shut off before going into the building. "All right," he said as he read his newest text message.

"Attali's finally located Bennington," he said. "We need to get a move on, because we're going to Fort Wayne. We have a long drive ahead of us."

The couple complied without saying a word and hopped in the car. Eytan pulled out and headed toward the highway.

As the cityscape receded behind them, Jeremy dozed off with his head against the window.

When he woke up, the sun was rising in the spot where he had seen the Baltimore skyline before falling asleep.

"What time is it? Where are we?" he asked between yawns.

"We've been on the road for four hours," Eytan replied without taking his eyes off the road. "Five more to go."

The bookstore owner turned around to find Jackie sprawled in the backseat.

"Everything all right, honey?"

"My whole body hurts," she complained, trying to stretch. "And you have no idea how excited I am to see Fort Wayne."

"Don't be so negative," Jeremy said. "I hear they have their own Coney Island. And a rock band called Grand Duchy even did a song about Fort Wayne: 'Once I was playing down in Fort Wayne/Lost in the grain, you know what I'm saying?'"

As his voice grew louder, the agent interrupted him with a forced smile. "Jeremy, come on, I need some peace and quiet."

"'Once we were kissing in the crowd/They cheered so loud, they'd come to listen...'"

Eytan began tapping his fingers on the steering wheel. "Cut it out. I'm serious."

"Hold on, there's a silly part in French," Jeremy continued, oblivious to Eytan's irritation. "Can you tell me what it means? *Vous vous rappelez/Dans la ville de Narbonne/Que nous avons embrassé toute la nuit.*'"

"That's enough, Jeremy!" Eytan raged.

Jeremy stopped singing, and no one said anything. Some time later, he stole a glance at his friend's stern profile.

"I'm sorry. I was just trying to lighten the mood."

He slapped his thighs and turned back to his wife. "Well, honey, at least we've learned one thing about our Jolly Green Giant. He's not a Grand Duchy fan."

Jackie bit her lip.

"What did you call me?" Eytan asked, hunching his large shoulders over the steering wheel.

"Jolly Green Giant," Jeremy replied. He was tensing up and beginning to feel very embarrassed. He tried smiling. "It's a term of endearment. Uh, I mean... It's way more endearing than Mr. Clean, right?"

Jeremy braced himself against the dashboard as the car came to a screeching stop on the side of the road.

"Okay, that's it," Eytan growled. "I tried real hard to warn you and Avi. Get out!"

Eytan stepped out of the car and stomped around to the other side. He grabbed Jeremy by the collar and dragged him to the back of the car. He opened the trunk with his free hand.

"You're blowing this way out of proportion!" Jeremy protested.

"*Get in!*"

"You're kidding, right? I get it. You don't have to..."

"Get in!"

Jeremy looked at his wife, silently pleading with her to intervene. She just shrugged. Okay, he was shit out of luck. If he didn't climb in now, he'd get punched and thrown in. So he got in and ducked as Eytan slammed the trunk shut.

Expressionless, Eytan slid behind the wheel again as Jackie took over shotgun. He handed her his cell phone and pulled back onto the highway.

"Call Eli."

Eytan listened to Jackie's short conversation with Eli, which confirmed that both he and Avi were fine. Jackie briefly mentioned that Jeremy was in the trunk. Eytan suspected that it wasn't so much to inform Eli but to shorten her husband's confinement in the trunk. She had to be feeling sorry for him, stuck in the back like some goon. Eytan was already feeling bad. He pulled to the side of the road again.

Ending the call, Jackie turned to Eytan. "He didn't do it on purpose, you know. He's intimidated by you. He only blurts out silly things because he's nervous. When you're not around, he doesn't act like a child."

"I feel something similar. Whenever your husband's not around, I'm not so angry and impatient."

"Exactly, and you just told us that patience is a skill that needs to be honed," Jackie reminded him.

Eytan accepted his defeat and smiled. "Go get him," he sighed. Sometimes he wondered if he would have liked Jeremy better when he was depressed. At least he would have kept his mouth shut.

CHAPTER 34

Leaning against the hood of a Mercedes parked on a dirt road that led to a small farm, Karl-Heinz was devouring his favorite sandwich, made to near perfection by his aide-de-camp. It consisted of a healthy chunk of braised pork flavored with a drop of port wine and cushioned between two thick and spongy slices of French *pain de campagne*. Of all the culinary delights that went with his SS colonel status during this time of restrictions, this was by far the best. Granted, the sandwich could have used a bit of butter. But it was wartime, after all, and beggars couldn't be choosers.

An unexpected breakthrough in his hunt had made his treat all the more enjoyable. Up until two days earlier, he had no appetite at all. He had made no progress in his search, and traveling across a country that he loathed revolted him.

Karl-Heinz hadn't been able to undertake his assignment from Reinhard Heydrich right away. Terrorists had attacked Heydrich on May 27, 1942, and the protector of Bohemia and Moravia had died from his injuries a week later. The assassination was met with a retaliatory mission supervised by Karl-Heinz. He had orchestrated the murder of nearly 200 men from Lidice and the deportation of the village's women and children to concentration camps. The entire town was then burned to the ground.

What followed was a gloomy summer, a boring fall, and a bone-chilling winter. For months, Karl-Heinz—along with the dozen man-hunting experts who made up his unit—scoured every inch of Poland in search of the Stutthof escapee. Using his best-known methods for cracking tight-lipped rats, he and his men had covered hundreds of miles, crossed scores of villages, and questioned countless farmers. All for nothing. Eytan Morgenstern had vanished. A child had outsmarted the Jäger. He would be ridiculed by the Gestapo and the entire Nazi Party.

But Karl-Heinz's ordinary determination had turned into pure obsession. He hadn't given up even after his superiors had suggested that he shut the search down. At this point, they were preoccupied with the defeat on the Russian front and the growing involvement of the United States. Sure, the higher-ups had good reason to be worried. And yes, the Reich would fall. It had been obvious ever since Churchill, backed by the entire British Empire, had refused to throw in the towel. But the SS colonel didn't care about any of that. To him, Nazism was a bullshit ideology created by a bunch of incompetent extremists. Göring was just a fat, corrupt, drugged-up psychopath. Himmler was a social-ladder-climbing zealot. And as for Hitler, he might have been an incredible speaker, but his tactics as commander-in-chief were ill-advised as soon as he strayed from the blitzkrieg method.

This was the bitter truth for which the people of Germany would soon be paying the price.

So why the hell would he follow a doomed leadership's orders to put his manhunt on hold and join a collapsing army? Never in a million years would he come home from a hunt empty-handed.

And because perseverance was always rewarded, fortune had finally smiled on him.

Two days earlier, his unit had been on the brink of giving up all hope. They had arrived at a small garrison held down by a low-ranking soldier named Reinke. The guy was showing Karl-Heinz and his men much less respect than he was used to receiving.

As an upstanding captain in the regular army, Reinke disapproved of the SS and made no attempt to hide his feelings. His honesty would have been risky if he had been talking with any other SS officer. But Karl-Heinz liked an honest man. A few well-chosen observations about the ridiculous policy of deporting the Jews and the absurdity of Operation Barbarossa had put the officer at ease. And while Reinke and Karl-Heinz would never be friends, they understood one another. A fugitive was more than enough for him to handle. He didn't need to get on the bad side of more than fifty men under the command of a throwback with an outdated sense of honor.

By this time, the Polish resistance had become a force to be reckoned with. They had recruited an extraordinary number of fighters and demonstrated unmatched determination. Acts of sabotage on roads and railways were cropping up everywhere. Not a week went by without a train getting blown up. Even more worrisome, the Armia Krajowa was wreaking havoc on the Wehrmacht's infrastructure. The skirmishes and losses along the frontier were having a devastating effect on troop morale.

Reinke himself had recently felt the wrath of the resistance. A few days earlier, a convoy carrying weapons had been attacked. He had lost fifteen good men, and the weapons in the trucks had vanished, along with the resistance fighters. The nature of the ambush proved just how formidable the resistance was becoming. Karl-Heinz knew the attacks would only become fiercer from here on out. Reinke had reluctantly acquiesced to Karl-Heinz's retaliatory measures: the execution of fifty civilians and the deportation of women and children. But he didn't hide his feelings that it wouldn't change a thing.

Karl-Heinz had asked the captain for information about the terrorist groups in the region, but no one in the German garrison seemed to know much about the fighters. One name popped up time and time again, though: the Tawny Bear. Specific details about this character's identity were unknown. He was simply described as a sort of Hercules on a savage mission to liberate Poland.

"Given his reputation, it would be a pleasure to eliminate this beast. Unfortunately for you, I'm rather busy with my current assignment," Karl-Heinz said.

"Eliminate him?" Reinke raised an eyebrow. "As far as the Polish people are concerned, this man and his gang are heroes. Kill a hero, and he becomes a legend. Kill a legend, and he becomes an inspiration. No one can kill inspiration."

"Everything dies sooner or later," Karl-Heinz responded. "And even someone with a reputation that's beyond reproach can be exposed. If you do get hold of that Bear, don't give him the opportunity to strut. Humiliate him. Make him out to be a coward. Persuade the people that he was working with you all along. You'll see what happens to this inspiration that you fear."

"Shrewd advice," Reinke said. "But catching him won't be easy. Considering the condition the sole survivor of the last skirmish was in when we found him, these men will put up a formidable fight even if we do locate them."

"Well, maybe this soldier has a piece of information that would help you smoke them out," Karl-Heinz suggested. He was already losing interest in the conversation.

"I don't know how reliable his information would be. The boy loses his cool in stressful situations. He says he felt like he was being chased by a wolf."

"First a bear and then a wolf? Your resistance fighters are a regular zoo." Now the Jäger was bored to tears. "Your soldier has too wild an imagination."

Reinke was quick to respond.

"If you think about it, all of Poland's a damned zoo—one filled with scavengers that have adapted to winters that no civilized human can stand. But on a more serious note, our soldier, Hanisch, said he saw the aggressor just as he pounced on one of our men. This is his description: 'tall, long blond hair that flowed in the wind, and ferocious blue eyes.'"

"Very interesting."

"Indeed," Reinke sighed, "A colorful description, but it's really not much to go on. One interesting thing: our soldier does seem to have a name for this wolf that attacked him."

"Let me guess: Wilhelm Grimm?"

"No, Colonel. Eytan."

"What?" Karl-Heinz was jolted out of his lethargy. "*Eytan?*"

"Hanisch claims he heard one of the terrorists yell his name. He said he sounded like he was calling a disobedient dog."

The wheels in the colonel's head were spinning. Eytan was a common name for Polish boys. These days, most of them were awaiting deportation in the ghettos and camps. Certainly Eytan Morgenstern, the boy he was searching for, would have looked like a child at the time of his escape. But the experiments could have enabled him to undergo a signif-icant growth spurt in the space of months. And his short hair would have grown out. What better for a Jewish fugitive than to team up with a band of underground fighters?

Although it was probably just a coincidence, Karl-Heinz intended to find out. He wasn't about to make any mistakes. He ordered Reinke to summon the soldier and insisted on meeting with him alone in the captain's office. The latter willingly complied. Once alone with Hanisch, Karl-Heinz showed him his only photograph of Eytan Morgenstern. Hanisch's reaction at the sight of the child in the striped prisoner's uniform left no room for doubt. "That stare!" the soldier repeated several times as he pointed to the image with a trembling finger.

Without causing any more drama, Karl-Heinz left the office and rounded up his men before asking Reinke for a map of the region. The hunt was back on track.

That was why the Jäger and his unit had been scoping out the surrounding farms for the past two days.

Karl-Heinz smiled as he swallowed the last bite of his sandwich. Thanks to a twist of fate, he would complete his assignment. And for him, it would be a double victory. He would not only capture Eytan Morgenstern, but also put an end to the dirty doings of that Tawny Bear, the one who was winning over the hearts of the Polish people.

Feeling protected by fate, Karl-Heinz picked up the succulent-looking apple sitting on the hood of his Mercedes. He took out a long dagger from his boot and began peeling the fruit. He removed the skin in one fell swoop and bit into the flesh. It took only three bites to devour his dessert.

Karl-Heinz threw the core to the ground. He wiped his fingers on a handkerchief embroidered with his initials before cleaning the sticky blade. He looked at the words inscribed in the metal: "*Meine ehre heisst treue.*"

"My honor is loyalty."

The official Nazi motto, as decreed by Himmler.

"My honor is victory," the Jäger corrected.

He put away his weapon and saw that one of his men was coming back from the small farm, that day's main target.

"Nothing of importance in the house, Colonel. But we found a secret hatch under a bale of hay in the barn," the soldier announced proudly.

"Interesting. Could be contraband or supplies for the resistance. We shall soon find out," Karl-Heinz mused as he slipped on a pair of black gloves and started walking in the direction of the barn.

"We've detained the farmer and his wife. If you want, I can question them, Colonel."

"And deprive me of my aperitif? No. What names do these people go by?" he asked as he stopped at the door.

"Jablonski, sir. Bohdan and Cecylia Jablonski."

"And how old are the Jablonskis?"

"I'd say they're in their sixties."

"What a shame," the Jäger lamented as he cracked his knuckles. "The younger ones always last longer."

CHAPTER 35

Eli had been cooped up in Frank Meyer's office for about an hour and was getting antsy. Avi, on the other hand, seemed right at home, with his nose buried in a book on anatomy and genetics, which he had found in the professor's pigsty of a workspace.

Eli felt a wave of relief wash over him when their host returned. Frank shoved a metal box in Eli's face, and he took it eagerly.

"Here's Eytan's supply of serum. Tell him I've been working on a new version that won't be as painful to inject. And while you're at it, please remind him that he *is* allowed to come visit me, even though I know he won't."

"You can't call the guy clinically anti-social, but I bet he'd be a real piece of work for a psychiatrist," Avi snickered.

"How well do you know him, Dr. Lafner?" Frank asked, glaring at Avi.

"How well can we really know anyone, Professor Meyer?" Avi replied, looking caught off guard. The sarcastic educator-scientist was now all seriousness.

"True, but that's a bit too philosophical for the point I was trying to make."

"And what point was that?"

"When you look at Eytan, you see a gutsy and determined man, right?"

"That's a pretty accurate description."

"Well that's your problem. When Eli and I look at him, we see a child. A child who hates what's happened to him. A child who's terrified of losing someone he loves yet again. That's why he keeps to himself. It's why he has never committed to a woman. It's why he's willing to stare danger in the face regardless of the consequences. Here's the truth, Avi. Eytan is still trying to escape Stutthof. He's still there in his head. So please, try to see under the surface and spare us comments like 'a real piece of work for a psychiatrist.'"

"I never saw him that way," Avi said. His tone had softened.

"It's okay, Avi. You don't know him the way we do," Eli interceded. He shot Frank a reprimanding look.

"No more jokes, I promise."

"If you can't understand him, at least respect his suffering, for the love of God," Frank pressed.

Eli leaned over the desk and placed a soothing hand on Frank's forearm. "Calm down. He gets it."

Frank took off his glasses and rubbed his eyes.

"I'm sorry. I take this very seriously."

"I think we've all noticed that," Eli said, trying to lighten the mood. "We snacked a little on the road, but how about we go for a real breakfast? As your punishment, you can pick up the tab."

Frank accepted the proposition. They walked to the faculty cafeteria in silence. With Avi embarrassed and Frank feeling guilty, Eli tried to break the ice by feigning interest in Frank's research. The latter took the bait, and soon he was back to himself. By the time the three had finished their eggs and hash browns, Avi and Frank were busy discussing medical subjects that were completely foreign to Eli. In fact, it seemed that the two were practically made for each other. Frank even suggested a possible collaboration in the event that Avi ever decided to leave the intelligence agency. Avi was intrigued.

Eli celebrated the first signs of a budding friendship. Frank and he would not live forever, and they would need someone to watch over Eytan once they were gone. During their flight to the US, Eli had latched onto an idea—an idea that seemed iffy at first but was becoming more conceivable in light of recent events. Jackie and Jeremy radiated an infectious zest for life and, more important, thought the world of Eytan. The same went for Avi. The three youngest members of the ragtag group seemed to get along and even enjoy each other. They appeared to be the perfect incarnations of what Eli had been dreaming of for a long time: successors.

A text message interrupted his thoughts. Eli leaned toward his breakfast companions and quietly interrupted their conversation. He didn't want to draw attention from the others in the cafeteria.

"Once we've received your students' results, we'll meet our friends in Fort Wayne. Operation Baltimore was fruitful, according to Jackie."

"Eytan was in Baltimore?" Frank asked.

"Yes, that's where the prosthetics company is headquartered."

"Makes sense," Frank replied, as if it were obvious.

"Why's that?"

"Baltimore: Johns Hopkins University, kid. It has the best school of public health in the country. It also has one of the top five medical schools and is right up there in the fields of physiology and biomechanics. That's everything you need to conduct research in the area of prosthetics."

"They've got your institution beat?" Avi asked.

"I wouldn't go that far. Sure, Johns Hopkins is ranked higher in certain fields, but those dorks have won only three dozen Nobel prizes, and we've got almost ninety. So who would you say is better?" Plainly, Frank wasn't waiting for an answer.

Eli, Avi, and Frank continued chatting for a couple of hours, until the three students turned up, tablet computers in hand. Frank joined them. He spoke with the students for a good fifteen minutes, his eyes glued to the screens of their devices. Finally, Frank gave each student a slap on the back and started walking back to his companions, bringing the tablet computers with him.

"You can thank my little friends for their good work. They may not look like much, but they're already extremely gifted in their field. So we can say this much about the prosthetic: it's imaginative—and insidious."

"I'm with you on imaginative, but what do you mean by insidious?" the doctor asked.

"The pulses sent by the brain and relayed through the nervous system to the muscles are analyzed by a microprocessor. It records the commands."

"You already explained that. Nothing unusual there."

"Oh yes, Dr. Lafner, everything's perfectly normal as far as that's concerned. But the program hidden in the standard code is much less so. I'm guessing that the military would find this feature fascinating. And it would be just as intrigued by the little gift I'm about to share with you."

CHAPTER 36

Janusz and Karol had left the campsite two days earlier to attend a secret meeting with other members of the Armia Krajowa. In the works for quite some time, the rendezvous would be a forum for new missions, the number of which had risen as the German position had weakened. According to reports, which were a bit slow to reach the middle of the forest, British Field Marshal Bernard Montgomery was pushing back Erwin Rommel's tanks in North Africa. America's intervention in the Pacific and the successive setbacks that the Wehrmacht was suffering in the USSR were giving the resistance fighters a surge of hope. At this point in the war, the role played by the resistance fighters was becoming increasingly important in preparation for what everyone was dreaming of: a large-scale landing on the Atlantic coast.

As was the case whenever Janusz and Karol were gone, the men in the camp were killing time. With his pince-nez resting on his nose, Marek was attempting to perfect a detonating pen that would be used to activate explosives. Pawel was dismantling the unit's supply of weapons and cleaning each piece with tender care. Piotr was doing push-ups, jabbing invisible opponents, and practicing strength-training exercises to stay in shape. Vassili, meanwhile, was checking his animal traps, hoping to bring back a little game that would add some variety to their meals.

Eytan was skimming the pages of a book that Karol had lent him. He hadn't mastered the German language well enough to fully grasp Stefan Zweig's prose, but he had a good sense of the author's depth, humanity, and suffering. Eytan had been reluctant to read anything by this Austrian writer, but Karol had insisted.

"The language does not belong to the Nazis," Karol had told him. "This writer is proof of that. A civilization that brought the world Goethe, Mozart, and countless others must not be reduced to a bunch of degenerate extremists. Speaking of which, can you tell me what the first country to be invaded by Hitler and his pals was?"

"Austria, I think."

"No, Eytan, it was Germany itself."

This was just one in a series of lessons that had helped Eytan fully understand what they were doing. By opening the doors to German culture, Karol was counseling Eytan to develop his powers of critical thought. Karol was saying that it was wrong to make all Germans bear the sins of just some.

"If you allow yourself to be consumed by hatred, it won't stop with just the evildoers," Karol had told him. "Your hatred will soon spread to others. If that happens, nothing will separate you from your enemies. You'll be one of them."

Faced with these thoughts and in light of the savage behavior he had exhibited during the attack on the weapons convoy, Eytan was full of remorse. He hadn't just let down those whom he now considered his family. He had lost respect for himself. He felt adrift, lost in a sea of doubt and darkness. He had allowed Bleiberg to change not just his body, but his very being. Once he had been a happy child who loved his parents and brother. That love had been replaced with a rage that would consume his soul if he allowed it to.

Piotr made no attempt to hide his distrust of the boy or the sadness he felt in seeing him on such thin ice. Janusz never mentioned the incident. Neither did Pawel, who continued his training as if nothing had happened, or Vassili, who remained silent as he calmly and carefully gave his knife-fighting lessons.

These men had welcomed Eytan into their group without asking for any gratitude in return. They had showered him with something he had been deprived of during the long, cold, and wet months at Stutthof: kindness. Amid the flames of war engulfing the globe, Janusz and his group had tried to reignite in him the embers of hope.

How could he turn his back on them? How could he let himself become a beast? What was the point in running away if he was destined to become the monster the barbarians wanted him to be?

Eytan rubbed his now-bald head. Karol had scolded him for shaving it. He viewed this as another renegade act. But Eytan didn't see it that way. It was a form of discipline. He was ridding himself of everything that was alien—including the blond hair—and proving his resistance to what Bleiberg had done to him.

But deep down, Eytan knew the first enemy he would have to defeat was himself.

~ ~ ~

By the end of the day, Janusz had returned. The joy of seeing their leader again—never a sure thing—vanished when they caught sight of two men following him. The first, who looked to be about fifty, was tall and thin. He had an ugly angular face and a long nose. He was carrying a suitcase that appeared to be heavy. The second was carrying two bags. This one was shorter and younger-looking. Like Piotr, he was muscular.

Instinctively, Piotr leaped up to retrieve his machine gun. Pawel and Marek followed suit.

"No need to worry. They're with us," the Bear assured his teammates.

"Who are they? And where's Karol?" Pawel asked, lowering his weapon and signaling Marek to do the same.

"Karol decided to spend two days undercover in Germany. This is..."

"Colonel Neville Wladowski," the tall, thin man said in perfect Polish.

"Second Lieutenant Stefan Starlin," his sidekick said.

"What the hell are they doing here?" Piotr spit out, ignoring the two newcomers.

"The British War Cabinet sent us to coordinate resistance activities in the region," Wladowski responded.

"Does Churchill really think these two hicks can help us destroy the Germans?"

"Relax, Piotr!" Janusz ordered. "Our job is conducting the largest attacks possible all over Poland. The Allies want to debilitate Germany's sphere of influence in preparation for a massive invasion from the Atlantic."

Wladowski dropped his suitcase and pulled a pack of cigarettes out of his jacket.

"We're from a special operations division. We're trained in close combat, sabotage, and infiltration."

"So basically you've come here to fix things that aren't broken."

"How's that?" the colonel asked as he lit a cigarette.

"What do you think we've been doing here? Throwing pebbles at the Germans and running away like little school kids?"

Piotr's face was turning red hot.

Marek and Pawel looked at each other and started laughing.

"Nobody said that," Wladowski responded. "The Armia Krajowa's accomplishments in Poland have been exceptional. Others out there are fighting with less training, fewer resources, and equipment that can hardly match your own. You're the ones we're using as an example for the other rebels across Europe."

The flattering explanation, plus the offer of a cigarette seemed to put the boxer in a better mood. Janusz took advantage of the cease-fire to introduce his unit to his guests.

"We haven't come empty-handed," Wladowski continued, pointing to the three pieces of luggage.

Starlin knelt down and opened each one. In the first suitcase was a two-way radio whose miniature size won a round of oohs and ahhs. The second bag contained several Ordnance Survey maps of Poland. But the last case garnered the most attention when Starlin proudly displayed its supply of US-made corned beef hash, chocolate bars, cigarettes, and a large box of cigars.

"And the party wouldn't be complete without..."

He raised a bottle of whiskey high in the air. Pawel and Piotr cheered as he unscrewed the cap. Even Vassili looked almost excited. Starlin filled the band's makeshift cups, carved from wood found in the forest. Marek, however, went straight for the radio, which he thoroughly examined.

Eytan was sitting off to the side and happily watching the scene. Janusz walked over to him, handed the boy a cup, and sat down.

"I don't know if..."

The Bear cut him off. "Drink up. It's an order! Who knows when your next opportunity to get sauced will be."

Without giving it another thought, Eytan swallowed the drink in one gulp. He handed the cup back to Janusz, who was scrutinizing the boy.

"Not bad," Eytan said, grinning.

"That's it? It wasn't too strong? Your throat's not on fire?"

Eytan shook his head.

"You never cease to amaze me," Janusz said. "Here's a second test. Smoke this."

The Bear handed Eytan a cigarette. He struck a match against the sole of a combat boot and lit the cigarette. Suspicious, the teenager brought it to his lips.

"Breathe the smoke in, and blow out," Janusz said.

Eytan complied.

"So?"

"It smells weird, but it's all right," Eytan said before taking a second puff.

Janusz roared with laughter and stood up.

"Don't be such a wallflower. Come join us."

"I'd rather watch from here. I feel like drawing."

"Another one of your many talents, although not exactly the most obvious," Janusz said as he started walking back to his friends.

"Hey, Janusz," Eytan ventured. "Are you happy?"

The Bear stopped and looked back at him.

"Those men are my only family," he said softly. "They're happy, so I'm happy."

Eytan smiled as he watched him rejoin the others. Then Eytan picked up the sketchpad and charcoal that Janusz had brought back from one of his visits to town. He quietly began depicting the scene before him. His fingers swept over the page smoothly and precisely, and the figures and faces took shape.

The party continued well into the night. When the initial rush subsided, Stefan Starlin gave them more information about the war and how it was progressing in the rest of the world.

"Some one hundred thousand Polish exiles are fighting alongside the Allies, and they're doing a hell of a job. The Germans sent to stop the advances of our troops in Italy know all about it."

"This war started with Poland, and by God, the Poles will put an end to it!" Marek shouted, his tongue loosened by the alcohol.

"Hear, hear," his cohorts replied.

"Let's raise our cups to those who've sacrificed their lives at Pearl Harbor and Stalingrad," Wladowski proposed. "The US has awakened from its slumber, and Stalin has decided to take on Hitler, as well. To Roosevelt and Uncle Joe," he cheered before raising his cup to his mouth.

The others repeated the gesture, and the conversation continued until fatigue set in. Vassili was the first to say goodnight. He needed to rest up before his morning watch.

~ ~ ~

The next day, as always, Eytan awoke with the sun. When he emerged from his hut—where he had to sleep alone because of his nightmares—he found the vestiges of the night's festivities. Empty bottles and cigarette butts covered the ground. Vassili came into the clearing, his arms loaded with tinder and logs gathered in the woods. He started to get the campfire going again. Eytan, meanwhile, began picking up the litter.

Janusz soon showed up and thanked Eytan. He yawned and ran his fingers through his unruly mop of hair.

"I've got the worst hangover."

"No shock there, considering how much you all guzzled last night," Eytan teased as he picked up an empty bottle.

"I don't know what makes me unhappier—this headache or discovering that we've completely gone through our stash of alcohol," the Bear joked. "Not that I'd want any at the moment."

He picked up a canteen of water, took several huge swigs, and poured the rest over his face.

"Vassili, get our equipment together. We'll be leaving for the Jablonskis," he said. "And wake up Pawel. He'll take over the watch while we're gone. Eytan, get ready too. You're coming with us."

"Who are the Jablonskis? What are we going to do?" Eytan asked.

"Some chocolate bars and a few cans of meat won't last very long, especially with two extra mouths to feed. We need more supplies. The Jablonskis own a small farm that's a two-hour hike from here. They help us. Our initial meeting was actually in their barn. It's time to apologize for what you did, don't you think?"

"I didn't mean to do any harm," Eytan replied, ashamed.

"I know," Janusz said. "I was teasing. But it is important that they get to know you in case you ever have to visit them without me."

Someone yelling interrupted their conversation. It was Pawel.

"I wanted one of you to wake me up, but I didn't need to get kicked in the ass, God dammit!"

Wearing a satisfied smile, Vassili emerged from the shelter that Pawel and Marek shared. He gave Janusz a thumbs up.

Ten minutes later, the Bear, the Siberian, and Eytan left the campsite and headed south to Bohdan and Cecylia Jablonski's farm.

~ ~ ~

At mid-morning, Pawel, who was nursing a cup of *ersatzkaffee*, sprang up at the sound of cracking twigs. He didn't have time to lift his weapon before a man in a German uniform came hurtling into view, as if he were being chased by a pack of wild dogs.

"Karol? For fuck's sake, you scared the shit out of me. Next time, warn me before you come bolting back like a madman. I could have shot you. Or had a heart attack."

Out of breath and dripping with sweat, the professor rushed to his comrade and grabbed him by the collar. Pawel had never seen him in such a crazed and panicked state.

"Where are Janusz and Eytan?" he asked several times.

"They left for the Jablonskis with that bastard Vassili. Why?"

"Oh no. Shit!" Karol shouted. "How long ago?"

"I don't know. At least an hour," Pawel ventured. "Calm down. What's got you so worked up?"

"We have to go help them."

"Help them do what?"

"Right now!" Karol cut him off, as if possessed. "Go warn Marek and Piotr. We don't have a second to spare."

"You wanna bring Marek? Are you nuts? He's not even freakin'..."

"We need everyone, Pawel."

"To do what?"

"I just came from Reinke's garrison. A special SS unit is sweeping the area in search of a child who's escaped from a camp. Sound like anyone we know?"

"They're looking for Eytan?"

"Yes," Karol said. "They've been spying on all the farms in the area for the past week, waiting for us to show up. Janusz and the others are going to fall right into their trap."

CHAPTER 37

The Audi was parked in the lot of a budget motel off I-469. Stretched out in the backseat, Jeremy was flexing his trader muscles as he analyzed the business plans he'd stolen from the H-Plus Dynamics accounting department. Jackie was in the front seat, studying the files she had swiped from the president's office. Meanwhile, Eytan was enjoying a cigar outside the vehicle while checking Simon Attali's text again for the location of General Bennington and his zombie commando unit.

From Eytan's cool demeanor, not a soul in the world would have guessed that only a few hours earlier he had destroyed part of a skyscraper, eliminated four guys without giving them a second to defend themselves, and stuffed one of his four closest allies into the trunk of a car.

Jeremy's brief moments of solitude in that dark cramped space had allowed him to collect his thoughts. His sense of humor, while bordering on abrasive, had always served as a defense mechanism. He often used it to hide his true feelings. He didn't mean to hurt anyone when he cracked a joke. Yes, he realized now that comparing Eytan—who had endured a lifetime of horrors, pain, and suffering—to the brawny man on a line of household cleaners or the guy in green on a box of frozen vegetables might have sounded cruel. But surely Eytan understood how he felt about him. And whether Eytan admitted it or not, he was, indeed, a giant man in green clothes. Wasn't there some humor in that? Besides, when it came to cleanup agents, Eytan was the champ. Hands down.

It would take more than a timeout in the trunk of an Audi to keep Jeremy from expressing his feelings for the Israeli agent in his own unique way. But for now, his role model was demanding serious work. And Jeremy would not let him down.

"Come on," Jeremy blurted to Jackie after a prolonged silence. He opened the door of the car to get out.

"Did you find something? Because I did!"

"All right, we'll both have our turns at show-and-tell," he said. He exited the car and hurried over to Eytan. "You wanted juicy information. Here it is!"

"You have my attention."

"I'd better have your attention! During my quick visit to the accounting department, I got my hands on the company's business plan from last year. It includes a twenty-year projection, which is an unusually long time frame."

"A projection?" Eytan asked. "You didn't dig up anything on their current status?"

"No need. We already know what the company makes. I figured it would be more useful to find out what their long-term goals are in order to gauge their strategy. Aren't war tactics all about anticipating your opponent's next move?"

"Yeah," Eytan admitted. "So?"

"So... It appears that our little friends are getting heavy funding from the US military. They won a military contract several years ago. But I haven't been able to figure out whether the money's coming directly from the Pentagon or a go-between in some kind of shadow arrangement."

"How big?" Jackie inquired.

"Three hundred and fifty million big."

"Yeah, that's pretty big."

"Actually, it's relative," Jeremy clarified. "Military contracts can run into the billions. To get a better idea, you have to put it into context. US military spending soared after the 9/11 attacks. The US got involved in Afghanistan and Iraq, as we know, and all those troops needed machinery and weapons. In addition, US weapons became much more sophisticated. The drone program, for example, really took off, because it eliminated so much of the risk of taking out targets. We could get rid of those nasty terrorists without risking any American lives. Lots of companies dipped their fingers in the arms honey pot."

"How do you know so much about all this military stuff?" Jackie asked.

"Most of the companies making the weapons and machinery are publicly traded. When I was on Wall Street, I had to have an idea of what they were doing. And for the most part, it wasn't a big secret. It was reported in the financial news. The US companies, by the way, aren't the only ones producing arms. BAE systems and Airbus, both European corporations, are among the world's top ten arms manufacturers."

"That's lovely. All out in the open," Jackie grumbled.

"Unfortunately, war is big business in the world we live in, honey. But there's something else about H-Plus Dynamics that's intriguing: the company's growth projection. Twenty years from now, they think they'll be selling two million units annually in the United States alone. It's interesting to note that the company is privately held but expects to go public sometime around 2025. That's probably because they'll need new manufacturing facilities—and an infusion of cash—to produce all those artificial limbs."

"They can't possibly sell all of the prosthetics to the military," Jackie said. "Sure, the wars in the Middle East cost plenty of young men and women their arms and legs. But the US is scaling down now, and I think most Americans don't have the stomach for another war."

"Not at the present time," Eytan said. "And don't forget, you're approaching this from a purely American viewpoint."

"Do you think this company is counting on another major war?"

"Why not? They've done it before, Jackie. The Consortium contributed to Hitler's rise in power. For them, World War II was just a way to further their own agenda."

"So you think they're prepared to start things up again?"

"That's what it looks like to me."

"I'm not so sure about that," Jeremy said. "Your premise has some validity. But in this document, they say that just five percent of their sales will be to the military. The civilian market will account for the other ninety-five percent."

"They plan to sell close to two million prosthetic limbs to civilians per year? Are there *that* many amputations in this country?" Jackie exclaimed.

"Maybe. All I know is that they're gambling big on it," Jeremy said. "Avi will be able to shed more light on this. As a doctor, he should have access to the kind of information we need."

"Well, Jeremy, I'm very impressed," Eytan said. "Good work. The Consortium is pulling a fast one here. That we know. We'll just have to wait and find out what it is. I'll call Avi."

Before he could pull out his cell phone, Jackie stepped closer and put her hands on her hips.

"I know I'm just a little girl in a world of macho men, but you could at least hear what I have to say before calling him."

"Sorry. I didn't mean to ignore you," the giant apologized.

"I'm just messing with you. Check this out," she said as she placed a stack of thirty-some loose papers on the roof of the car. "I'm curious to hear what you think."

Intrigued, Eytan flipped through the papers one by one. Each page had the same format. There was a photo of a man in uniform. Under each photo was a résumé of his military position, a description of his skills, and—less customary—his medical statistics, including blood type and heart rate, both resting and at maximum exertion. The bios were stamped with either a "pass" or a "fail." Eytan slid three of the profiles out of the stack. The first two looked like the men they had confronted in New York. The third one was Sergeant Tim Terry, the sniper who had shot down Titus Bramble.

"Here's our special unit. Attali wanted evidence. This is it. Irrefutable evidence."

"Yeah, it'll be hard to top that," Jackie said. "Unless a little detail bites us in the butt."

She pointed to the top corner of one of the profiles. "There, see that?"

Jeremy and Eytan peered at the corner. "It looks like this information has been sent by fax, but the tiny characters are impossible to make out," Jeremy said, looking at Eytan. "Don't you have superior vision, too?"

"That's another one of my powers," Eytan muttered. He looked closely at the documents and placed them back on the pile, letting out a bitter laugh.

"What's going on?" Jeremy asked.

"He read the date the files were sent," Jackie said. "Just as I did."

"So?"

"H-Plus Dynamics received the files on these soldiers a few years before they disappeared in battle," the Kidon agent explained. "These soldiers were deliberately chosen and approved by a company that's developing prosthetics for the military, and as chance would have it, they all magically vanished on the battlefield. Isn't fate funny?"

"You don't seriously think..."

"I certainly do, Jeremy. I can't imagine a Marine ever volunteering for an amputation. Someone was in charge of making sure they'd lose their limbs."

Jackie shivered and zipped up her jacket. "That's disgusting," she said. "One day, you'll have to tell me how you keep your faith in the human soul."

"It's a daily struggle."

CHAPTER 38

Armed with their rifles, the three men hiked along the edge of the forest.

They had left the camp more than an hour and a half earlier, and they had almost reached the Jablonski farm. The Bear appeared more relaxed than usual, his hangover finally gone. Even the Siberian had shed his typical gruff demeanor. Eytan was reveling in the warmth of the springtime sun and picturing a future for himself. For the first time, he could envision an end of the war.

"Do you know these farmers well?" Eytan asked Janusz.

"Cecylia and Bohdan? Yes, I know them very well. I grew up around here. When we were kids, their son, Josef, and I were as close as brothers. We lost touch when he enlisted in the army, and I left to go work in Warsaw. When I came back after joining the Armia Krajowa, the Jablonskis didn't think twice about helping us."

"What happened to their son?"

"They haven't heard from him," Janusz said. "They're still hoping he'll come back."

Eytan nodded sympathetically. Vassili's voice startled him out of his thoughts. Until now, the Siberian had been silent, as usual.

"He's not coming back," Vassili said. "No one's coming back."

"Yes, I know Josef's not coming back," Janusz said. "But Bohdan needs to believe that he is."

The Bear pressed on, leaving Eytan and Vassili trailing behind. The boy couldn't remember ever having heard Vassili speak, and he had chosen to respect his silence. Even their knife-handling and stealth-assassination training sessions were done wordlessly.

"How come you never say anything?" Eytan asked.

"I don't talk if I have nothing to say. Besides, no one at the camp ever asks me any questions."

"How did you learn Polish? And what do you mean 'no one's coming back'?"

"No Polish officer is coming back," Vassili clarified as he stepped over the trunk of an uprooted tree. "As for the language, I've lived in this country for four years. I learned by interacting with people, first with help from Red Army interpreters. Later, Karol taught me."

Eytan would never have guessed that his instructor could be so chatty. Now he seemed like a natural conversationalist. The boy decided to push further.

"And how did you end up here four years ago?"

"I came to Poland with my unit in September of 1939, two weeks after the German invasion. Stalin and Hitler divided your country in two. The fascists controlled the land west of the Vistula, and we—the communists—took the eastern half.

"I had no idea. My parents never told me any of this."

"It's not the kind of thing you tell a child," Janusz said. Eytan and Vassili had caught up with him.

"This alliance seems a little contradictory to me," Eytan said. "Why did you leave the Red Army?"

Janusz sighed and turned to Vassili. "Tell him about Kharkiv," he said.

"In 1940, I was sent to Kharkiv in Ukraine, where many Polish soldiers had been deported. When we got there, agents for the Soviet secret police, the NKVD, handed us gloves and butcher's aprons. They were a dark stiff leather that smelled like decayed carcass. In groups of three, we went down to the underground cells where your fellow countrymen were rotting away. I can still remember the gurgling of the water seeping into the cells, the clanking locks, and the squeaky hinges. My two partners would enter a cell, grab a Polish prisoner, and tie his hands behind his back. Then we would take the prisoner to a remote part of the cellar. Every man behaved the same. They all walked with their heads held high and with a proud look in their eyes. They were ready to brave what was in store for them. These men were not afraid of torture. They were true fighters. We weren't. When the guy entered the room, he knew as soon as he saw the blood on the floor and the sacks of sand against the walls. Some fought. Others closed their eyes and prayed. My job was to hold the man down while an NKVD agent shot a bullet in the back of his head. Between all of us, we killed three hundred that first night. And I know that several thousand more of your people were treated the same way."

Eytan froze."Are you serious?" he asked.

Vassili stared at Eytan. "Always," he replied. He continued walking, his student on his heels.

"But why? What for?"

"Poland had a conscription system that required all university graduates to serve in the army," Janusz said. "The men the secret police executed were scholars, physicians, lawyers, professors, politicians. Hell, there was even a prince. If you want to enslave a country, you start by eliminating the elite."

"But how did Vassili end up here with us?"

"Because, as Karol would say, bumps in the road are not as important as where the road leads us."

"I don't get it."

"Listen to the rest of his story. You'll understand."

"After four days of nonstop executions, I was ordered to interrogate a young elementary school teacher who was accused of working with a resistance network" Vassili said. "The political commissar asked her the same questions over and over, and each time she gave the same response: 'I didn't do anything.' At one point, he got up and grabbed her by the hair so forcefully, he pulled out a huge clump. He started hitting her with a stick—first on her body and then on her face—until she fell out of her chair. She cried and moaned as he kicked her. He told me to do the same."

"Don't tell me you listened to him."

"Oh, I listened! I did exactly what he told me to do. But not in the way he expected. I took that bastard by his hair and dragged him away from the teacher. Then I turned him toward me so I could look him in the eye while I broke his neck. I picked up the girl, and we fled the prison together. That's how I became a deserter."

"And how did you meet Janusz?"

"The teacher really did work for a network of resistance fighters. After putting me in isolation for a short period to make sure I wasn't a spy, the fighters introduced me to Janusz and the others. And you know the rest of the story. I'm indebted to this country, and a Siberian always pays his debts."

"We live in a complicated world, Eytan," Janusz said. "Alliances can change overnight. Today's allies could be your enemies tomorrow. Between black and white, there are infinite shades of gray. You have to remember that if you want to survive."

Eytan marched on, revolted by Vassili's story and confused by his confession. Until now, his sense of morality had been simpler; there was good and there was evil. But the more time he spent in the resistance and the more he learned about the world and human nature, the more the line became blurred. His way of thinking no longer matched up with reality.

After another half hour of hiking, they spotted the Jablonskis' little house on the other side of the green. Vassili went to examine the dirt road leading to the farm. Following Janusz's orders, Eytan climbed a tree to survey the surroundings, a task usually assigned to Pawel. From his high position, he had a clear view of the area. The property was a strip of land a few hundred feet wide between two woods. Chickens pecked the ground in a pen attached to the house. Sixty-some feet away was the barn where Eytan had hidden months earlier. A handcart stood beside the double doors. Other than the clucking of the hens and the crowing of a rooster, the property was silent.

Vassili came back a couple of minutes later, visibly concerned.

"No tracks in the dirt," he announced.

"So what's the problem?" the Bear asked.

"The ground is too tidy. I think someone swept it to erase the tire tracks."

"Ah..."

"I don't see anything from up here, no movement anywhere," Eytan whispered.

Startled by the proximity of the voice, the two men looked up to see the bald youth dangling upside down, his legs hooked over a limb of the tree. The boy laughed at the surprise on his partners' faces. Using only his abdominal muscles, he lifted himself into an upright position.

"You think soldiers came by and tried to cover up their visit?"

"Yes."

"Are they still here?"

"Why else would they hide their tracks?"

"I agree. Fuck!" Janusz spit out. "This isn't good. The smart thing to do would be to get out of here, but we have to see if Cecylia and Bohdan are safe. I'm going in. Cover my back if things turn sour."

"In broad daylight? That's crazy!" Eytan said, lowering himself again. "I'm the stealth operations expert. Plus I run faster than you. Either we wait until nightfall, or you let me go instead of you."

"Definitely not! There's no way I'm sending you on a doomed assignment."

"The kid's right," Vassili insisted. "If we need to get out quickly, it'll be easier to do when it's dark. And if somebody gets caught, it should be Eytan, not you. You're too important. You know too much about the resistance."

"Do you really think I'll talk if they torture me?" Janusz said, offended.

"Yes. You'll try like hell to keep your mouth shut, but I've seen tough men crack under pressure," Vassili said. "Eytan won't have anything to tell them. And I'm Russian. They'll kill me on the spot. No questions asked."

~ ~ ~

On the other side of the farm, concealed by the woods, Karl-Heinz Dietz and his dozen men were observing the Jablonskis' modest home and its surroundings through binoculars. They were in green camouflage and waterproof ponchos. They were also wearing black, gray, and green makeup to keep their white faces from standing out. For two days straight, the pack had been roughing it in the woods and keeping constant watch. His men shared his passion for hunting and never complained about staying quiet. It was an inherent requirement for the assignment. Unfortunately, the same couldn't be said for Captain Reinke.

Karl-Heinz wanted five soldiers positioned in the barn. Reinke had agreed on the condition that he be able to camp out with the SS unit. For the past forty-eight hours, he had witnessed the daily routine of a rather unusual troop. Despite his obvious good intentions, he couldn't hide his impatience, which was driving Karl-Heinz up the wall. When the first signs of movement appeared, the Jäger was relieved to finally have the captain off his back.

"Look," he said to Reinke as he handed him the binoculars. "On the other side of the farm, at the edge of the woods."

The captain looked through the binoculars. "I don't see anything," he said. Karl-Heinz's men rolled their eyes. "Oh yeah, I can see those tall leaves moving."

"Someone's hiding in that tree," Karl-Heinz informed him. "The idiot can't stay still and keeps shaking the branches. Your resistance is here, and they're trying to decide what to do."

"You mean they know we're waiting for them?"

"I didn't do anything to hide it."

"So then... My men are in danger! We have to act."

"I wouldn't do that if I were you."

Before the captain had time to question or answer, Karl-Heinz had the chilly blade of his dagger against his throat.

"To catch big game, you need good bait," Karl-Heinz calmly explained. "Do you understand?"

CHAPTER 39

Fortunately, the motel's decrepit façade wasn't a good representation of the rooms inside, each of which had a nice sitting area, a comfortable double bed, and an impeccable bathroom.

Enjoying a hot shower, which relaxed his muscles and cleared his head, Eytan smiled as he recalled his friends' latest display of humor.

Jackie and Jeremy had told the clerk behind the desk that they were working for a major movie studio and were scouting locations for a remake of *Dune*. The clerk had excitedly told them about the beach at Fox Island Park. A perfect place for filming, he said.

Still grinning, Eytan left the bathroom with a towel around his waist. He did a deep side stretch to test his ribs and put on a pair of black boxer shorts and his trusty cargo pants. He plopped down in front of the television and started watching CNN.

The news anchors were providing unemotional commentary interspersed with superficial analysis. At the moment, they were focused on Greece and its austerity measures. Eytan was taking note.

Here was a nation impoverished and humiliated by poor policy on the part of the European Union. The country had undergone a steady economic decline after years of negligent leadership. Now it was a breeding ground for fanatic nationalists.

As if to echo the death camp survivor's alarm, the CNN commentators were assessing the steeply rising power of the far-right party, Golden Dawn. Party members had been accused of patrolling the streets of Greece in black shirts, attacking immigrants, and racketeering. They denied being neo-Nazis, but the symbol on their flag resembled the swastika. And their salute was like the fascist salute. Eytan, who had been feeling good just minutes earlier, was now despondent.

"A world with no memory." He switched off the TV.

An incoming text rescued him from his defeatist musings. "Here. Meet us outside."

Eytan threw on his T-shirt and jacket, left his room, and started walking toward the parking lot. Avi and Eli were waiting by their Ford.

The doctor waved when he spotted Eytan, but the giant didn't acknowledge him. Instead, he pounded on the door of the adjacent room. "They're here," he yelled before heading toward Eli and the doctor.

A few seconds later, Jackie and Jeremy joined them for their minireunion.

Eli opened the door of the car and took out Frank's gift and the serum. He also pulled out a tablet computer containing information on the software found in the prosthetic's microprocessor.

~ ~ ~

Jackie was quietly watching Eli and Eytan. They looked like they were up to something. Something terribly bad, judging by their smiles. Avi, meanwhile, was grilling Jeremy about his stay in the trunk.

"I'd be careful if I were you," the bookseller warned. "You're next on his list."

"Thanks for the heads up. But don't worry. Eli's brother has already given me a good spanking," Avi replied. "He really put me in my place. I'm still embarrassed."

Jackie badgered him for the details of their encounter with the infamous Frank Meyer. Avi happily complied. He recounted the adventure with a great deal of embellishment and kept her entertained until Eli and Eytan interrupted the one-man show.

"We need your brilliant insight, Dr. Lafner," the Kidon agent announced.

He brought them up to speed on all the details gleaned from the stolen H-Plus Dynamics documents. Eytan shared the questions that had arisen from the revelations. Avi excitedly soaked up the data. At the end of the presentation, he closed his eyes for almost a whole minute. He exhaled as he opened them again.

"I've got an idea, but I need a computer to see if my theory is correct," he said.

"Here, take our key card and go get our laptop," Jeremy said. "Our room's closer."

"I'd love to, but I'm not that kind of guy," Avi responded as he headed toward his own room.

"What are you talking about?" Jeremy asked.

"I'm not into threesomes," Avi hollered back before breaking into laughter. He disappeared around the corner of the building.

When she saw the pissed-off look on her husband's face, Jackie began giggling. She knew what Jeremy was thinking. But really, Avi wasn't a jackass.

~ ~ ~

Avi sat down at the computer to begin his Internet search. The first link confirmed the doctor's suspicions, and the following ones only reinforced them. He closed the private-mode browsing window and rejoined his companions in the parking lot.

"Don't worry, guys. The Consortium's not counting on a war. There's no need."

"Finally, some good news," Jeremy said. "But don't leave us hanging. Spit it out."

"Flesh-eating bacteria. Bone cancer. Vascular disease. Diabetes."

"I thought you had some good news," Jeremy said.

"Sorry, Jeremy. We're onto something here. But it's not good news. These are leading causes of limb loss in the United States, and the incidence is rising. Thousands of cases of bone cancer are diagnosed every year. Many of those patients require amputation. And we've all heard about flesh-eating bacteria. Sometimes amputation is the only way to stop the progression of an infection."

"This is where it can get very scary. Eytan, you, Eli, and I know that the Consortium has been up to its elbows in the development of biological weapons. It's conceivable that the organization could see a bright future in unleashing flesh-eating bacteria on all of us just to sell more prosthetics."

"But let's leave that out of the equation for the moment and just look at diabetes. At present, more than 350 million people around the world are afflicted with diabetes. That figure is expected to rise to 592 million by 2035. With those numbers, you could easily call it a pandemic. And it's developing at an incredible speed, with obesity rates on the rise and lifestyles becoming increasingly sedentary. In the US alone, nearly thirty million people—almost ten percent of the population—are diabetic. That's not counting the undiagnosed cases. Just think about all the money the Consortium stands to make on this population."

"It's all that junk food," Jackie said. "One of my uncles lost a toe because it's all that he eats."

"When you think about it, the strategy's brilliant," Jeremy said. "I'm sure the Consortium is up to date on pharmaceutical treatments for diabetes, as well as cancer and bacterial infections. They could easily thwart any new approaches, buttressing the foundation for their market."

"And right now, the Pentagon is financing all the research and development," Avi agreed. "The military is always on the hunt for the latest combat technology. It's an ingenious scheme, for sure."

"While they're at it, the Consortium's jumping at the first opportunity to tell the military about Eytan and his *unique* condition," Jackie added. "Most likely to get rid of him, because he's a threat. Just look at what he's already accomplished. I don't know this Cypher character, but the guy runs a tight ship."

"The irony is that they're not doing anything that's against the law by developing prosthetics and making them available to the military," Eli said. "Sure, it's morally questionable. But I don't see anything illegal about it. They can do it right out in the open."

~ ~ ~

A stone-faced Eytan listened to his teammates as they debated Avi's conclusions. The pieces of the puzzle were falling in place with merciless clarity. Since the Bleiberg affair and his discovery of the Consortium, his own fate had become entangled with the secret organization's. Jackie had no idea how correct her assessment was. Cypher was an intelligent, manipulative, and formidable opponent. Most of all, he was a villain. The kind that any good fighter wound up facing sooner or later.

Eytan wondered if he would ever break free from the hellish bondage he had been in since childhood. Would he forever be someone's guinea pig? First Professor Bleiberg, then Karl-Heinz Dietz, Cypher, and General Bennington. In his past life, Eytan Morgenstern had been the plaything of a group of fanatics. Now he was battling white-collar criminals backed by extremists with the means to satisfy their thirst for power and world domination.

A question began forming in his mind. His cold-blooded enemy was always one step ahead. And more important, Eytan was sure there was a larger objective behind the vendetta against him and his closest friends.

"Your analysis is a good one," he said, breaking into the conversation. "By placing Bennington and his commandos in my way, Cypher knew there'd be a showdown between us. He also knew that I'd have to eliminate Bennington to protect Jackie and Jeremy. If I fail, if I fall into their hands, we know what they have to gain. Research conducted on me would allow the military to improve the performance of its future soldiers. But if I succeed, would that really hurt the Consortium? Or might that give them an advantage? Why would they put their perfectly legal operations at risk?"

"I understand your concerns," Eli said. "But we have to do something. We have to get our friends away from this seething wasp nest."

"I hate not having choices."

"I don't want to sound selfish, but Jackie and I would like to get back to our quiet little life," Jeremy said. "The Consortium, the Marines, the White House—all this is too much for us to handle. I don't think we have the wherewithal to take on Cypher's hidden agenda."

"Jeremy's right," Jackie insisted. "Whatever he has in mind is way over our heads. Let's just finish with Bennington. If other problems arise, we'll cross that bridge when we come to it. And Eytan, I miss my baby girl."

"We could take care of everything if I secured your safety by turning myself over," Eytan said.

"You really consider that an option?" Jeremy said. His tone was icy. .

Eytan silently acknowledged the tension but chose to return Jeremy's angry stare instead of acquiescing. He could see Eli waving off Avi, who seemed ready to intervene.

"You think we would actually stand by and allow you to hand yourself over to those people?" Jeremy continued. "You know what, Mr. Mossad? Screw you!"

"Excuse me?" the giant shouted. He wasn't used to this kind of treatment from people he considered his friends.

"You're such a moron!" Jeremy fumed. "You can threaten to throw me into that trunk again all you want, but that won't stop me from saying what's on my mind. Let me ask you something. Do you like wearing those blinders?"

"What?" Eytan couldn't believe what he was hearing.

"You may be a strong guy, but your skull is empty!"

Eytan saw the stunned faces all around him. But Eli was actually cracking a smile.

"Now you've gone too far. I..."

"Oh, I'm just getting started. You can be a huge jerk sometimes. Just own up to it, and accept the fact that the other people here have feelings too. We're in this mess because you always insist on shutting everyone else out. And why's that? Because Mr. Tough Guy is too scared of getting attached to anyone, of having any kind of real relationship."

"Come on, Jeremy. I don't need any lectures right now. Listen, I was just offering..."

"What you're offering is a huge crock of shit," Jeremy yelled.

"A hypothetical," Eytan corrected. He closed his eyes to cool down and explain himself.

"Well, it's a dumbass hypothetical."

"The five of us can't take on a base filled with expertly trained and fully equipped Marines. The only way to get to Bennington is to give me up. Well, at least *pretend* to give me up. You believed it. They'll believe it."

"Huh?" Jeremy let out, looking sheepish. "So that's your plan?"

"I like you all a lot, but not enough to go back to being a guinea pig. You understand, don't you?"

"Uh, yes. Of course…"

"Let me explain what I'm thinking," Eytan told his teammates before turning back to Jeremy. "As for you, my friend, one of these days, you and I are going to have a little chat about *blinders* and *empty skulls*."

Over the next fifteen minutes, Eytan detailed his strategy for the coming battle.

"Our success rests solely on expert coordination. We'll synchronize our watches just before taking action. Everyone understand what needs to be done?"

They all nodded.

"Okay, back to the car. Bennington and his men won't be making it to sunrise."

CHAPTER 40

For the first time since the bombing that had killed his wife and children a few months earlier, Janusz felt completely lost. His temptation to go and see if Cecylia and Bohdan were all right was at odds with his caution and the need to protect his men.

Vassili was right. Janusz could not run the risk of getting caught. He would put an entire section of the Armia Krajowa in danger if he broke under torture. What's more, his capture would be a huge blow to the morale of his troops and fellow countrymen. The more his influence and reputation had grown, the more the Bear understood that there could only be victory or death for him. That was why he never left the camp without a grenade in his pocket.

Honor had always guided his actions, but he bitterly realized that whatever he did now, he would be disloyal—disloyal to the Jablonskis if he abandoned them without even trying and disloyal to Eytan if he sent him into the trap. And yet, if anyone could handle the assignment, it was the boy with the shaved head. Janusz had watched him throughout his training period. The kid excelled in everything and could handle workloads that were well beyond the capabilities of the strongest men in his group. Further, he had a knack for every style of combat. Simply put, he had surpassed his instructors. And the Bear was convinced that Eytan was hiding the real extent of his superior skills. Why, he didn't know. But the facts spoke for themselves.

These certainties, as well as the telling tattoo on the kid's forearm and his mysterious notebook full of chemistry equations had Janusz convinced that Eytan was the one member of his group who should never fall into the Germans' clutches.

"We're leaving," he decided with a heavy heart.

"There's movement in the barn!" Eytan warned.

"Are you sure?"

"Yes. I can see men in uniform through the cracks in the barn siding. At least three of them."

"Can you get a good shot?"

"Negative. There's too great a risk of missing and attracting attention our way."

Vassili signaled Eytan to climb down from the tree. He moved closer to Janusz, who was stroking his beard.

"We could turn the trap around on them," the Siberian proposed.

"I know what you're going to suggest," the Bear said. Already, he wasn't keen on the idea.

"So you know it could work," Vassili continued. "Eytan and I climb onto the roof. We go in through the hayloft. Once we're there, we jump down on them. By the time they realize what's up, they'll be dead. Meanwhile, you'll be covering us from outside. In and out. Over in a minute."

"That's running a lot risks, all to wind up killing how many soldiers? Three? Five? Ten? If Bohdan and Cecylia are in the barn, they could get killed too."

"And what do you think will happen to them if we do nothing?" Eytan intervened. "Let's give this a shot. I know you're dying to try it too."

"Thanks for putting in your two cents, kid, but you don't win a war by acting on whims. You do what needs to be done."

Eytan, however, refused to give in. He looked to Vassili for support.

"The Bear is right. A leader who acts on his whims is no leader," Vassili said, seeing the disappointment on Eytan's face. "But trying to do something for these people, who are our friends and allies, is no whim. We don't have a choice. We're disobeying orders!"

"I'm forbidding you." Janusz said.

"You're not going to stop me," Vassili said, giving Eytan a nod and starting toward the barn. "If you don't approve, you can always shoot me in the back."

Janusz quickly grabbed his rifle. It was now his duty to cover these two pigheaded men as they slunk off. And even though he was angry as hell, he couldn't help smiling. He actually admired the initiative of these two renegades. In the end, it made his job that much easier.

~ ~ ~

Eytan and Vassili quickly made their way from the woods to the barn. Eytan was in the lead. When he got to the structure, he hoisted himself on a pile of wood stacked against one of the walls. He started climbing. At the top, he used his arms to raise himself up, and without making a sound, he swung his legs onto the roof. Crouching, he silently made his way to the opening and looked inside the barn. His partner joined him half a minute later and questioned the boy with his eyes. Eytan made a fist with his left hand and then opened it up to reveal five fingers—the number of soldiers he had detected. He pointed to three men sitting together and then pointed at Vassili. The Siberian agreed without saying a word. Using the same sign language, he told Vassili that he would take care of the two other targets, who were leaning against posts in the barn. The Siberian propped his machine gun against his back and took out his hunting knife. Eytan did the same with his hunting knife.

The two shadows slipped into the barn and stretched out in the hayloft. On their stomachs, they crept slowly, like two snakes.

Eytan had almost made it to the end of the hayloft. Once directly above the targets, he stopped and winked at the Siberian, signaling the attack.

In perfect synchronization, the two resistance fighters leaped. Vassili landed full force on the shoulders of his first victim. The man let out a gasp that sounded like a balloon rapidly losing air. The soldier Eytan pounced on had no time to react. Determined to avoid repeating his past mistakes, the young man had carefully calculated his strategy for breaking his opponent's neck in one clean snap.

The element of surprise worked like a charm. The German soldiers were not only caught off guard, but also unprepared for savage hand-to-hand combat, because they hadn't been trained for it. Eytan stabbed his second target straight in the heart. His move was strong and blunt. His task accomplished, he pivoted toward Vassili just as the latter slit the final soldier's throat. The man dropped to the ground, choking on his own blood.

In fifteen seconds, five men had taken their last breaths without making the slightest yelp.

"Good work, kid," Vassili congratulated. "Strike hard and don't look back. That's it in a nutshell."

"I think I got it."

"I want to know something. When you murdered those guys who fled the convoy assault, did you enjoy it?" the Siberian asked as he wiped his blade against the jacket of one of the dead soldiers.

"No, I was hoping it would make me feel better, but it didn't," Eytan replied.

"That's a good thing. Killing an armed and hostile enemy—that's war. Getting pleasure from it is twisted. I remember the face of everyone I've killed. It's a heavy weight to carry around, but if you don't, you're not human. Don't ever forget that, kid."

"Will do," Eytan promised before pointing to the open hatch where the Jablonskis kept their hidden reserves. "That's why the Germans set up their trap here."

Eytan approached the ladder the couple used to get into their hiding place. He aimed his gun at the opening and leaned in. He felt the blood drain from his face when he peered inside.

"What?" the Siberian asked.

"See for yourself," Eytan said, looking away.

Vassili approached and looked into the dark space. Bohdan and Cecylia were lying lifeless in a revolting mix of dirt and dry blood. While the old farmer's face was still recognizable, his wife's was a deformed mass of swollen flesh.

"Fuck!" the Siberian shouted before spitting at the closest dead soldier. "They're lucky to be dead."

"Yeah, because for them, this war is over," Eytan agreed.

"Let's get outta here," Vassili advised.

~ ~ ~

Karl-Heinz had planned his strategy to the last detail. After spotting the approach of the resistance fighters, he deployed his men along the edge of the forest so that they could watch over as much land as possible. Four shooters situated in the center and on the right were covering the house. Four others positioned on the left had a view of the barn and the barnyard.

Reinke was anxiously pacing back and forth and fidgeting with his cap.

"There's no reason to be worked up at this point," Karl-Heinz said, observing the barn through his binoculars. "Your soldiers are already dead."

"Thanks to you," Reinke railed.

"With such deduction skills, you could end up as a Reich minister," Karl-Heinz chuckled. He was gratified to hear his officers laughing along with him.

"I swear..."

"...that I never give a second warning," Dietz sighed. He put down his binoculars. Turning toward Reinke, he thrust his dagger into the officer's sternum. The man gave Karl-Heinz a look of disbelief before falling to his knees, a trickle of blood at the corner of his lips. Reinke let go of his cap. It dropped to the ground, landing on a blanket of leaves.

Karl-Heinz picked up his binoculars again and resumed his observation without paying any attention to the dying officer.

"How sad. If only you had been more patient, you could have seen your band of terrorists get captured."

He stopped talking when he saw a liaison officer come running toward him.

"They're about to leave through the roof," the officer told him. "Three men have a good shooting angle."

"Permission to open fire. Wound them, but don't kill anyone until I decide otherwise."

"On your orders, Colonel!"

The messenger ran off to relay the orders. Karl-Heinz stuck two fingers between his lips and, turning toward the SS officers at his right, let out a deafening whistle. He signaled to them to join the other officers. Karl-Heinz leaned over Reinke's body, pulled out his dagger, and put it back inside his boot without even wiping it off. Then he joined his men.

As he arrived at the shooters' post, the first bullets were already being fired.

~ ~ ~

Safely crouched behind a tree, Janusz was shifting his focus from the barn and the house to the woods and back again. The eerie calm was not a good sign. And so a huge wave a relief swept over him when he spotted Eytan and Vassili leaving the barn, by way of the roof. Together, the two men jumped to the ground and started running toward the Bear.

The crack of gunshots shook him to the core. He got a grip immediately and began shooting back, showering the trees on the other side of the farm with bullets. He couldn't determine the exact location of his opponents, so he kept up a steady fire, praying that he would be able to protect his vulnerable friends. His prayers didn't work. Eytan keeled over, blood gushing from his thigh and hip. His head crashed to the ground. Vassili grabbed him by his collar and dragged him as quickly as possible. But the Siberian swiveled on his heels when a bullet hit him in the shoulder. With a beastly growl, he tightened his grip on Eytan and continued to pull him forward.

Giving up on the bolt-action rifle in favor of his German machine gun, the Bear sprang out of the forest and let the ammunition rip. He spewed curses as he fired.

~ ~ ~

Janusz's desperate initiative bought Vassili some time. He was able to haul Eytan to their commander. He retreated into the forest, dragging the boy with him.

The firing picked up again.

The Siberian let go of the unconscious boy.

"I'm going to carry him," he shouted to Janusz.

No response.

He turned back toward the farm. The Bear hadn't withdrawn with them. He was on his knees, with one hand on the ground. Vassili headed back toward him. As he helped his comrade up, dozens—hundreds—of bullets began whizzing through the air, hitting the trees and the earth all around them. Clumps of dirt were flying in every direction. Amid the chaos, the Red Army deserter heard a throaty cry.

"We've got you covered. Bring him back!"

Vassili placed an arm around Janusz's chest and dragged him toward the forest. After a few halting steps, he spied Karol, Piotr, and Pawel frantically emptying round after round. Marek and Colonel Wladowski were there, as well. A little farther away, the powerful Stefan Starlin was hoisting Eytan—still knocked-out—over his shoulders.

"Retreat!" Karol roared as he drew back.

Vassili and Janusz sank deep into the woods, surrounded by Wladowski, Marek, and Starlin. The loud blasts lost their intensity the farther they went. Pawel and Piotr remained behind to keep up the protective barrage.

"Withdraw! Now!" the professor yelled at the two remaining shooters.

It was too late.

The boxer tumbled backward like a flicked domino. Seeing his fallen friend, Pawel stopped shooting. He leaned down to grab Piotr's leg but wasn't able to complete the act. A bullet struck him in the middle of the chest.

Vassili didn't have to be told. Pawel and Piotr were gone. Taking a bullet himself wouldn't have been as bad as this. All of a sudden, fighting seemed absolutely absurd. The price was unacceptable. And a thought flashed in his mind. What if their only chance of finding freedom was in death?

CHAPTER 41

Trailed by the Ford, the Audi was racing along the few miles separating the motel from downtown Fort Wayne. The team was taking comfort in the prospect of bringing their escapade to an end. It was also giving them fresh energy.

Eli, in fact, was showing no signs of fatigue, even though he had spent many hours driving halfway across the country. The endurance of this man with the rugged face was impressive. A tenacious spirit certainly seemed to be a character trait shared by Eytan's closest friends. Avi was driving the second vehicle so that Eytan could get some needed rest. The team felt revived, but the Kidon agent had done more than his fair share of the work.

"I think I'm starting to hate this Audi," Jackie said. "This is the second time I've been on a road trip with Eytan, and the itinerary is always the same: traveling across a continent, tossing explosives here and there, and getting a backache from spending too much time in a car."

"I totally agree, sweetie, but Avi and Eli have covered quite a few more miles than we have," Jeremy said. "How do you manage to have the energy for this?" he asked, turning to Eli.

"I don't have a choice. It's a requirement of our profession. But compared with some of the other unpleasant tasks that Eytan and I have had to deal with, driving isn't so bad."

"Have you been working together for a long time?" Jackie asked.

"That's a loaded question."

Eli began recounting his story, from the death of his mother to his rise to keeper of the archives at Mossad, from his first meeting with Eytan to their partnership as trackers of war criminals. Jackie and Jeremy—who had believed that nothing could be as shocking as Eytan's incredible confessions—listened in awe as Eli summarized his own extraordinary experiences. His was a life of sacrifice and solitude, which had all the elements of a Shakespearian tragedy but was described as a thrilling adventure. He touched on his failed marriage, weakened by the constant traveling and risk-taking. He also talked about his daughter, Rose, who lived in Boston with her little boy. Now that he was a grandfather, he was seriously thinking about retiring and moving to America.

By the time downtown Fort Wayne loomed on the horizon, the couple had learned that Eli Karman, Frank Meyer, Avi Lafner, and Eytan Morgenstern were a family—in spirit if not in blood. And they were more alike than they appeared to be. They weren't all that easy to get to know, but anyone who managed to peel back the layers would find that they all had big hearts. At the same time, they were forces that someone would be foolish to mess with.

And judging by the protective way Eli and Avi were treating them, Jackie and Jeremy had also realized that they were now part of this odd little family.

~ ~ ~

As arranged, they parked their two vehicles in the lot of the first big-box store they came across, which happened to be a Wal-Mart. Customers were streaming out of the store, their shopping carts full of groceries. Jeremy wondered how many of the bags were stuffed full of diabetes-friendly junk food. The Consortium was betting that the unhealthy diet of many Americans' would persist and even worsen.

The five members of the group met in front of the store. The giant asked how they were all feeling. Their mental state would play a decisive role in the next few hours. He then scanned the parking lot.

"What are you looking for?" Jackie asked.

"I need a motorcycle," Eytan replied distractedly.

"Why do you want a motorcycle?"

"It's part of my routine. I need to go scout the area."

"What about us?" Eli asked. "What should we do in the meantime?"

"You'll wait for me here. I have a hunch Avi wouldn't say no to a nice cup of coffee."

"You're a clever one, my friend," the doctor said. "Coffee at a Wal-Mart. There's a first time for everything."

"Hey, you drink coffee from a vending machine. Remember? Get your nose out of the air. Ah, I believe I've found just the right bike. I'll be back in an hour, tops. Stick with the coffee and stay away from the doughnuts while I'm gone." Eytan gave Jeremy a wink.

"Ha, ha. Very funny. You think you can read my mind now?" Jeremy yelled back as the Kidon agent strode away.

Eytan headed toward a large red and white power cruiser. He fiddled with the bike before straddling it and revving the engine. Embarrassed, Jeremy looked away as the giant took off.

"I guess after taking out two special forces units, instigating a shootout in the middle of Manhattan, and destroying part of a Baltimore building, stealing a bike is a minor offense," Jackie said.

"I don't know much about the law," Avi replied, "I only believe in two things: medicine and Charlie Parker."

"Bird? You like jazz too?" Jeremy asked.

"I *worship* jazz," the doctor corrected.

And on that note, the group headed into the supercenter.

The foursome found a table in the food-concession area. Jeremy picked up his jazz-centric conversation with Avi. Jackie, who had never shared her husband's passion, turned to Eli. He was interested in how she had met Jeremy and, by extension, Eytan. She was becoming fond of this man, and without hesitation she opened up, recounting her issues with her abusive father, as well as her time spent with the intelligence service. She couldn't help thinking how differently she would have turned out if Eli, so patient and attentive, had raised her instead of her father. The time flew by as Eli and Jackie shared more and more about themselves. Avi and Jeremy, meanwhile, hadn't exhausted their treasure trove of jazz knowledge. Before they knew it, the hours had slipped by, and they saw Eytan making his way toward them.

"If I were to depict serenity, I would paint the four of you exactly as you are right now," the giant said with a smile.

"Then pull up a chair and join us. You're allowed to take a little break," Jackie said.

"I'd love to, but we've got a job to finish."

Frowning, they left their safe haven and followed Eytan out the door and around to the back of the building. The stolen motorcycle was parked near a delivery bay. Eytan walked up to it and opened the top compartment. He pulled out a map of the region and unfolded it over the seat of the cycle.

"Okay, I've found a wide-open stretch a good distance from Bennington's base," he said. "There's not a single home within a mile radius and no hills that would allow Tim Terry to take up an elevated position. We'll probably come into contact with the others, but Terry will be watching from a distance. He's our main threat. Frank's little present, though, gives us a big advantage."

"According to Frank, the effects of his device are radical but limited," Avi said. "We can only use it once."

"I'll make sure our enemies are grouped around me," the Kidon agent said.

"Unfortunately, that's what has to be done," Avi said. "Once you give me the green light, I'll start counting down from thirty. That way, we'll have enough time to get back to the Ford. The car will be a sort of Faraday cage, protecting us or at least lessening the effects. Afterward, it'll be dysfunctional."

"You sound like you're not all that positive about this," Jackie said. "It doesn't inspire a lot of confidence."

"I'd be lying if I said there's no risk. We're not dealing with an ordinary machine. And Frank doesn't use it for the same purpose that we need it today. As for you, Eytan, after the explosion, your earpiece will be useless, so we'll no longer be able to communicate. By the way, I don't know the exact effect it'll have on your metabolism."

"What's your best guess?"

"I'm hoping your unique physical condition will allow you to withstand the shock better than the soldiers. But it's possible that the waves will cause your body to overheat. If that happens, you'll have to administer an emergency dose of serum."

Jeremy took a pack of cigarettes out of a pocket of his jacket. He lit one, inhaled, and passed it to Eytan after seeing his outstretched hand.

" I understand." The Kidon agent exhaled a cloud of blue-gray smoke.

"Jeremy, hand me a smoke too," Eli said. "And Avi, you be quiet. Right now I need one."

"Anyway, if something bad happens, I'll help you," Jackie told Eytan. "Considering the distance between us, I'll be able to reach you in less than sixty seconds. Assuming you get out with no problem, I'll stay back to protect the boys in case Bennington has sent out troops to lock down the perimeter."

"And I'll be covering with a sniper rifle as soon as the device is triggered," Eli said.

"Your priority will be to locate Terry and take him out," Eytan ordered. "He'll most likely be focused on me, which will give you a clear advantage."

"Sounds good."

"Meanwhile, Avi and I will run to the Audi parked outside the device's range and bring it back," Jeremy said. "Then, once all the bad guys are dead, we'll meet up and get the hell out of there,"

"I'm impressed," Eytan said. "I love the optimism. Well, since everyone knows what they've gotta do, let's get to it! In less than fifteen minutes, I'll be sending out the invitation."

"How do you plan to do that?"

"The same way I always do," the giant replied, folding the map. "As politely as possible."

CHAPTER 42

Spread out in the undergrowth, the SS unit was waiting for instructions from Colonel Dietz. Five minutes had passed since the gunfire had stopped and the Polish insurgents had run off. Bullets in the tree trunks, shattered windows in the farmhouse, two bodies at the edge of the woods... It was clear that a battle had taken place here. A surreal silence enveloped the area.

Karl-Heinz was the first to get up. He adjusted the shoulder strap of his rifle as he walked toward the lifeless bodies. The pack leader's nine men followed a few steps behind.

Karl-Heinz looked at the barn just long enough to spot the open eyes of a young soldier lying with a bloody cheek against a bed of fresh straw.

"Throw Reinke's corpse in with the bodies of his men," the Jäger ordered as he continued walking." And burn the whole lot up."

Two SS officers obeyed and rushed to retrieve the remains of Bruno Reinke. Observing his officers' diligent obedience, Karl-Heinz smiled. He prized the cohesiveness of his group. They were of one mind. What chance did a clan of amateur yokels with nothing but a pathetic sense of bravery have against his experienced unit of trained and meticulously organized professionals? Obviously none, he thought as he inspected the bodies of the men he had personally conquered.

"One to the head and one to the heart. Beautifully done, Colonel," his aide-de-camp said.

"Not bad considering the distance and the relative state of confusion."

"I was wondering why you chose this strategy. Why eliminate only two of them?"

"Good question," Karl-Heinz replied. He liked being the instructor. "I was still unsure of the number of men we'd be dealing with, as well as their strength and stamina. And without such crucial information, I wasn't going to attempt a direct approach. I needed to know more about our main target, and on that score, our mission was a huge success."

"What do you mean?"

"I'm now absolutely certain of Eytan Morgenstern's present-day appearance. He's not only gotten much bigger, but also taken up shaving his head and eyebrows."

"I see, but what about the others?"

"I want to chase those animals out of their hideout. After this, they'll be on the defensive, and you *never* blindly pounce on a wounded beast. Let's recap. Their leader—the Bear, I'm guessing—has been hit. Morgenstern too, along with that brute who joined him in the barn. That means their resistance will be considerably weakened when we go in for the final kill. Plus their ability to move is now restricted, and their morale, I'm sure, has suffered considerably. To really drive it home, I killed these two," he said as he kicked the resistance fighters' bodies. "To sum up, I'm laying the groundwork for a flawless victory. I play to win. Strategy over bravery. That's what separates the vanquishers from the vanquished."

~ ~ ~

Marek led the way, his tears blurring his vision. He was praying silently for his fallen comrades and asking the Lord to welcome them. As the devout clockmaker trudged on, he pictured Jesus bearing the cross to Calvary. Supported by Neville Wladowski and Vassili, whose face was getting whiter as the blood drained from his pierced shoulder, Janusz was pressing a hand against his stomach to stanch his bleeding. It took superhuman effort to complete each step. Lagging slightly behind, Stefan Starlin was carrying Eytan, who was bigger and heavier than he was.

Karol was the rear guard. He looked punch drunk.

The wounded men's groans marked their steady trudge through the forest. They jumped at the slightest noise, expecting to be attacked at any moment. But the anticipated ambush never materialized, and they made it back to their camp.

Marek immediately scaled a tree to search for followers. Thanks to their location, it was tricky for intruders to enter and easy to detect threats. The clockmaker's heart tightened when he remembered that this had been Pawel's job.

Stefan placed Eytan on a wooden table next to the camp-fire just as the boy was beginning to regain consciousness.

"Tend to them as well as you can, and quickly too," Wladowski told him.

The latter complied, relying on the medical training he had received during his time with the SOE.

"How do they look?" Karol asked.

"Vassili and Janusz are lucky," Stefan said. "The bullets didn't do any serious damage. They have flesh wounds: serious but not deadly. I've cleaned them up."

"What about Eytan?"

"He wasn't as lucky. He was shot in the hip and leg. It won't be too big a deal in the long run. But the bullets are still in there. I have to get them out."

"Better not dawdle then," Karol said. "We need to leave as soon as we can. Do your best to get him back on his feet."

Stefan ran to get one of the suitcases he had brought with him the night before. He came back with a medical pouch from which he pulled out a pair of scissors, a knife with a long thin blade, some cotton, a clean cloth, and a bottle of clear liquid.

"This ether will make you woozy," he told Eytan, who was now fully awake. "You'll hardly feel a thing."

"Don't bother. It won't work," the boy said.

"The kid's got guts. I've seen plenty of guys panic at just the thought of getting cut up."

"That's not his style," Vassili said. He had come over to sit beside the boy.

"We'll talk more about it after you wake up, champ," Stefan promised Eytan, a smile on his lips.

Stefan applied the anesthesia-drenched cloth over Eytan's nose and mouth and turned his head as he counted to ten. When he turned back, the boy was looking at him, still conscious.

"Hmm... Can you try sniffing this?" Stefan asked Vassili.

The Siberian brought the cloth to his nose and breathed in heavily.

"How do you feel? Dizzy? A bit sleepy?"

"Both! I also feel like punching you in the face for asking me to do that. We need every conscious soldier that we have."

"It wasn't a prank. I couldn't test it on myself. I wouldn't be able to operate. But why isn't it putting him to sleep?"

"I already told you. This stuff doesn't work on me. Just get on with it and pull out the bullets."

"Don't be silly!"

"He's telling you the truth. Go ahead and operate," Karol said. He placed a protective hand on Eytan's forehead.

"What?"

"Operate on him. I'll explain afterward."

"But the pain..."

"Do it!" Eytan ordered. "I know exactly what to expect. Just fix me."

Karol picked up a piece of wood and wiped it off. He gave it to Eytan, who clamped it between his teeth. Eytan brought his wrists together and held them out to Vassili, who grabbed them. Karol gripped his ankles.

Stefan took a deep breath. The procedure would require speed and precision. He plunged the knife into the boy's thigh. After a brief moment of calm, the moaning began.

~ ~ ~

Colonel Neville Wladowski had his back to the operation and was busying himself with the radio. He was trying to block the sounds, but could still hear them well enough to imagine what was happening on the table. The creaking of the wood as Eytan shook, the heavy breathing, the squish of flesh being torn and manipulated. And the encouraging words of the men at the boy's side. The colonel had seen and heard it all before. He had witnessed similar surgeries on the frontlines. Such scenes were impossible to chase from his head. They were locked in there for life. Once you stripped away the exaggerated tales of glory and the propaganda, you were left with cold reality. The battlefield was a slaughterhouse.

"All right, the first one's out," Stefan declared. "Hang in there, kid. We're almost finished."

Wladowski was focused on another priority, which was just as crucial as Stefan's valiant efforts to get the bullets out of the boy. As he fiddled with the radio, he was trying to figure out a way to save their mission. With two men dead, another three weakened—one of whom was their leader—and a cohort of SS troops on their heels, pulling off a successful escape would take a miracle. And yet Wladowski refused to believe that he had parachuted into Poland only to wind up in the hands of the Germans.

"Done," Stefan sighed as he dropped the second bullet on the ground.

Hearing the announcement, Wladowski turned off the radio to save its precious battery life. They needed to discuss their next move.

He swung around to look at his comrades. Stefan's face was red and wet with sweat. He was leaning on the table where Eytan lay. The boy's chest was rising and falling evenly. Karol was stroking his forehead and wiping the dribble off his chin. The expression on the professor's face had all the tenderness of a father.

"Now can you tell us what's going on?" Janusz grunted. "How did you know that we had walked into a trap? And what did you find out about Eytan?"

"When I arrived at the garrison, I heard soldiers talking about a raid at some farm where there was a stash of equipment and supplies. The farmer had been tortured into confessing that his wife and he were helping the resistance."

"We saw their bodies in the barn," Vassili confirmed.

"It's hard to distinguish fact from rumor, but from what I heard, it sounded like a Colonel Dietz—an expert manhunter—was going after a boy who had escaped an SS research facility. After Reinke left the garrison, I ducked into his office. That's where I found a file."

"*My* file," Eytan interrupted. Grimacing, he sat up. "Here, I go by Eytan. In Stutthof, they called me Patient 302. For about a year, this German scientist—Bleiberg—conducted medical experiments on children in hopes of creating a superhuman. Every week, they injected us with stuff that was supposed to propel us into the next stage of human development. And every week, another guinea pig croaked. They couldn't handle it. By the time I escaped, all the kids with me had died a painful death. The lucky ones suffered just a few hours. I heard Bleiberg say the other ones had some sort of aggressive cancer. Only one survived. Me."

"At least you're alive," Wladowski said.

Eytan shot him a scornful stare. He took off his jacket and let it fall to the ground. Then he removed his T-shirt to reveal a chest full of deep puffy scars. He turned around to show his back, which had the same scars.

"When Bleiberg realized that I was withstanding his experiments, he expanded his research. He started evaluating my resistance to pain. On good days, I only had to put up with a few lashings and trials that tested my memorization skills. On bad days, I'd get the whip, the stick, the knife. Sometimes they'd burn me with a torch. Afterward, I didn't get any medical attention. They wanted to see if I would heal on my own. They starved me. No food, no water. They injected me with what they said were viruses that made me so sick, I wanted to die. *You* weren't a guinea pig, Colonel, so don't tell me I was lucky to survive."

Everyone was dead silent.

"I'm sorry," Wladowski said. "I could never imagine."

He turned to Janusz.

"Do you realize how serious this information is?"

"Obviously,"

"Eytan should have told you this the day he joined you. Him being here with you, with *us*, compromises our missions, both the ones we carry out ourselves and the ones that involve other units. It's clear that Eytan is a complication. A big complication."

"The boy is one of us. You take him out, you take all of us," Vassili threatened, spitting in the dirt.

"The colonel's right, Vassili," Eytan said. "I should never have stayed with you. I've put you all in danger. Piotr and Pawel should have died fighting for our country, not trying to save my butt. And I can't get captured by the Nazis. Imagine what they'd do with an army of men like me."

The men fell silent until Eytan spoke again.

"If you want to kill me, I won't stop you."

"Piss off!" Stefan shouted. "I didn't work my ass off carving those bullets out of you just to see you take more of 'em."

"The first man to get behind that idea will answer to me," Vassili yelled, tightening his grip on his knife.

The men nodded in unison to signify their unanimous rejection of the boy's proposal.

"What about this," Janusz asked as he pulled out Eytan's notebook. "What is it?"

"From what I understand, once I'm done growing, my body will go through phases of overheating. Professor Bleiberg developed a serum that would counteract it. The formula's in that notebook. That's why I snatched it before I ran away."

With a sad smile, Janusz walked over to Eytan and handed him the notebook. The boy hesitated a moment, but with Janusz's insistence, he took it.

"You misunderstood me," Wladowski said. "I wasn't talking about eliminating Eytan, or handing him over, or anything else of the sort. We've got to get him to London, as far away from the Nazis as we can. There's another group of resistance fighters—assembled by the English—about thirty miles from here. I can contact them to determine a meet-up point. Once we've joined them, we'll arrange to get Eytan out of the country."

"I want to stay here," Eytan said. "But I'll do whatever you think is necessary to keep my friends out of danger."

The men gave each other resigned looks.

"Colonel, arrange the meeting," Janusz ordered. "We'll move out in five minutes."

Neville Wladowski turned the radio back on and sent a distress call as Stefan and a limping Eytan hastily gathered a few items. While they were doing that, the professor took the Bear and the Siberian aside.

"Can you believe that trap those guys set for us?" Karol asked. "This Dietz character and his gang are more clever than anyone else we've gone up against. So why didn't they finish the job?"

Janusz thought it over a few moments, but Vassili gave the answer. "To kill a pack of wolves, you have to find their cave. It's possible they're watching us right now."

He started scanning the woods.

"If they were that close, Marek would have spotted them," the Bear objected. "Marek, you see anything?"

His question was met with silence. Janusz asked again, and again he got no answer. He walked over to the watch post and looked up.

"Grab your weapons!" Janusz yelled as soon as he spotted the clockmaker. His friend was still seated on the limb of the tree, with his rifle across his lap. And a knife thrust deep in his Adam's apple.

A second order rang through the air. And this time the order was in German: "*Feuer!*"

Gunshots rang out.

~ ~ ~

Eytan ducked. Bullets hit the dirt all around, forcing him to shut his eyes. When the gunfire finally stopped, a gloomy silence descended on the forest. Eytan felt compelled to leap up, grab a machine gun, and fight. But the sole of a boot came pressing down on the back of his neck.

"Stand up, 302. Slowly." The voice sounded delighted, almost singsongy.

The boy complied, wincing as he rose. Time seemed to stand still. Clouds of dust and the afternoon sun piercing the branches of the trees distorted his vision. He raised a hand to block the light. He looked down to discover Wladowski slumped over the radio, his body riddled with bullets. To his right, lying on a bed of moss with his knife resting in his open hand, Vassili was gazing at Eytan. But his eyes were devoid of any life. By his side, Karol was resting peacefully, his arms folded strangely across his bloody chest.

Between two SS men in camouflage, Janusz was on his knees, hands behind his head. Seven other officers came out of the woods and lined up behind the vanquished resistance fighter.

"The Tawny Bear and Patient 302. What prized trophies," said the man with the singsong voice. "Colonel Karl-Heinz Dietz, at your service, gentlemen."

With a twisted smile, he saluted Eytan and Janusz and clicked his heels. He put his pistol back in its holster and inspected Eytan. He looked astonished.

"It's hard to believe you're still a child. I can only imagine what you would look like if you had the opportunity to reach adulthood. I see now why Heydrich wanted you eliminated."

"You didn't come to take me to Stutthof?" Eytan said.

"No, my precious. I came here for a fight. I'm anxious to see if you deserve a place among my most prized hunting mementos."

"I won't fight you," Eytan said. What was the point? "Kill me now. Just get it over with."

"I'm afraid you don't have a choice if you want to save your leader," Karl-Heinz replied, pointing to Janusz. "Give me what I want. An entertaining fight. A valiant resistance. You'll be dead in no time, and I'll allow your friend to rejoin his renegade compatriots. If you refuse, I'll execute him on the spot. In either case, you have my word of honor."

Karl-Heinz took off his jacket and dropped it to the ground. He leaned down and pulled a dagger from his black boot. He walked over to Vassili's body and picked up his knife.

"Perhaps fighting with this will give you a little boost of courage," the colonel said as he threw the weapon at Eytan's feet.

Eytan squatted and picked up the knife. It was covered with the Siberian's blood. The boy grunted in disgust and stood up, the pain ripping through his leg. He glanced at Janusz, who was powerless and incapable of understanding a single word of what was said because they were speaking German.

"What if I win? What will your soldiers do?" Eytan asked.

"That's a bit presumptuous, don't you think? I've hunted wild beasts much fiercer than you and battled the bravest men, but never before have I had the privilege of killing a monster." Karl-Heinz faked a jab, forcing Eytan to step back, wincing again.

Eytan took a fencer's stance, transferring his weight to his right leg to relieve the pressure on his injured hip. This position lessened his exposure to his opponent but eliminated the possibility of switching to attack mode.

"I'm not a monster," Eytan spit out as he swept the air with his blade to keep the SS officer at a healthy distance. "What's the glory in vanquishing me when I'm wounded?"

"I don't care about glory. Winning is all that matters."

Karl-Heinz circled around Eytan, rolling his shoulders and neck. He faked several strikes. Eytan guessed he was testing his reaction. But the colonel's excitement seemed to be wearing off. Was he thinking that the fight wouldn't be any fun? Eytan was fatigued and out of breath, and he was losing his will to survive.

Karl-Heinz executed a series of blade twirls, which forced Eytan to back up even farther. He awkwardly dodged his opponent's assaults. Before Eytan knew what was happening, the Jäger squatted, and with a perfect spin, the man swiped at his leg. Eytan fell backward. The colonel rushed in, ready to stab Eytan in the heart. In an act of desperation, Eytan grabbed his assailant's wrist.

At that second, a blast went off. Shocked, Karl-Heinz looked up. Eytan used the distraction to his advantage. Using his good leg, he pushed himself off the ground and stood up. He glanced in Janusz's direction. An SS officer was keeling over, struck in the throat. Another officer had taken a bullet in the brain.

Stefan Starlin! Eytan realized that Starlin had escaped the hail of bullets that had killed his comrades.

Seizing his opportunity, the Bear stood up with a nasty grin plastered on his face. He head-butted one of his guard dogs, smashing the man's skull. Gunfire continued to crack through the air. Eytan couldn't tell where it was coming from. In no time at all, the invisible enemy had gunned down three more Germans. Then the firing stopped. The remaining soldiers were shuffling clumsily around the liberated Janusz.

Eytan tightened his hold on Vassili's knife, and ignoring the pain, he hurled himself on Karl-Heinz. He struck his opponent with all his strength. The Siberian's blade bit through his shoulder, inciting an icy shriek from the colonel, who dropped his dagger. Reinvigorated by the Englishman's intervention and the Bear's newfound energy, Eytan twisted the steel deep into Karl-Heinz's flesh. He blocked the man's increasingly mad screams. Bones, muscles, tendons, and ligaments all ceded to his furious assault.

When a bullet went whizzing past Eytan's ear, the officer pushed back. He kicked Eytan. With an animal-like howl, he pulled the knife out of his shoulder and threw it down. Rolling in the dirt, Eytan grabbed the colonel's dagger and crawled back toward him, picking up Vassili's knife on the way.

Another blast went off.

He turned around. An SS officer had shot Janusz in the stomach. He and the other officers were circling around the Bear as he held his abdomen. Janusz looked at Eytan. He smiled and plunged his free hand into a pocket of his jacket.

"Stay alive, and don't forget us."

"Janusz! No!" Eytan yelled, understanding what his leader, mentor, and friend intended to do.

The explosion from the Bear's grenade blew up the surviving men. Eytan was lifted off the ground like a leaf caught in the wind. When he came to again, he realized that Stefan Starlin was carrying him away from the scene on his shoulders. In the distance, through the branches of the trees, he could make out three men whose uniforms were ablaze. He could also see Colonel Dietz convulsing on the ground. His mutilated right arm didn't even look like it was attached to his body.

Eytan let out a cry amplified by hate and grief—a cry that rose to the heavens like an unstoppable promise.

"I'll find you again, Dietz! I don't care how long it takes. I will find you!"

CHAPTER 43

Eytan had finally found the checkpoint where vehicles entered the facility. For five minutes he had been driving slowly along the barbwire fence that surrounded the Marine base. A security guard in black uniform was talking to a man in a large Mercedes. He gave the man his ID and waved. The car entered the facility and disappeared at the top of a hill. Whistling, the guard ducked inside his post, a small guardhouse marked Gate 1.

The Israeli agent slowed down and lifted the visor of his motorcycle helmet. He smirked as he read the dozen or so signs posted on the swath of land that separated the base from the state highway. The US military was always overdoing it with the warnings: "Danger," "Alpha Division, Minefield," "Drive Slowly, Unsafe Area," and on and on.

Someone who wasn't familiar with Marine Corps bases might have seen some irony in the fact that just a single person was guarding the front entrance. Most people didn't know that the friendly guard was simply a human face welcoming visitors and politely sending nosey passersby on their way. Cameras all along the fence and on the guardhouse roof were doing the real work of surveillance. Their images were directly transferred to a security post that was fully prepared to respond to a dangerous intrusion. Eytan knew from experience that the actual perimeter was way beyond this checkpoint, several miles back in some cases. It was this surveillance would allow Eytan to send his invitation.

Eytan arrived at the security gate. Before guard could even ask Eytan about the nature of his business, the agent had pulled out his Glock and pumped the booth full of lead. The protective glass shattered, and the security guard threw himself to the floor. The agent put down his kickstand, dropped his empty magazine, and replaced it with another. He walked closer to the guard, who had already placed his hands behind his head, and gave the surveillance camera a coy smile.

"I have a message for General Bennington and I needed your full attention. What's your name?"

"Steve."

"Do you have a good memory, Steve?"

"Yes," the man stammered.

"Wonderful. I would like you to tell dear Benny that Eytan Morgenstern—that's me—will be waiting for him at the following coordinates."

Eytan gave him the longitude and latitude of their meeting point and had him repeat it three times.

"Oh my, you *do* have an excellent memory. Please let him know that my peace talk proposal is only good for an hour."

"Whatever you want, sir."

"Thanks, Steve. Have an excellent rest of the day. It was a pleasure doing business with you."

Eytan congratulated himself as he hopped back on his cycle. Jackie wouldn't be chastising him for his lack of manners.

He turned on the ignition just as he heard engines roaring in the distance. It was the security team.

Ten minutes later, Eytan reached the clearing where he had arranged to meet Bennington and his Marines. He parked on the grass and took his earpiece out of his jacket so he could get in touch with Eli. They needed to go over the last details of their operation. Before he could make the call, though, his cell phone started ringing. He planned to ignore it, but he changed his mind when he saw the caller's name on the screen.

"Well, well, Jenkins, my boy. Got any news for me?"

"I'm afraid our dear Jenkins cannot come to the phone right now. Reception is very poor at the bottom of the Thames."

Eytan recognized the sugary voice and English accent. It belonged to a man whom he knew only by nickname. It was the man who controlled the Consortium.

"Cypher. Or should I call you Jonathan Cavendish, president of H-Plus Dynamics?"

"Wrong again, Mr. Morg. Poor Cavendish is no longer with us either. It's true that I'm listed at the top of my company's masthead, but Fergus Hennessy is a pseudonym. I get a kick out of little jokes like that."

Eytan thought about it for a few seconds.

Fergus Hennessy. Hennessy Fergus. Sy-Fer...

"That is a little joke, isn't it. Not a great one. A little one. Glad it gives you a kick."

"Some humor never hurt," Cypher replied. He sounded annoyed. "I won't keep you too long. I understand you have an important meeting with General Bennington."

"I'm assuming you're the one I should be thanking for getting me into this mess."

"You give me too much credit. Let's just say I alerted the Marines and the White House. You know how dogs behave whenever you throw them a bone."

"After Elena's death, you promised to get your revenge by exposing me. I see you've followed through on that promise."

"I'm hurt by your insinuation. Do you really think, Mr. Morg, that I'm a man who bases his decisions on anger?"

The plan within the plan, Eytan thought.

"By sending the military after you," Cypher continued, "and getting your friends involved, I've forced you to..."

"...do your dirty work."

"Exactly."

"I saw that coming," Eytan said.

"You saw it coming? Then please inform me of my intentions. I'm curious to see if your mind is still just as sharp."

"You no longer need Bennington, or H-Plus Dynamics, or money from the Pentagon. You've already been compensated for your research and development of the prosthetics. You have the prototypes and the plans. You were counting on me to clean up after you."

"Spot on, Mr. Morg. Bennington chose the front men for our program. He then prepared them for our prosthetics by sending them into well-orchestrated battles. Unfortunately, he knows too much and needs to disappear. Our business with the military will continue, but on completely legal terms. You see, Mr. Morg, you will further my ambitions and serve as my best agent."

Eytan laughed.

Cypher's voice had lost its sugary quality. It was becoming harsher and more threatening. "You lost the match before it even began. To be honest, you lost it the day Bleiberg turned you into what you are."

"You're not the first person to think he had me beat. And I'm still here, more determined than ever. What'll happen if I expose your little scheme to General Bennington? If I tell him about the surprise software inside the processors? And what'll happen, Cypher, when I've demolished your organization?"

"Absolutely nothing will happen on Bennington's front. He's a very stubborn man. He won't give you the time of day. As for the Consortium, it has existed for centuries, and it will live on much longer than you. Our group is more important than you'd ever believe. It exists for one simple reason: to oversee human destiny by guiding its evolution. In the massive chaos that's our world, this is no easy task. The human race needs direction. Otherwise, only the Law of More will prevail: more powerful, more affluent, more intelligent, more cynical, but never more human. You and I both know a lot about that."

"Your organization paid Bleiberg to genetically manipulate children. You caused epidemics. You encouraged human mutilation. You played with lives. How can you seriously consider yourselves paragons of wisdom?"

"We're realists!" Cypher replied. He sounded angry. "We're not cruel and greedy. And we don't seek to dominate the world. We just take advantage of man's little quirks to achieve our objectives; we don't create them. You may think we're schemers, but you're wrong. We're planners."

"Plans. That's not what people need."

"And what is it that people need?"

Eytan looked at the phone in disgust, then ended the call by throwing the device in the grass. He observed the landscape in front of him and quietly muttered.

"Dreams."

CHAPTER 44

On this late-autumn afternoon, the field stretched as far as the eye could see to the north and the west. The air, devoid of the slightest breeze, gave the Midwestern scenery a sense of calm before the storm. To the southeast, a forest of trees rose above a lake whose smooth surface shimmered in the mellow light of the setting sun. A flock of brown birds raced in the sky, forking off suddenly and swooping to the ground like crazed arrows.

Standing beside his motorcycle in the middle of the prairie, Eytan soaked in the beauty of his surroundings. The occasion called for a cigar, but he was fresh out of his favorite guilty pleasure and had to settle for a cigarette.

He heard Eli's voice in his earpiece. "We're positioned safely within the forest."

"I'm in position too, but not undercover."

"I know. I've got you in my rifle sight."

"Be careful where you aim."

"I should have clocked you on the spot for having come up with such a dangerous plan. I believe Jacqueline agrees with me."

"Do you have a better solution?"

"No."

"Then stop complaining. Is our little toy working properly?" the giant inquired.

"Avi is activating it as we speak, with Jeremy's help. He says it looks like a big microwave."

"Technically, he's right, it *is* a big microwave."

"That's what Avi's been trying to tell him for the past five minutes."

Eytan scanned the road for signs of his guests' arrival. The sound of an engine caught his attention. It was a sound he knew all too well.

"Chopper's approaching," he warned. "The land convoy won't be far behind. Make sure you're hidden. We can't let them see you."

"Okay, here we go. Good luck."

"We'll need it."

The helicopter's thumping was getting louder. Eytan closed his eyes and silently counted the blades' rotations to determine how far he was from the aircraft. Stefan Starlin had taught him this trick during his MI6 training. When he opened his eyes again, the helicopter was within sight and flying at a low altitude.

"Eli, they've sent an undercover Huey. Are your skills still sharp?"

"UH-Y1, standard model. Two men in the cockpit, one shooter at the side door. He's got a 7.62 mm."

"Perfect. You get an A plus!"

"Thanks! They're taking you seriously, but not enough to use some fancy-pants type of aircraft. This model doesn't have the latest on-the-ground detection technology."

"Well, we won't complain about that. The Marines' most advanced equipment is in the Middle East. Since Bennington is leading a secret operation, he can't use the more sophisticated gear without justifying it and attracting unwanted attention."

"They're coming. I suggest we cease communications until you give the green light. I'm making sure everyone's undercover. You'd better come back alive."

Eytan didn't say what he was thinking: at this point, it was out of his hands.

The Huey hovered above the Kidon agent and then swept over the lake, disrupting the birds. The blades of the chopper sent them flying in all directions.

The aerial survey was lasting too long for Eytan's liking. If one of the men onboard picked up the slightest movement on the ground, the Marines would rain bullets down on his friends, giving them no chance of survival. The metal hummingbird stationed itself above the treetops. Eytan instinctively reached behind his back to take out the weapon wedged inside his belt. From this distance, about a thousand feet away, a bullet wouldn't do major damage to the aircraft but could reach the pilot and thus compromise the vehicle's stability, as well as the shooter's aim.

The giant calculated the angle he'd need to maximize the bullet's impact. He released the safety on his weapon and tightened his grip. The Huey took flight again, positioning itself closer, one hundred feet away. The machine gun was pointed in his direction.

Eytan slipped his hand along the bottom of his jacket and into his pants pocket. Then he turned his attention to the road to the west. Three SUVs and a light brown Humvee soon appeared.

The vehicles headed into the field and sped toward Eytan. When they were about forty feet from their target, they formed a circle around him.

Four men in black jumped out of each SUV, assault weapons in hand. Exiting the Humvee were two men whom Eytan quickly identified as the pair Jackie and he had fought in the alley during the High Line incident. They took their positions beside the passenger door of the vehicle. A man in his fifties emerged. He had buzz cut, bulging pecs, and a broad build, and he was wearing green cargo pants that perfectly matched the Israeli's jacket.

He walked up to Eytan and eyed him from head to toe.

"General." Eytan greeted him with a salute that was too stiff to be sincere.

"Morgenstern," Bennington replied calmly. "I knew you'd show up, but I was expecting a confrontation, especially after your exploits in Baltimore. I watch the news like everyone else. A fire engulfing the very building where our supplier is headquartered? That couldn't have been a coincidence. You don't tread lightly, and I like that. But a man as determined as you, a man who executed an explosion of that scale wouldn't be turning himself in so easily. So I'm sure you have something up your sleeve."

"You're right. Surrendering isn't my thing. I've come to negotiate."

"Negotiate? Other than your body, what do you have to offer?" The general was leering.

"Sorry, sir, but you're not my type. I actually have some valuable information concerning the prosthetics that you've equipped your men with. It's a little surprise concocted by H-Plus Dynamics, and I'm sure it will upset you. I've got the proof, and I'm prepared to hand it over."

Bennington was clearly intrigued. He rubbed a finger over his lips.

"And what are you demanding in return?"

"That you forget about me, and you also forget about Jacqueline and Jeremy Corbin."

"And where exactly is the lovely couple?"

"Far away."

"I see. And this proof you speak of is obviously being kept safe?"

"Obviously."

"Of course. So, if I understand correctly, you're telling me that our friends at H-Plus Dynamics have given us unreliable equipment, and you'd like to use this information as a bargaining chip."

"That sums it up nicely."

"Okay, but tell me this. Now that you've alerted me to the problem, I'm perfectly free to lead my own investigation and have our experts figure out what's what. That considerably diminishes my interest in your offer."

"I forgot to mention that I also have proof that the men in your unit were deliberately mutilated so that you could make them part of your little Robocop program. I wonder how they'll react when they find out what you did to them."

"And who do you think they'll believe? The man who saved them and gave them back their lives or the one who's considered a threat to the nation's security?"

Bennington paused to gauge the weight of his words. "Progress requires sacrifice. There's never growth without pain. My unit represents a decisive step toward the emergence of a new kind of soldier, a new order of fighting men and women."

"So you're admitting your involvement," the giant pressed, exhaling a cloud of cigarette smoke.

The general squinted. Eytan knew he was sizing him up.

"I don't believe you have any proof. All you have is a hunch. Yes, I knew about it. I even selected them myself." Bennington smiled coldly. "The higher-ups at the Pentagon would have never okayed my program if I hadn't provided subjects with the required attributes. I chose my men according to criteria specified by H-Plus. Then I did what had to be done. It was my duty."

"A soldier's duty is to be loyal to those who fight alongside him. You're just one name on a long list of whack jobs," Eytan spit out before throwing his cigarette butt on the ground.

"You have no right to judge. My loyalty is to my country. I'm providing a means by which the lives of our young men and women can be spared."

"Blah, blah, blah. I've heard sickos like you spout that garbage a million times over. Sacrifice a few to save the rest. It's bullshit. I admit I don't care about your creepy little shenanigans or your ass-backwards morality. You can chop up your young men and women all you want. Every general has blood on his hands. I'll ask you one more time. Think about your answer very carefully. Do you accept my proposition, yes or no?"

"You're surrounded. Some very heavy weapons are aimed at you at this very moment, and you think it's a good idea to use that tone on me? Your friends will be eliminated, just like all the other annoying snoops who tried to stop this project. As for you, Morgenstern, my scientists are going to dissect you like a bug and analyze every inch of your body. I'm going to enjoy watching them do it."

"Do you know much about electronics?" Eytan asked, ignoring the general's threats.

"What?" Bennington replied. For the first time, he looked confused.

"Of course not. You're like the sorcerer's apprentice. You play with powers that you know nothing about. *Now!*"

"Now what?" the general said, clearly frustrated.

The Israeli agent didn't answer. He took a step closer to the general, who was forced to back up.

"Take him out!" Bennington ordered.

The soldiers advanced cautiously, their eyes glued to the sights of their weapons. They closed in on Eytan. He froze and then turned his hands upward, as though he were pleading with the heavens. This seemed to confuse Bennington even more.

At the same moment, the grass in the field went flat. Swept off their feet by an invisible force, the men, all of them equipped with prosthetics, fell to the ground and squirmed like earthworms. They cried out in agony and failed in their attempts to get on their feet again. Even the general was brought to his knees. The helicopter blades stopped rotating. The engine went dead, and the chopper crashed.

Eytan wobbled. His vision was fuzzy. He struggled to remain standing and continue walking. Wiping away a trickle of blood dripping from his nose, he bent over the general, took him by the chin, and forced the officer to look him in the eye.

"It's hard to imagine the effects of an electromagnetic pulse on the ground if you've never experienced one," Eytan said, panting. He removed his earpiece. The device no longer functioned, just as the rest of the electronic equipment within range of the microwave generator provided by Frank no longer worked. "To answer your question, *now* I'm going to eliminate your precious command unit," he said as he took out his weapon. "Then I'll take care of you."

With those words, Eytan's muscles started to tense up, and his heart began to beat so fast, he feared it might fly out of his chest. He couldn't breathe. He searched frantically inside his jacket and took out the case containing the syringes filled with the serum that kept him alive. His muscles were becoming stiffer by the second. He fell to the ground and felt himself convulsing. With his teeth clenched and his temples dripping with sweat, he struggled to maintain control. In a final effort, he tried to open the small case. No dice.

With his heart reliving the pain he had felt so many times during Bleiberg's experiments, Eytan closed his eyes, and, just as he had years earlier, he begged for a quick death.

CHAPTER 45

Tensions were rising inside the sedan as Avi began his count-down. The crucial moment for setting off the electromagnetic pulse generator was fast approaching. With their eyes closed, the four people in the car were as wired as a team of astronauts preparing for a shuttle launch. Avi had only added to their stress by revealing the possible effects of the weapon. But Jeremy, in fact, had asked for the information.

"We've known about EMPs for a long time," Avi had explained as he took out the big black carrying case and began setting up. "Lightning, for example, is a type of EMP. It's a burst of electromagnetic activity. Scientists began studying EMPs in earnest in the nineteen forties, when they discovered that they were a side effect of nuclear explosions. The pulses would mess with and even destroy all nearby electrical equipment and electronic devices."

"The consequences of using EMPs on a highly industrialized country could be catastrophic," Eli added. "No more means of communication, no more power. And for a very long time too. A collapse of all significant communications and energy systems could lead to chaos and a financial catastrophe. The world's major power brokers have been developing EMPs in secret for years. Now countries like Iran and North Korea are threatening to use them."

"We're about to launch a small atomic explosion? Are you out of your mind?" Jackie exclaimed, terrified.

"No, we're not nuts," Avi said. "There are nuclear EMPs and non-nuclear EMPs. The device Frank gave us is the latter type. It would take too long to explain how it works in detail, but basically, it'll create a pulse that's strong enough to cover the area where Eytan is located. The soldiers equipped with prosthetics can say good-bye to their fake limbs. The toll on the rest of their bodies will be pretty rough too."

"And what the hell is a college professor doing with this kind of contraption?" Jeremy asked.

"I also was surprised that Frank had this," Avi said. "I'm sure the US government is quietly funding research on these things at major colleges across the country—at least the smaller versions. But even the smaller ones can do a lot of damage. That's why we need to take cover inside the vehicle."

They slid into the car, which would act as an improvised shield. Once there, they experienced the longest thirty seconds of their lives.

A sharp sound pierced their ears. A deep boom followed, and the car rose from the back to the front as if being carried by an invisible wave.

"Whoa, what was that?" Jeremy yelled, clinging to his seat.

"The shock wave," Avi replied. "The mere fact that you've asked the question means the Faraday cage phenomenon wor..."

Before he could finish his sentence, the helicopter plunged from the sky and crashed.

"It worked," Jeremy said as his wife silently slipped her hand into his.

"That was crazy," she gasped, gaping at the wreckage.

"Great," Eli said. "If everyone's all right, we'll move to phase two of the operation. Go!"

They all got out of the Ford. Eli leaned against the hood as he used his riflescope to check on Eytan.

"Come on," Jeremy said to Avi. "We need to make sure the Audi's still working."

"It should be fine, as long as Frank was right about the wave's range," the doctor answered.

Sticking with the plan, Jeremy and he dashed through the forest while Jackie, pistol in hand, planted herself beside Eli to protect him in case any intruders showed up.

"So how does it look out there?" Jackie asked as the Israeli veteran scanned the area around his fellow Kidon agent.

"Eytan's alive," Eli sighed in relief. "He's walking toward a man who's on his knees, probably Bennington. I see a dozen soldiers on the ground."

"What are they doing?"

"A few are moving. Others are writhing in the grass."

"What a mess."

"That's the nature of the beast. Hold on. Eytan is squatting in front of Bennington. Our little general doesn't have much longer. Everything's going perfectly. Now I have to find that sniper, assuming he's in the area." Eli widened his surveillance. "I'm sure he's nearby."

"In addition to the aerial support, they've got land coverage. That's pretty standard for recon units, right?"

"Right," Eli said absently, fully focused on locating the last enemy who posed a threat. "Got him. I found Terry!"

"Is he aiming at Eytan?"

"No, he's moving to a new position. The Huey crash blocked the bastard's line of fire. Good Lord, he's running too fast."

"His file mentioned serious leg injuries. He's equipped with prosthetics. But I don't understand why they're working. He had to be out of range when we used the EMP."

"Yes, they're working, dammit," Eli cursed. "I won't be able to take him down at that speed."

"Where's Eytan? Is he okay?"

Eli pivoted slightly and straightened up. He pulled away from his riflescope for a brief moment and then looked through it again.

"What do you see? What's going on?" Jackie asked.

"Eytan is on the ground," Eli said. "The shock wave must have triggered an attack. He wasn't able to inject his serum."

"How much time does he have?" she asked.

"Ninety seconds, tops."

"A hundred feet, ninety seconds. Here we go," Jackie let out as she set off in a sprint.

Eli tried to localize Tim Terry. No success.

"Dammit," Eli muttered.

Everything had turned on its head. Avi and Jeremy were gone. Jackie was off on a desperate foot race. Eytan was knocking at death's door. For a second, Eli was at a loss. But only a second. He sprang back and decided to kill two birds with one stone. He'd clear the field for Jackie while attracting the sniper's attention. The circle formed by the SUVs and Humvee partially obstructed Terry's line of vision but not enough to provide ample coverage for the Kidon agent.

The Israeli veteran inhaled as deeply as his weakened lungs would allow and mentally ranked his targets in order of importance, excluding General Bennington. Eli couldn't take aim at him because he was behind Eytan. Game on.

He shot round after round, taking men out left and right. Those who tried to get up were executed first. In the space of seconds, four of them bit the dust, shot cleanly in the head. To eliminate all risk, Eli then took aim at the soldiers lying on the ground. Maybe they had already died from the pulse, or maybe they had just passed out. He couldn't take the chance. Thanks to the precision and confidence gained from years of training and practice, Eli Karman continued to shed blood.

He spotted Jackie in her full sprint as she approached the zone.

He scoped the area. No sign of Terry. The man had to be crouching somewhere. Taking his speed into consideration, Eli determined the area where the sniper was most likely positioned and began examining each inch of it in order to flush him out.

Not even a car zooming into view from across the field was enough to distract him. Avi and Jeremy were on their way back, pedal to the metal. At least that was good news.

The Audi did a race car-style skid and stopped a few feet from Eli.

"I've always wanted to do that," Avi shouted as he opened the car door.

"I'd just like the chance to drive the thing," Jeremy complained. "Where's Jackie?"

Without taking his eye off the riflescope Eli summed up the turn of events.

"Let's take the car and get her out of there!" Jeremy responded. His eyes were filled with panic.

"Negative! As long as Sergeant Terry's still alive, we're sticking with the plan," Eli ordered with finality.

~ ~ ~

Some eight hundred feet away, Jackie was pumping her legs and swinging her arms as fast as her little body would allow. Driven by the sole desire to reach Eytan in time and confident of Eli's ability to protect her from the sniper, she was determined to push herself to the limit while ignoring the blasts going off behind her.

As she approached the circle of vehicles, all she could see were bloody corpses. She rushed to Eytan's immobile body. Beside him, General Bennington was trying to lift himself up.

For a hot second, Jackie made vague eye contact with him. She pointed the pistol at him and coldly lodged a bullet between the eyes. He fell backward like a bowling pin. The young woman released her weapon and threw herself beside Eytan. He was wearing a serene expression that she had never seen on his face before.

This was no time for serenity. She grabbed the case that held the syringes and yanked it open. She took out a dose and pushed up the sleeve of Eytan's jacket. A shiver ran through her as she felt his icy skin, and her heart sank when she saw all the puncture wounds on his arm. No time for feelings, either. She set her eyes on the biggest vein, which ran through the 302 inscribed in black ink, and jabbed him with the needle.

Jackie injected the entire dose of green fluid just as another bang went off. She felt a burning sensation in her leg. She looked at her thigh. Her jeans were covered with blood. It was too soon to tell, but she thought it was just a flesh wound. It was stinging, but not really hurting.

Fearing that she would be shot again, she grabbed Eytan by the shoulders and used all her strength to roll him over. Thank God the Humvee was at least partially shielding them.

~ ~ ~

"Target detected. Terry at three o'clock!" Eli shouted as he pivoted to his right.

Through his scope he could see Terry, along with his rifle and tripod. The weapon was pointed directly at Jackie and Eytan.

"Who's he shooting at?" Jeremy yelled hysterically.

"At Jackie, but he didn't get her," Eli lied. "*I'm* not going to miss, though."

He pulled the trigger twice.

"Did you get him?" Avi asked.

"I'm not sure. All I can see is the tip of his gun."

Eli paused. His opponent's tripod was rotating slowly. It was now pointing in the Israeli veteran's direction.

~ ~ ~

Behind the improvised shelter, Jackie squeezed her fingers around the butt of her gun, fully expecting to take a second bullet at any moment. There was still no sign of life in Eytan's pale face. She put a hand on his smooth skull. It was burning hot. She almost jumped when the giant opened his eyes.

"You scared me half to death," Jackie said, sighing in relief.

He didn't seem to be listening as he tried to sit up.

"What happened?" he mumbled, shaking his head.

"Eli killed all the soldiers, and when we saw that you were down, I came to help, as planned. I took Bennington out while I was at it."

"How bad is it?" he asked, pointing to Jackie's bloody jeans.

"It's superficial. Terry shot at me once, then stopped."

"That means he's decided to go after Eli. Shit! Eli doesn't have what it takes to go head-to-head. Stay covered. I'm on it."

"Wait, do you think you're in any condition to..."

Eytan leaped to his feet with cat-like agility and grabbed an assault rifle. He scrambled to the Humvee and jumped on top of it. Taking advantage of a clear view, he turned toward the spot where Eli was positioned to determine his friend's line of sight. He shouldered his weapon and spun around. He spotted Tim Terry with an eye glued to his scope and his finger on the trigger. After taking a second to adjust, he pulled. Two simultaneous shots went off.

CHAPTER 46

From improvised bleachers made of cinder blocks and wooden planks, kids cheered as their favorite players fought their hearts out. The sun in the clear-blue sky was beating down on both teams and the hundred or so spectators. The soccer match had pinned two neighborhoods against each other. The green jerseys were beating the reds by a single goal with only a few seconds left. The heat, combined with the crowd's enthusiasm, had brought the energy level to a boiling point. Maybe this was just a neighborhood game, but in Brazil, soccer was the national religion.

The final whistle sounded. The victorious team members leaped and hugged. The players on the other side straggled off the field. The kids waited nearby, hoping to get in a word or two with their favorite players.

Eytan watched the scene run its course. This was his first time in Brazil. Despite the vivid colors of the houses and the lush vegetation, what he saw all around him was the poverty.

And what he had felt since arriving the previous night was the heat. He was doing his best to stay in the shade, but that didn't help much. He was exuding sweat from every pore in his skin.

Two young women, walking casually hand-in-hand, flashed the giant flirty eyes as they passed him. Entertained by their coquettish ways, he simply smiled back. Over the course of the last few years and numerous work-related trips, he had picked up on his effect on women. His teacher and mentor, Stefan Starlin, never missed a chance to tease him over his distant attitude toward the female species.

"If I were tall like you, I'd be heating up bedrooms all over the world," Stefan sometimes told him.

"You mean there are some bedrooms you still haven't set ablaze?" Eytan would reply. It wasn't flattery. The man had quite a reputation with the ladies.

The giant grinned as he remembered the man who had watched over him for almost a decade.

He turned his attention to the winning team's coach. He was Eytan's sole reason for visiting the country. Of average height and in his fifties, the man with graying hair was wearing light-colored cotton trousers and a white shirt. He was congratulating his players with his left hand. His right arm was dangling by his side.

~ ~ ~

The loose gravel in the courtyard crunched under the tires of the black convertible driven by Karl-Heinz Dietz. The man got out of his flashy new car and shut the green entry gate. He paused at the front steps of his opulent-looking abode in the high hills of Rio de Janeiro. He had been living a beautiful life here for more than five years and had never tired of it.

He had bought this land for next to nothing as soon as he was absolutely certain of the Reich's downfall. For another ridiculously low sum, he had built his two-story provincial home amid the lush vegetation. A jungle of exotic plants kissed the ocher walls. Wild orchids grew from tropical trees whose broad branches stretched above the tile roof. But the home and its location weren't what he prized most. His true treasures were Juliana, his wife, and Milene, his daughter. They were the only people who mattered to the man who was now going by the name Carlos Diaz.

Karl-Heinz entered his house and placed the soccer ball, which he had been carrying under his good arm, on the tile floor. He headed into the dim living room, where shutters on the windows filtered out the sunlight. He called for his wife and daughter but got no response. He switched on the ceiling fan and opened a cabinet door in search of a glass.

"There's already a whiskey awaiting you on the coffee table, Colonel Dietz."

Karl-Heinz jumped. He hadn't heard a word of German in ten years. And no one in Brazil was aware of his past, not to mention his standing in the SS. He turned around slowly to peer into the sitting area where the mysterious voice was coming from. He could make out a massive silhouette that was taking up practically all of the green loveseat.

"Come sit down. It's your home, after all," the stranger said. "I took the liberty of pouring myself a drink too. I'd feel bad making you drink alone."

"Who are you?" Karl-Heinz asked, regaining some of his composure.

He closed the cabinet door and walked toward a high-back chair that faced his visitor.

"I'm the sum of all your victims."

The stranger leaned forward to let Karl-Heinz see his face. "Morgenstern?"

"Let's toast, Colonel!" Eytan replied as he picked up one of the glasses. "Let's toast like two old combatants who've survived the horrors of war."

Karl-Heinz sat down and picked up his own drink. He clinked his glass against Eytan's.

"You've become a man," Karl-Heinz remarked. "More than a man. And yet I can still see your childish features. So tell me. What have you been up to all these years?"

"After our encounter, I left for England with Stefan Starlin."

"Who's that?"

"He's the Brit who snatched me from your claws when you attacked our camp. He also happens to be the man who gave me this spiffy ensemble."

Eytan showed off the cargo jacket he was wearing.

"Starlin had it on him when he made me part of the SOE. It's important to him, so it's important to me. Anyhow, with some help from the Polish resistance, he got me to London. Then he brought me into the MI6, where I have autonomous-agent status. The intelligence agency provides me with files on war criminals. I study them. I choose my targets. And I go after them. Some have to be put on trial. Others..."

"I see. Can you believe the irony?"

"It'll be even more ironic by the end of the year. The British want to disband their cleanup brigade. So I'm getting transferred to Mossad, where I'll enjoy logistical advantages while keeping my autonomy."

"A Jew-turned-Aryan will be working on behalf of a Jewish state to hunt the very war criminals who created him. The Nazi regime perfectly embodied all that is absurd in this world. So you ended up a hunter just like me. Have you taken many of them down?"

"Yes."

"What do you get out of it?"

"Nothing other than the satisfaction of doing my job."

"You can't be serious. Aren't you enjoying the sweet taste of revenge?"

"There's nothing sweet about revenge."

"You're lying. I bet right now you're getting off on just the thought of killing me. I bet no woman could ever give you a hard-on like the one you've got at this very moment."

"Was that your motivation?" Eytan asked. "Pleasure?"

"Yes," Karl-Heinz grunted. "I miss the exhilaration of taking on a fierce beast or a worthy warrior. I don't care about politics, or ideologies, or any of the other fantasies that phony prophets spit out in order to establish power. That first encounter, the perfect moves, and the victory are all that I care about. I wanted to slit your neck like a butcher slaughters a cow. Missing that opportunity is still my biggest regret. But I did get to kill your friends."

"Your attempts to provoke me are useless. I'm here with one very specific goal, and nothing you say or do can stop me from accomplishing it."

"All right then, kill me if that's what you want, I'm no longer in a position to defend myself. But killing me won't do anything for you. All your life, you'll be driven by the lust to kill. And all your life, those you love will suffer."

"That's why I keep them at a safe distance," Eytan replied. "And I always will. It's for their own good. And mine too."

Eytan rose to his feet and loomed over Karl-Heinz, watching the man tense up. Karl-Heinz understood the rules of the game. The winner lived. The loser died.

Vae victis—woe to the vanquished, Eytan thought.

Eytan knew it wasn't just the fear of dying that the man was feeling. He was thinking of Juliana and Milene and all the moments they would never share. Perhaps he was wondering if they, too, would die on this day.

Eytan pulled an impressive knife from his belt. He knew the sight of it was reawakening the pain in Karl-Heinz's dead arm.

"You plan to finish me off with the same weapon from Poland?"

"I don't use it in your honor, but in memory of the man it belonged to."

To Karl-Heinz's surprise, Eytan put the knife back in its sheath.

"Relax. I didn't come here to kill you, Dietz, or to bring you to Israel for trial. I wasn't given authorization. But that doesn't matter, because I'm a free agent and can do as I please. The truth is, your death wouldn't be good enough for me."

Eytan checked his watch. He rummaged inside his jacket and took out a colorful braided bracelet, which he threw on the coffee table. Karl-Heinz picked it up with a trembling hand.

"That bracelet belongs to..."

"Your daughter, I know. Her name is Milene, I believe."

"You didn't..."

The former colonel's voice was lifeless. Eytan responded with a snarky smile.

"I would never separate a daughter from her mother," he announced as he threw Karl-Heinz a gold wedding band, which the man instinctively caught on the fly. Eytan imagined the heartache and insane rage he was feeling.

"You're right, Colonel. Those who are closest to us pay the price for the lives we lead. And now, if I may..." Eytan reached over and took the bracelet out of Karl-Heinz's hand. "I'll still be needing this. You can keep the ring."

"How could you," Karl-Heinz sobbed.

The giant walked over to the French doors, opened them, and pushed back the shutters as he rattled off a list of names.

"Janusz, Karol, Vassili, Piotr, Pawel, Marek. It was for them that I *could* have done it," he said.

"*Could* have?" Karl-Heinz repeated.

Eytan left the house and closed the doors behind him. He walked over to Karl-Heinz's car, where Juliana and Milene were standing. When he reached it, he turned around and saw Karl-Heinz looking out the window, the relief evident on his face.

Eytan gave the child her bracelet. She slipped it back on her wrist. He smiled at the child and patted her blond curls. He turned to Juliana and reached into his jacket. Karl-Heinz was expecting him to pull out a gun—Eytan knew this. But Eytan pulled out a cigar instead. Juliana wasn't following the agent's movements anyway. She was looking at the window. She flashed a cold, suspicious look at her husband. Juliana was holding something, and when she caught his eyes, she threw it in his direction. Karl-Heinz's photo was on the cover of the document. In his SS uniform, he was standing in front of the destroyed village of Lidice.

Eytan could already hear the words running through the former SS officer's head. "That was the past. Those were different times. I'm not that man anymore." Had he really talked himself into believing all that? Eytan picked up Juliana's suitcase and led the mother and daughter out of the courtyard. He opened the green gate. The three of them walked out to the street.

~ ~ ~

Karl-Heinz felt his legs give out. He slid to the floor. He was torn between the torment of losing his family and his anger at himself. He had let the young Eytan slip away all those years ago. Karl-Heinz had been above it all. Life had been sweet. He had never expected the world to come crashing down around his ears. He cried, laughed, and cursed the bastard Patient 302.

"It has been and will be the fate of all those who cross your path, Morgenstern, to feel pain and sadness! Even with one arm, I'll become a hunter again. For the rest of your life, everyone you love..."

His obscene promises bounced off the walls of his living room. Seconds later, the house he had shared with his beautiful wife and daughter burst into flames.

CHAPTER 47

With his weapon wedged in his armpit, Eytan was examining Tim Terry's corpse. Blood was flowing from the Marine's head and forming a dark puddle around the barrel of the gun lying next to him.

"It's done," Jackie said, her hand on the giant's arm.

"Almost," he corrected, grabbing Terry's legs and pulling the body toward the circle of military trucks.

"Quick, go join the others," he ordered. "I'm going to inspect the vehicles and bodies. You don't have to be here for that."

"Your call," she replied, fully aware that no arguments could sway the Kidon agent when he had made up his mind. "But aren't you forgetting something?"

"Am I?" he asked in surprise as he continued to heave the dead weight.

"Unbelievable," she sighed.

She turned her back and started limping away.

"Thanks?"

"About time," she hollered.

"I thought I already said that."

Jackie stopped. She turned around to face Eytan. The disarming wink he shot her was worth all the thank-yous in the world. She turned around again and continued to limp away. She was eager to hold her husband in her arms.

~ ~ ~

Jeremy was pressing as hard as he could against the bullet wound. He couldn't feel his fingers anymore. They were red with blood. Actually, he couldn't feel *anything*. He couldn't understand anything either. He could hardly believe he was still standing. In fact, he was kneeling.

Beside him, Avi was ripping open a packet of compresses with his teeth and unscrewing a bottle of antiseptic with his free hand. The doctor's calm behavior bewildered Jeremy, but he surrendered to Avi's unquestionable expertise.

"Eyes on me. Keep your eyes on me," he instructed Eli in a reassuring tone that sounded almost melodic. It infused Jeremy with hope. "I'm going to disinfect the wound and put pressure on it. It will hurt, but that's a good sign. And don't stop looking at my handsome face."

Avi shooed Jeremy's hands away. He applied a thick square of soaked gauze to the bluish skin swollen from the bullet and began to clean Eli's injury.

The trembling man struggled to stay conscious. Every time his eyes started to roll back, he refocused on Avi's face. The doctor kept trying to make him smile.

"Don't talk," Avi whispered when Eli started to articulate something. "Everything will be all right."

Tim Terry's final bullet had struck Eli in the shoulder, shattering his clavicle. Jeremy had rushed to Eli, catching him to cushion his fall. Just as quickly, the blood had started shooting out of him in huge spurts. Springing into action, Avi had grabbed the backpack filled with first aid supplies, which they had bought after fleeing the High Line. He had emptied out its contents and given Jeremy his instructions.

"Tear open Eli's sweater, and apply pressure to the wound."

Since then, Jeremy had watched in fascination as Avi performed a graceful dance with his skilled fingers. He had come to believe that they would make it.

"I need you to cut four strips of tape to hold the gauze in place," the doctor ordered.

Jeremy fumbled to execute the task. But before he could finish, Eli's chest started heaving.

"He's having a heart attack," Avi said, sounding just as composed. "Secure the tape while I start CPR."

With extreme effort, Jeremy contained his growing sense of panic. It seemed as though they had gone through their allotment of good luck.

Avi placed the heel of his hand on Eli's sternum. He placed his other hand on top of the one on the sternum, and with straight arms, he began a series of compressions.

Jeremy observed the old man's face. Eli was staring at him with eyes that looked pleading. Jeremy didn't know what to make of it or how to respond. As the seconds passed, Eli's expression became more insistent. His eyes gleamed with energy. He took Jeremy's hand and squeezed with unexpected strength. Then he released his grip. And Jeremy understood.

After thirty compressions, Avi placed a hand on Eli's forehead and pinched his nose. With his other hand, he lifted Eli's chin. Avi put his own mouth over Eli's and blew twice.

Back to chest compressions. Then mouth-to-mouth again. Jeremy searched Eli's face for the slightest sign of recovery. Avi continued his rotation, the sweat dripping from his forehead. Two sequences, then three. The fourth was his last.

With his hands joined on Eli's chest, Avi stopped his thrusting. The doctor remained motionless for a second, then slumped and took his head in his hands. Numb, Jeremy watched as Avi began to weep. Unable to look at him any longer, Jeremy stood up and turned away. He ran his fingers through his hair. His eyes misty, he peered at the heavens. The ground was swaying under his feet. Dozens—no, hundreds—of conflicting thoughts were colliding in his head.

In stark contrast to Avi's sobs, the birds were chirping wildly in what sounded like celebration. They had reclaimed their turf in the sky.

"Boys, we got lu..."

Jackie stopped when she spotted Jeremy. Her smile faded. Tears rolling down his cheeks, Jeremy rushed to meet her. He took Jackie in his arms and held her tight.

"No," she whispered, tearing herself from his hold.

Seeing Eli, she fell to her knees beside Avi. Jeremy joined them without uttering a word. Jackie caressed the old man's forehead. He had died in what seemed like excruciating spasms, but now he was peaceful, at rest. Pain, it appeared, was only for the living.

Jeremy, Avi, and Jackie remained huddled around Eli's lifeless body for some time. When he heard a twig snap behind him,

Jeremy looked over his shoulder. Frozen in his tracks, Eytan was standing mute a few feet away.

Jeremy, the reader and bookseller, found himself struggling to find the right words. Soothing, comforting words. He searched Jackie's face, hoping she would know what to say. She couldn't find the words either. They didn't exist.

The three of them rose to their feet and joined Eytan. Jeremy could see all the emotions of a man whose walls were crumbling. And even though the man wasn't shedding a tear, he could recognize the aching father and abandoned son in his eyes.

CHAPTER 48

The odor of cooking oil and grease invaded the foodie's nostrils. The only vegetables that this establishment offered were the tomatoes and iceberg lettuce that garnished the burgers dumped on the tables with mugs of beer. Truck drivers and construction workers made up the clientele at this pit stop off I-95, just south of the Beltway. The décor consisted of old rural landscapes in plastic frames. Complementing the artwork were the country hits blaring from the loudspeakers.

Simon Attali was seated in front of a meager salad of the same tomatoes and lettuce that went with the burgers. Although salads weren't on the menu, he had talked the manager into having the cook throw the vegetables in a bowl. And the cook had succeeded in scaring up a packet of Italian dressing to go with it.

The United States would never cease to amaze the master spy. Americans liked to think of themselves as the glamorous leaders of the free world. But this restaurant was another side of the country. In truth, America was a colorful hodgepodge of wealth and poverty, English and multiple other languages, many faiths, healthy athletes and young adults who shot up heroin, optimism and cynicism. And without a doubt, the American dream, so obtainable just a decade ago, had taken a hit, except for those born with a silver spoon in their mouths. One of those people was the pudgy man in the black raincoat who had just entered this dive.

Attali watched the man, whom he silently called Mr. Potato Head at the occasional Mossad meetings that concerned the pathetic loser. He was walking toward him with the awkward smile often exhibited by the well-off when they found themselves in surroundings that didn't meet their criteria. Of all the jackasses who haunted the White House and

Pentagon hallways, *he* had to be the one heading the case that had brought him to the United States.

Travis Lamont pulled back the chair across from Attali and sat his flabby ass down.

"Sorry I'm late," he apologized. "I couldn't break away, and then the beltway traffic was miserable. But I don't need to tell you about the beltway. You've had some experience with it. So here we are. How's it going, my man?"

How's it going, my man? Did they offer courses in Washington on how to be ingratiating and hip at the same time? Attali could see right through Lamont's attempt to create an artificial rapport. Idiots who fell into this trap would bitterly regret it. But Attali had a trick or two of his own, and now he was using one that Eytan Morg had taught him when he joined the intelligence service.

"Play the fool. No one ever suspects the fool," the assassin had advised him. And Eytan was a master in the art of passing himself off as a dumb jock.

It was time to respond.

"Oh, same as you, I'm sure," Attali said. "Always hustling to get some politician out of a mess that he's made."

"Tell me about it," Lamont snickered. "Right now I'm stuck with one who'd rather drop his pants in front of secretaries than write up reports, which the government pays him a pretty penny to do."

"I trust you'll use your typical discretion to fix the situation."

"You know me too well," the potbellied government worker laughed as he pointed a playful finger at Attali. "Let's say I have some photos, and in exchange for keeping them a secret, I've made a new friend. In a vultures nest the size of DC, it's important to have friends."

Attali tried to keep himself from showing his scorn.

"True, friends are important, but also fickle," he said, slapping the thick file beside his plate.

"The purpose of your visit?" Lamont questioned as he looked ravenously at the document with a red cover.

"This? No, this is a gift, a token of goodwill."

"Simon, you're something else. You know what a kid I become when I'm presented with a pile of candy."

"If I were you, I'd limit my sugar intake," the Israeli joked. "Speaking of which, you don't have diabetes, do you?"

"I don't like it when people make fun of my weight," Lamont said, offended. "It's not very nice."

"I'm not making fun of you. I'm worried about your health, especially in light of some information I acquired a few days ago."

"I'm touched by your concern, but I don't see where you're going with this."

"Did you know that nearly 2.5 million diabetics in the United States suffer foot ulcers and that as many as five percent of them will have to undergo leg amputations?"

Lamont ran his fingers through his hair. Attali was clearly making him nervous.

"No, I had absolutely no idea.

"Fortunately, they make miraculous prosthetics these days," Attali continued. "I learned this recently, and I've been finding out more about these devices."

Travis Lamont's smile disappeared. His shell was cracking, and Attali was reveling in it. His hatred for this man had reached a new high after he had gotten Avi Lafner's detailed report, accompanied by the doctor's resignation.

"Don't beat around the bush," the White House envoy said, plainly angry.

"Sending the hounds after Eytan Morgenstern? That was not a good idea!" Attali declared, shaking his head. "And all for what? To enhance the performance of soldiers that you yourself mutilated?"

"What? That *we* mutilated? I had no idea!" Lamont shouted, placing a hand over his heart. He calmed down and adopted a conspiratorial tone.

"It was one general who devised the whole scheme behind our backs. I swear! All I did was attend a Pentagon meeting."

"A meeting in which you decided to track and kill Titus Bramble."

"No!" Lamont rose up. "That was not *my* decision."

"No need to lose your temper. I believe you, Travis. I just hope the media believe you."

Lamont was pale and fidgeting in his chair.

"You don't plan to... Come on, Simon. We've been friends forever. I must have two or three things that would interest your government."

"I'll get to that. But first, I'd like to give you this," he said as he slid the file toward Lamont, who took it immediately and began flipping through the pages. "The company that developed these prosthetics for your Marines incorporated software. You see, each artificial limb has the capability to transfer a Marine's health stats to his command unit in the same way that members of a Grand Prix team follow their driver's heart rate, respiration, and blood pressure during a race."

"That was all included in the project's statement of scope," Lamont said as he continued to leaf through the pages.

"Statement of scope? I find it very disturbing to hear you talk with such indifference about the lives of the young men and women who defend your country," Simon sighed.

"Spare me your morality lesson. Neither of us has much credibility on that score. This situation has given me more shit in two weeks than I've had to deal with in a whole year. Anyway, why are *you* complaining? Your superagent was able to get out just fine, and the program's creators were eliminated. And you've got your hands on the plans for those damned prosthetics."

"Damned right, we have them. By the way, I need to thank you for that. I'm sure we'll put them to good use. However, if you don't mind, we won't incorporate the software that allows for long-distance control."

"What?"

"I'll say it again so that you get the whole picture. H-Plus Dynamics inserted software that allows them to keep the prosthetics from working at any given time. Don't you see? A war zone, gunfire, heated man-to-man combat... Your forces get the upper hand, then bam! Your troops are immobile. That's all it takes to lose a battle. Maybe even a war. Funny, isn't it?"

"Are you sure about what you're claiming?"

"Experts who know much more about this than I have weighed in. It's all there in the file. It's up to you to investigate these bad people who are prepared to play a dirty trick on you."

Attali watched Lamont with a mocking smile. The man crossed his legs and stuck the document between his knees.

"Why would you give me this?" he asked.

"I've already told you. It's a token of goodwill."

"What do you want in return?"

"I'm asking that you leave Jacqueline Walls and her husband, Jeremy Corbin, the hell alone. As of now, they're out of the game."

"That can most likely be arranged."

"You're not understanding me. If they're involved in so much as a car accident, I will hold you personally responsible. I will make sure that the press, as well as a number of the friends you've acquired during your career find out the full extent of what's written in that dossier."

"Okay, okay," Lamont said. "You have my word."

"I don't give a shit about your word. I'm not giving you a choice."

"But you're not asking me to stop looking for your agent, Eytan Morg—or Morgenstern?"

"He no longer belongs to my agency. In fact, he never belonged to anyone. This mission has cost him," Attali said as he pushed back his chair. "Eytan Morg is off the grid. If I were you, I'd be happy about that. If a man like him knew your name and your involvement in this, you'd be sleeping with one eye open."

Lamont didn't respond.

"Well, I believe we've reached an agreement," Attali said as he got up and put on his coat.

"Hold on. Can you at least tell me a bit more about this former agent of yours?" the White House envoy risked asking as he grabbed the Israeli's sleeve.

"What for?" Attali spit back as he shook off the man's hand. "You wouldn't understand. Cold-blooded creatures never do."

EPILOGUE

With a lump in his throat, Jeremy watched a flock of sparrows swirl in the clear blue sky. A warm breeze brushed his face, bringing some comfort to his aching spirit. On the horizon, beyond the trees, the sun was finally setting on a day that had taken too long to die. Jeremy understood that his grief wouldn't subside with the setting sun. His pain would ease eventually. But some kinds of pain hurt more intensely than others.

Jeremy had been gazing into the distance for several long minutes and putting off the inevitable. Actually, he was scared. Scared of coming face-to-face with the grave. Scared of reliving the hopeless battle against death that Avi and he had waged for the sake of their friend. But from the depths of his affection for Eli, Jeremy found the courage. At last, he lowered his head and brought his eyes to the coffin.

Rose intended to follow Jewish custom and wait a year before putting a tombstone on Eli's grave, but she had given Jeremy the inscription that would be on it: "Show me a hero and I will write you a tragedy."

Jeremy tried to hold back the tears as he thought about those words.

The sound of tires on the cemetery's gravel road brought him back to reality. He needed to stay strong in order to help the others deal with their own pain. Jeremy dried his cheeks and turned to Jackie, who was pushing the stroller. Annie was playing quietly with a toy car.

"I still can't believe it," Jackie said softly.

"Me either," Jeremy said, clearing his throat to regain his composure.

"He didn't say anything before he... "Her voice broke off before she could finish the question.

Jeremy recalled Eli's face, the feel of Eli's hand squeezing his. What he had mistaken as an expression of suffering or fear was actually his final request, his final wish.

"I think he wanted—wants—us to take care of Eytan."

"How can we take of him now that he's gone?"

"By living, sweetheart. By cherishing everything he's given us. And most important, by being there for him," Jeremy responded with conviction. "There will be a day when he's ready, and he'll come back."

Jeremy stopped himself when he saw Avi walking toward them. The doctor put his cell phone back in the pocket of his raincoat.

"I was just talking to Simon Attali," he said. "He says the case is closed for good. You won't have to worry any longer."

"Can you thank him for us?" Jackie asked.

"I won't have the opportunity."

"So you're really leaving Mossad?" Jeremy asked.

Avi nodded. "I no longer have a taste for the job."

"What will you do now? Start your own practice?"

"I've been offered a research position at the University of Chicago. Frank pulled a few strings for me. I'd like to work on Eytan's serum. Frank's coming today, by the way."

"So you'll be in the United States," Jeremy said.

"As a matter of fact, I'm going to start house hunting tomorrow. I'm sure wherever he is, Eli would be happy. And Chicago is much closer to New Jersey than Tel Aviv. With the help of an expert bookseller, who also happens to be a fan of good music, I might learn a thing or two about men in tights. And a sheriff's deputy friend can always come in handy."

Jeremy and Jackie smiled at each other.

"Don't get too excited," Jackie replied. "My influence is limited to my county in New Jersey."

"And you won't win this bookseller over by referring to the heroes in the serious genre of graphic novels as men in tights," Jeremy said.

"Okay okay, don't gang up on me," Avi said. "I'd happily exchange a cop and a bookshop owner for a couple of friends. But only if you promise to make me a strong pot of coffee when I visit."

"In that case..." Jeremy began.

Jackie finishes his sentence. "You can count on us."

~ ~ ~

ON AN ISLAND OFF THE COAST OF IRELAND

The rusty hinges of the old chest creaked as he lifted the top. Plumes of dust hovered in the air before settling on the earthen floor of the hiding place. He rummaged in the messy heap of papers, weapons, and uniforms that would have made a museum curator quiver with excitement. Finally, he found the sought-after item.

Eytan left the dark and narrow room and walked away from the stone structure that was his place of refuge. He headed toward the rocky coastline on this island, isolated for centuries from the rages of humankind.

He closed his eyes and let the wind beat against his face.

The ghosts from his past were rising. His father, his mother, his brother, Roman. He could feel Vassili's rugged hand on his shoulder and Janusz's protective embrace. He could hear Karol's voice reciting Stefan Zweig. And then he heard Eli's laugh.

The giant opened his eyes again to face the ocean that crashed against the rocks at the bottom of the cliff. The smell of seaweed swept by sea spray filled his entire being.

He looked with disgust at the dagger and reread the inscription engraved in its blade.

"*Meine ehre heisst treue.* My honor is loyalty."

"I've given a new meaning to these twisted words. Eli, please forgive me for taking so long. Today, I'm breaking my chains," he said as he threw the weapon. The dagger swirled in the air before sinking into the waters that would swallow it forever.

Eytan Morgenstern sank his fists into the pockets of his black jeans and walked back home.

By the power of the word
I regain my life
I was born to know you
And to name you.
Liberty
—Paul Eluard, 1942

Now this is not the end. It is not even the beginning of the end. But
it is, perhaps, the end of the beginning.
—Winston Churchill

In memory of Edith and Valérie.

~ ~ ~

Thank you for reading The Morgenstern Project.

We invite you to share your thoughts and reactions on Goodreads and
your favorite social media and retail platforms.

We appreciate your support.

ABOUT THE AUTHOR

David Khara studied law, worked as a reporter for Agence France Press, was a top-level athlete, and ran his own business for a number of years. Now he is a full-time writer. Khara wrote his first novel—a vampire thriller—in 2010, before starting his Consortium thriller series. The first in the series, *The Bleiberg Project*, became an immediate bestseller in France, catapulting Khara into the ranks of the country's top thriller writers.

ABOUT THE TRANSLATOR

Sophie Weiner is a freelance translator and book publishing assistant from Baltimore, Maryland. After earning degrees in French from Bucknell University and New York University, Sophie went on to complete a master's in literary translation from the Sorbonne, where she focused her thesis on translating wordplay in works by Oulipo authors. Growing up with Babar, Madeline, and The Little Prince, Sophie was bitten by the Francophile bug at an early age, and is fortunate enough to have lived in Paris, Lille, and the Loire Valley.

ABOUT LE FRENCH BOOK

Le French Book is a New York-based publisher specializing in great reads from France. It was founded in December 2011 because, as founder Anne Trager says, "I couldn't stand it anymore. There are just too many good books not reaching a broader audience. There is a very vibrant, creative culture in France, and we want to get them out to more readers."

www.lefrenchbook.com

CPSIA information can be obtained
at www.ICGtesting.com
Printed in the USA
FSOW03n0611280415
6744FS